A CHRISTMAS KISS

Wetherby gave his cravat one last inspection in the mirror, then started for the door. Leaving the room, he noticed that Millicent had just entered the hallway and was standing under the kissing bough. She looked lovely in a bright blue velvet dress. He wanted to take her in his arms and smother her with kisses. But—he reminded himself that he was a reformed man now. Nothing on earth could move him to do anything to give her a dislike of him.

"Good evening, Mrs. Copley," he said, looking up for one whole minute at the clump of greenery above them. "Our hostess has very attractive decorations, would you not say?" Her gaze followed his, he was glad to see. Now, she would realize what a true pattern-saint he was.

Millicent stared at the mistletoe. She knew full well what his lordship was thinking to do. Did the man have no idea of how humiliating it was to be grabbed and kissed with no more than a by-your-leave? A gentleman might—but a rake of Wetherby's ilk—no, never. If a man were so assaulted, he'd undoubtedly wish to place a facer square in the mouth of the offending party.

His lordship needed to be taught a lesson.

Millicent threw her arms around Wetherby's neck and pulled his head down until his lips met hers. She was not very strong, but she was determined—and—she had the advantage of surprise.

She kissed Wetherby until she had no more breath in her and had to let him go . . .

Books by Paula Tanner Girard

LORD WAKEFORD'S GOLD WATCH

CHARADE OF HEARTS

A FATHER FOR CHRISTMAS

Published by Zebra Books

A FATHER FOR CHRISTMAS

Paula Tanner Girard

Zebra Books
Kensington Publishing Corp.
http://www.zebrabooks.com

ZEBRA BOOKS are published by

Kensington Publishing Corp.
850 Third Avenue
New York, NY 10022

First Printing: December, 1996
10 9 8 7 6 5 4 3 2 1

Printed in the United States of America

One

Millicent Copley raced toward the rear of the country manor just a pace in back of her exuberant son. Like a kite, her bonnet flew behind, held only by the ribbon tied beneath her chin.

With all the enthusiasm of a six-year-old, Master Rupert threw open the heavy oak door and burst into the warm kitchen. "I won! I won!"

An elderly, pumpkin-shaped woman turned from stirring a pot on the stove and eyed the muddy prints following him. "Well, ye certainly have now, haven't ye? And brought in half the outdoors while ye were doing it."

Millicent, her cheeks pink from the crisp December air, stood in the doorway and looked down at her mud-splattered clothing. "Oh, my! Mrs. Woodstock will think us unredeemable, I am afraid."

Of course, Mrs. Woodstock, quite used to the young mistress' lighthearted ways, thought no such thing. All who knew her considered Mrs. Copley to be kind, pretty, and self-effacing. However, as was expected of her, the cook placed her hands firmly on her hips and clicked her tongue, "Tch! Tch! Well, ye better take off yir wet wraps before ye catch yir death. There's hot chocolate in the pot and scones fresh from the oven on the table."

Rupert had already pulled off his scarf and mittens and was climbing onto a stool alongside the wide working surface. He grabbed a scone and smeared it with raspberry jam. "You may have won, Momma, if you had not fallen in the mud puddle," Rupert said solicitously.

Laughing, Millicent removed her soiled pelisse. "Yes, I just may have done."

From the look of condescension on Rupert's face, it was plain to see that he really didn't think that possible. But not one to give in to such arrogance, even in an adored son, Millicent challenged him back. "I dare say, young man, I can still give you a run for your money any day."

"But not for long, Momma. Soon I shall be a man and then you will not be able to keep up with me."

For a moment a twinge of anxiety struck Millicent, but the tug at her heart was quickly dispensed as the inner door opened and a plump freckle-faced girl looked into the kitchen.

"What is it, Sukie?"

"A letter came for you in the post half an hour ago, ma'am."

Millicent quickly pulled off her soggy half-boots and padded into the main house. "It must be a letter from your grandmama," she called back to Rupert. "Mayhaps your Aunt Cissy has had her baby."

It was a letter from her mother, all right, but it wasn't the news she'd expected.

Jedburgh Border

Dear Millie,

 The doctor says he does not know how he miscalculated. He now thinks the baby will not arrive for another three weeks, so your father and I cannot possibly be back before Christmas. Since this is Cissy's first lying-in, she begs us to stay on until end of Twelfth Night. Your father said that because we took our traveling coach, it would be impossible for you to come all the way to the Scottish border by yourselves. It distressed me to think that you and Rupert would have to spend the holidays alone, but do not despair, dear, for as I was writing this I had the most inspired idea. I shall write to your brother-in-law, Lord Copley, in London, and ask if he can arrange to fetch you to the city to spend the holidays with them.

Mrs. Huxley wrote more about Cissy's home in Jedburgh and about their new son-in-law, and ended saying how pleased she was that she was able to think of something that would keep Millicent and Rupert happily occupied during the holidays. They would exchange presents when they returned in January.

Millicent had been a widow now some five years since Captain Bertram Copley had been killed in the Peninsula. Her only solace was that before his death, her sweet husband saw their baby christened, and knew his son showed no signs of the disfiguring facial birthmark which had marred Bertie's short life. Rupert was perfect, eyes the color of chestnuts like his grandfather Huxley's, and the blond curls of the Copley men which wreathed his cherubic face. An angel and the joy of her life, or so his mother viewed him. In fact, it was the way Millicent saw most everyone—as warmhearted as herself.

The next two weeks passed without a word from Baron Copley, and Millicent despaired that she and her son were faced with the dismal prospect of being alone in the large house on Christmas. Rupert had always had his grandparents and his Aunt Cissy around until Cissy's marriage the year before. Millicent, her spirits never for long on the down side, determined to do everything in her power to give her son a special present to make him happy. Rupert was a practical lad and had never been one to ask for expensive or useless gifts, so Millicent had no fear that he would overstep the boundaries of sensibility and wish for something she couldn't acquire in the village.

They had gone outside to make tracks in the first light

snow when she asked, "Rupert, what would you like more than anything else for Christmas?"

Delight filled the boys eyes. "Oh, Momma, do you really mean I can have anything I want?"

With a smile and a nod of her head, Millicent assured him that she did.

"I want a father."

That wasn't the sort of thing Millicent had had in mind, and she was at a complete loss as to how to reply.

"Robert has a father, and Pokie and Beenie. All four Dowser boys share one, but they don't mind. Why can I not have a father, Momma?"

Unexpectedly, Millicent felt her cheeks burn. "I would have to get married."

"How does someone get married?"

Millicent bit her lip. She'd try to explain it simply. "Well, when two people like each other well enough, they go to a clergyman and tell him they want to live together for the rest of their lives. Then, he has them sign a piece of paper which says it is all right."

"Is it hard?"

"Not if you love someone."

"I am a little young to get married, am I not?"

"Yes, I believe you are. It is better to wait until you grow up."

"Oh," said Rupert, losing interest in the subject the minute a rabbit bolted from the hedge and ran across the yard. Off he scampered after it.

Letting out a sigh of relief, Millicent watched him go. Dedicated to educating and raising her son, she'd accepted none of the proposals which had come her way over the last five years. Besides, how could any man really be of interest to her after her gallant and humorous Bertie? She would have to think carefully how she could sway her imaginative son to make a more realistic choice, but then it was still four weeks before Christmas. Surely by then she'd persuade him to think of something more feasible.

Some twenty miles north of Cross-in-Hand at his country estate in Kent, Ernest Lance, Marquis of Wetherby, oldest son and heir of the Duke of Loude, called his valet. "Jespers, prepare my things. We shall be going to London."

Used to his master's quixotic decisions, Jespers asked patiently. "Is it to be a long stay, your lordship?"

To tell the truth, Wetherby hadn't thought of why he was even making the trip. His spirits were not much for doing the pretty of late, and now that all four of his happy cohorts—the Merry Five, they'd called themselves—had betrayed him by tying the knot, life had lost much of its flavor. None of his new acquaintances had half the imagination for derring-do escapades as he and his friends had hatched.

Wetherby was quite aware that the *ton* considered him to be a handsome devil. He was brown-haired, brown-eyed, medium-tall, of athletic proportion, carefree, and good-tempered. He prided himself on being a sportsman, a bruising rider. However, all these attributes did nothing to assuage his growing boredom.

Upon the death of his mother, the marquis inherited her Orchid Hill estate near Tunbridge Wells, and a small income. Although it wasn't a great deal of money, he didn't need his father's largess anymore to meet his bills. The house had fallen into disrepair over the last three years, but Wetherby had kept on a small staff in case he wished to use it during the hunting season. Now it seemed he stayed longer and longer.

"No, I don't suppose I'll spend more than a few days, Jespers. Just long enough to catch me up on the latest news."

Sir Jonathan Bridges told him on passing through that he'd heard that his last paramour, Mrs. Hawthorne, had taken up with Lord Hazelton's second son. Wetherby couldn't blame the widow. He hadn't been to town for several weeks and he couldn't expect so affectionate a lady to wait for him to call.

Perhaps Genevieve was still available for a few evenings of fun. Dancing girls from Drury Lane were more easily entertained and not in the least demanding. A bauble or two satisfied them.

Wetherby called for his groom. "George, have the coach readied." His mother's old traveling carriage was small and compact. It suited him well enough to transport Jespers and himself back and forth from the city, enabling him to leave his more fashionable coach at the mewes in London. In good weather or foul, he preferred to handle the ribbons himself and usually rode up with the coachman. So his lordship set off for London with very little direction of what he should do with himself once he got there.

Upon arrival at Loude's Hall in Grosvenor Square, he found a letter awaiting him.

> *Roxwealde Castle, Devonshire*
>
> *My dear Wetherby,*
>
>   *I hope this finds you well. Sarah wished to spend our son's first Christmas in the same place she and I met and married. Her parents are coming from Elmsdale to be with us. Since you are the only one of the Merry Five who is yet footloose and fancy free, perhaps you will be able to come for the holidays. Unless of course you have far more exciting escapades on your calendar.*
>
>   *Your friend,*
>
>   *Andersen Copley*
>
> *P.S. I am sure you will be pleased to know that I have not asked Lord Favor or his daughter Lady Caroline to join us.*

Wetherby snorted and thought back to the party the baron had invited him to nearly two years ago at his ancestral castle in Devon. The five merrymakers had planned on taking their pretty lightskirts for a week of fun. Aspiring actresses, they'd called themselves. Instead of the out and out frolic they had all anticipated, it had ended up being a matrimonial pit for four of his best friends. Only he and Lady Caroline remained unattached. Once she'd been the most sought-after debutante of the *ton*—and the target of Wetherby's own pursuit for two years as well—but his interest diminished substantially when she humiliated him by openly snubbing him in favor of the baron.

Lord Copley, however, had surprised them all by marrying his hostess Sarah Greenwood, the daughter of a country squire. Caroline had returned to London, and instead of licking her wounds from her failure to capture the baron, renewed her flirtation with Wetherby. He thought he'd expressed his feelings quite fully when he'd said he wished to have nothing further to do with her, but Wetherby found that Caroline could be a very determined woman when she wanted something badly enough.

Now as he again ran down the letter, a positive thought struck him. A few weeks in Devonshire could very well provide an escape from Caroline's unwanted attentions. It would also give him a good excuse not to have to spend the holidays at his sister Evelyn's house in Warwickshire with her placid husband and their tribe of children. Where, no doubt, he'd also have to take another raking over the coals by his father. "Find a woman of good bloodlines, settle down and produce an heir. That's an order, you do-for-nothing!"

Wetherby began to feel much more the thing. "I say, Jespers, how does Christmas at Roxwealde sound to you?"

The valet maintained his usual noncommittal mask, but the good servant remembered with a definite acceleration of his heart the beautiful old castle which had been the center of a colorful party not two years ago. Of course there was the baron's lion, Dog, who caused Jespers some apprehension, but that was a mere trifle compared to the draw of good food, lively spirits, and a certain pretty little maid belowstairs who had caught the servant's eye. "Whatever suits you, my lord."

The marquis hit the palm of his hand with his fist. "That is it then, by God! We shall go."

Wetherby grabbed some paper and penned off a quick acceptance to Baron Copley. Then with his father's wiggings ringing in his head, the marquis set out for White's, whistling.

The club proved rather quiet that afternoon. A light rain had been falling all day. Wetherby handed over his hat and damp coat to one of the footmen and accepted a brandy from a passing waiter.

Two gentlemen sat in the bow window, Lord Alvanley and Poodle Byng. The former called to the marquis. "Come sit down, Wetherby. Deuced dull day if I do say so myself. Nobody has slipped on the pavement and I had a bet with Poodle here that someone was bound to take a spill in the next ten minutes. Half an hour has gone by and not one soul has taken a tumble. No fun in that."

Wetherby glanced out the window in time to observe two young women of obviously questionable reputation—because they wouldn't have otherwise been on St. James Street—pull up their skirts to avoid dampening their hems in a puddle. The sight sent the blood surging through the marquis's veins. What a pity, he thought, that they weren't allowed to entertain women in their clubs. Liven things up a bit.

"I say, Wetherby, do sit down," Byng rasped. It was considered a privilege to be asked to share the seats in the front window at White's where Beau Brummel himself held sway. Whereas not long ago he would have been amused by their banter, the marquis now found the men's shallow remarks only annoyed him. He made the appropriate excuses to leave their company and wandered into the gentlemen's gaming room. Three men dozed before the fire, while a foursome sat at a table playing whist. From their intense expressions and rumpled clothes, he took it they'd been at it for some time. He stood wondering whether he could find enough men to get up a game, or whether he should amble over to another club. Before he could make such a momentous decision, he was greeted from behind.

"Your lordship, what brings you to London?"

Wetherby turned to face the Honorable John Teagardner, his jovial face and several chins snuggled into his high collar like a red hen on its nest.

"Teagardner," the marquis said, delighted he'd found at least one affable face. "Actually, I was contemplating going over to Waitier's for a good meal."

"Why don't you join Filmore and me at Grillon's. I promised Mrs. Teagardner we'd meet her for lunch." John stepped aside to reveal a slightly-built, nattily-dressed man standing behind him, smiling, not in the least offended by being dwarfed by the young giant. But then John dwarfed everyone.

Teagardner had been another of the eligibles who had succumbed to the edict of his parents to get married and start his nursery. He always did everything in as generous a manner as he was oversized, and started off by having twin sons. The bets that his wife was again increasing were circulating in the clubs, but no one could tell for sure because Mrs. Teagardner was as big around as he.

Filmore stepped forward and extended his hand, his deep voice belying his small stature. "Are you here for the holidays, your lordship?"

"Not really. I've just accepted an invitation to join the Copley family in Devonshire."

"Zounds, Wetherby! In those godforsaken moors?" Teagardner expounded. "Ain't that dangerous? I hear his lordship has wild beasts wandering all over the place."

Wetherby's good humor took a turn for the better. Knowing he wouldn't find anyone with better dispositions than the two men in front of him, he readily agreed to have lunch at the famous hotel. Still, he couldn't resist one backward glance at the card players.

"You won't be able to join them," Filmore said, shaking his head. "Raggett says they've been at it for over thirty-six hours, and Kendale seems to be cleaning up as usual. He took me for two thousand pounds last week. I was lucky. Most of the members think it's dashed unfair that he be permitted to play. They don't consider him *ton,* y'know, but he still manages to get himself invited. They say if it weren't for Lord Blackmere's patronage, the man wouldn't be allowed to set foot in any of the clubs."

Wetherby looked over at the expressionless face of the hawkeyed player who was accepting a note from the Earl of Markham. "I see nothing wrong with the fellow, only that he seems to win every contest he enters. I would like to have a go at him myself sometime." A good confrontation with a worthy opponent, Wetherby thought, might be just the antidote he needed to restore his spirits. However, if the man had been playing for a day and a half now, there would be no challenge in it.

By the time they arrived at Grillon's, their party had swelled to six, because Mrs. Teagardner had invited Lord Boswick and Mr. Elroy Bennington. "I found them languishing at Hatchard's Bookstore," she claimed. "They looked like they needed a good meal."

Wetherby was only slightly acquainted with Boswick's family, but he felt he knew Mr. Bennington quite well. It was at the infamous party at Roxwealde Castle where his sister Anne Bennington had eloped with Henry Smith, one of the original Merry Five. It was at the same soiree, Wetherby remembered with a bit of male pride, that he'd introduced young Bennington to the delights of his first *affaire de coeur* with one of the little doxies.

The meal proceeded in a most pleasant manner, the food excellent and the conversation friendly. The afternoon would have been a complete success had not Wetherby spotted Lady Caroline sitting with friends at a nearby table. She waved, but he acted as though he didn't see her. She was proving to be a real thorn in his side, but the more he ignored her, the more she did to gain his notice. This time she fluttered her handkerchief high above her head. Only Caroline could make such a gesture look charming instead of ill-mannered. Wetherby made a great show of brushing an imaginary spot from his sleeve. Finally, with a certain sense of satisfaction, he caught a sideways glimpse of her raising her nose, and with a sniff, she turned back to her partner.

Mr. Teagardner rapped the marquis on the arm. "I say, Wetherby, you're not listening. M'wife asked you a question."

"Oh, I am sorry, ma'am," the marquis apologized.

Mrs. Teagardner, with a glance toward Lady Caroline, laughed. "I only asked if you are having Christmas with your family, my lord."

Reprimanding himself for letting the termagant make him forget his manners, Wetherby gave Mrs. Teagardner his full attention. "As I told your husband, I am going to Devonshire. However, I do plan to be in town for a few days. I hope we can get together again. The day has been most pleasant."

Teagardner scraped the last spoonful of pudding from his plate. "Wish we could, but we leave for our house near Haslemere tomorrow. Plan to be there for the holidays, y'know. Expect the whole family down from Cambridgeshire."

Wetherby turned to the viscount. "Surely you will be in town a bit longer, Filmore."

The young lord ran his finger around his collar. "To tell the truth, my family wants me home before the week is out. The Bandit King, y'know."

Wetherby frowned and looked at the other two men. "How about you?"

Boswick shook his head. "My father says the same. I'm not to go out at night unless I am accompanied by the four men he has hired."

Only Elroy Bennington answered with a cocky grin.

Wetherby raised his eyebrows. "You don't seem to be afraid of the notorious bandit," he said facetiously.

The young man sat back and folded his arms across his chest. "Why should I be'?"

Mrs. Teagardner gasped. "Elroy, how can you ask that? Your father is one of the richest merchants in England."

"Don't make no difference. The Bandit King only kidnaps sons of noblemen."

Eyes wide, Teagardner looked at the marquis as if the horror of it all had just dawned on him. "I say, Wetherby. You ain't thinking of making that long journey to the Devonshire moors all by yourself, are you? Never know where that jackanapes is going to strike. If you remember, the first Christmas he snatched Lord Brett's son in Yorkshire. The year after, it was two kidnappings, one in Cheshire, the other in Norfolk. Last December he grabbed Baron Duffmire's son right off a street here in London. No telling where he'll choose to do his mischief this year."

The marquis laughed. The chance of meeting up with the Bandit King held little terror for him. He felt confident that he could hold his own with any vagabond. All the victims had been foolish young men from wealthy, titled families. Fearing harm to their sons, their parents had paid the ransoms before notifying the authorities, and the victims had returned telling tales of the polite, masked man whom they had named the Bandit King.

"He always wears a black hood and no one can identify him," Filmore said. "He prints his ransom notes and his only signature is the black pearl he sends to his victims' homes."

"Well, I am not taking any chances with my sons," Teagardner exclaimed. "We'll be at home for the holidays."

Seeing the startled look on Mrs. Teagardner's face, Wetherby said reassuringly, "He doesn't kidnap babies, John."

"One never knows with scoundrels, does one?" the big man said defensively. "I'd be careful if I were you, Wetherby. Why don't you leave a few days early and stop off at our house on your way? Should be much safer than staying at a public place."

"Kind of you. I may just do that."

So arrangements were made and dates set, and although he laughed about it, the marquis was encouraged by friends he ran into to accept their hospitality at their country estates on his journey to Devonshire. Knowing that all the inns along the way would be crowded this time of year, Wetherby humbly acquiesced. Especially when he was assured that several of the households included charming young daughters.

The next few days proved so busy with visits to the bootery and his tailor and the purchasing of Christmas presents that Wetherby found little time to socialize, let alone visit Drury Lane. Genevieve would have to wait. He sent her a small bottle of perfume with his regrets and returned to Orchid Hill. Early Boxer gifts of money went to his staff, and Jespers packed his new wardrobe. With a sense of accomplishment, Wetherby realized he had four days before he was due at the Teagardners'. The trip to Haslemere would only take one full day, which left him three days to relax at Orchid Hill.

Meanwhile in the Huxley manor outside Cross-in-Hand, Millicent had all but given up hearing from Lord Copley when a special messenger arrived bearing a letter. She quickly tore open the seal.

> *Roxwealde Castle, Devonshire*
>
> *My dear sister-in-law,*
>
> *Forgive the long delay in writing to you. Your mother's letter was sent to our London address long after we had removed to Roxwealde. I have just now received it.*
>
> *She explained your circumstances, and though we will not be in London, we insist that you join us for Christmas. However, I would not think of letting you travel over two hundred miles alone with a child when the weather is so unpredictable and bands of thieves lie in wait ready to rob unsuspecting holiday travelers.*
>
> *Therefore, I am making arrangements for you to be escorted by my good friend, Ernest Lance, the Marquis of Wetherby—a most honorable gentleman—whom I*

*would trust with my own life. I have every confidence that
he will see you safely to our door. I have sent a missive
to him by special messenger also, so you should be hearing from him shortly. You met his lordship in London when
Sarah and I came to town after our marriage a year and
a half ago. I am certain you remember him.*

Truly yours,
Andersen

Millicent dropped the letter and clasped her hands to her
burning cheeks. Did she remember the marquis? How could
she forget the handsome rogue and the passionate kiss they
had shared outside in the darkened garden at Lord Copley's
ball?

"Oh, my goodness! How can I face him?"

Two

Millicent took a deep breath and closed her eyes. While the humiliating remembrance of that evening flooded her memory, she tried valiantly to persuade herself that it had been a terrible case of mistaken identity. Or was it? After all, she was the one who had run straight into the circle of Lord Wetherby's arms. From the tales that Millicent had heard of the marquis's character, he was quite used to having women throw themselves at him. It probably had not bothered him one tittle to kiss another woman until his real ladylove turned up.

Millicent picked up Lord Copley's letter and stared blankly at his words, envisioning the large mansion on the River Thames.

The large crush that night at the ball had proven to nearly suffocate Millicent, and she'd sought a moment of solitude in the vast park that ran down to the water. In the daytime the gardens had seemed inviting, but at night, even with the gaslights set at intervals, the twisting paths and maze of high shrubs proved quite confusing. Blackness had engulfed her. She'd found herself impossibly lost and had turned to retrace her steps when she ran head-on into the solid form of a man. Their impact knocked the breath from her. Then, without a by-your-leave, the rogue caught her up in his arms and kissed her.

He broke the embrace and whispered in her ear, "Where have you been, my enchantress?"

Although they'd met only briefly in the receiving line, Millicent had recognized his voice instantly. Ernest Lance, the Marquis of Wetherby. Before she could speak, he'd pulled her full against him and kissed her once more with such intensity that Millicent thought she'd never catch her breath again. She'd not been held by a man like that for over three years, since Bertie. She'd responded and kissed him back. Oh, the shame of her wanton actions would stay with her the rest of her life.

Her lips were still shamelessly pressed to his when a desperate voice—a very feminine one—came from the other side of the hedge. "Your lordship?"

The marquis raised his head slightly and with a voice, husky with passion, whispered in her ear, "Who are you?"

Before Millicent could do more than gasp, the other woman repeated, "Your lordship? You know who I am, but I cannot find my way through the hedge."

With her heart pounding wildly, Millicent had taken advantage of Wetherby's distraction to break loose. She rushed toward the house, but her path led her under the yellow arc of the gaslight, and she thought he might have recognized her. She was sure her fears were well-founded, for when the marquis returned to the ballroom half an hour later his gaze fell upon her. Instantly he made his way toward her. She'd tried to get away, but to no avail. He'd cornered her, and with more charm than it was fair for any man to possess, asked, "My dear Mrs. Copley, may I have the pleasure of this dance?"

What a loose woman he must have thought her to be, to have succumbed to his wiles so readily. She had darted away and sought the refuge of her room. For the remainder of her stay in London, Millicent had done her best to avoid the marquis.

Then and there, Millicent had decided that the hustle and bustle of the big city was not for her, and with a great deal of relief, she returned at the end of the Season to the tranquility of her father's home in Sussex.

Yet as remote as the little village was, gossip about the Quality filtered down to Cross-in-Hand, and Millicent heard that the marquis hadn't married. The rumors had it that he continued to pursue—or was pursued by—half the great beauties of the *ton*. Now here it was a year and a half later, and heaven help her, his lordship was coming into her life again.

Wetherby was taking a turn about his mother's small conservatory. The pale winter light filtering in through the unwashed glass covered the statues and leafless plants in a shroud of fog. The orchids were gone now, the baskets hanging empty. A few potted palms drooped sadly, and ivy vines climbed most everywhere.

He was lost in contemplating how it had once looked when Jespers hurried in. "A messenger from Devonshire just arrived with this missive for you, my lord."

It was another letter from Lord Copley, and began as the other had done; but as the marquis read on, a growing sense of uneasiness settled over him.

My dear Wetherby,
 You remember making the acquaintance of my sister-in-law Millicent in London. I told her you would be happy to escort her and her son Rupert to Roxwealde Castle when you come. It should not pose any undue inconvenience, since they live but a mere twelve or so miles south of Orchid Hill. I have written to her to expect to hear from you in the near future.

Wetherby stared at the letter. "Good God, Jespers! How can he do this to me?"

"Do what, my lord?"

"Lord Copley has asked me to escort his sister-in-law and her son to Devonshire."

"Is that a problem?"

"She lives in Cross-in-Hand. That is south of here by far more than twelve miles, I'm afraid. Also the roads will be muddy ruts this time of year. Haslemere is due west and a day's ride. If we are to be at Teagardner's on time, we shall have to leave a day earlier than I had planned. That will mean Mrs. Copley will have to be ready in two days."

"Can you not inform her of that, my lord?"

Wetherby looked at his valet in utter amazement. "Notify a lady to be ready to leave on a two-hundred-mile journey in two days when she thinks she has two weeks to prepare? You must be mad, Jespers."

Jespers looked suitably corrected. "Yes, my lord, I see your meaning."

The marquis came back into the main house and headed for his study. It was outside of enough that he was being asked to play nursemaid to a country matron and her child.

"Blast! If I'd known this ahead of time, I would have had my family coach sent down from London. 'Tis too late now, I left orders for it to be repainted while I was gone. No telling how many trunks she will have. Just think what that will mean for you, Jespers."

The valet, who had just begun to regain some of his composure, asked apprehensively, "Me, my lord?"

Wetherby seated himself at his desk and pulled out a piece of paper. "You will be crowded inside the carriage with a woman, her child, a maid, and most likely a nurse for the boy."

Jespers's eyes enlarged alarmingly.

In the meantime, while Wetherby was hunting a decent pen, he tried desperately to conjure up a picture of Mrs. Copley. For the life of him he couldn't recall what she looked like. He believed her hair was brown. When he'd been introduced to her, she kept gazing at the floor, and when large groups formed, she would disappear. In deference to his friend, the baron, he'd promised to seek her out at the ball and ask her to dance.

He'd had a devil of a time all evening trying to find her.

It was as though she had been deliberately trying to avoid being seen, but when he finally approached her and asked her to stand up with him, she'd bolted like a cornered animal. He wondered what could have attracted a lively fellow like Captain Bertram Copley to such a mouse.

If Wetherby remembered correctly, that was the evening he'd begun his affair with the willing Mrs. Hawthorne, a pretty widow of good *ton* but of little means. She'd agreed to meet him in the maze, and he thought he'd found her when a surprisingly enticing morsel came flying into his arms. At first he had believed the mysterious woman to be Mrs. Hawthorne, and when he'd received such a heated response to his kiss, he'd congratulated himself. Several men had courted Mrs. Hawthorne, but only a few were fortunate enough to be the recipient of her charms. Then to his shock he discovered that it wasn't his paramour he held in his arms—but another. A strange, warm fairy creature who then vanished as quickly as she appeared. Many times he'd wished he could find her again, but he never did. He began to think perhaps she'd not been real at all. She had to be Venus sent to give him her blessing, because in those few stolen moments, she'd so inflamed his blood that he'd found himself quite easily persuaded to Mrs. Hawthorne's wishes to form a liaison.

Wetherby remembered more vividly Master Rupert. Lord Copley had insisted, "Come Wetherby, you must meet Bertie's beautiful son."

They had gone to the third floor nursery, where Andersen introduced him to his blond, curly-headed nephew. Rupert was the baron's spitting image, except that the child's eyes were brown instead of blue. Wetherby had remembered staring into those dark eyes much the same color as his own, regarding him gravely.

After the baron had taken his leave, Wetherby stayed on to play a game of swords with the boy. He remembered letting the lad win the duel, much to the child's merriment. In fact, finding a willing audience for his wild tales of adventure of knights and their fair ladies—which the marquis had loved to make up since childhood—he had spent, much to his own surprise, the entire afternoon engaged in nonsensical games abovestairs with a four-year-old. Afterward, Wetherby remembered feeling that the time in the nursery was far more satisfying to him than the social chitchat going on in the salons below.

However, he had no illusions that a few hours in a playroom with a child were anything like spending several days with one in a coach. For the first time since he'd received Copley's letter, the corners of his mouth turned upward. Heaven help Jespers.

Now having found all he needed to write a note, Wetherby smoothed out the paper on his desk. "Children are perpetual motion machines, Jespers. Master Rupert will be all over you. You know I always take over the ribbons and will be riding up with John Coachman."

His valet's voice had taken on a decided tone of anxiety. "Perhaps I can sit behind in the rumble seat with the groom."

The marquis dipped his pen in the inkwell and began to write. "What, and have you sick with pneumonia by the time we arrive in Devonshire? You will stay inside. There is nothing for us but to make do. I shall send the baron's rider back immediately to Cross-in-Hand with a note for the widow Copley telling her to be ready in two days."

Master Rupert straddled one of the brick pillars which flanked either side of the entrance gate leading to the Huxley manor. His gaze did not leave the road. He'd been there since dawn, swathed in his winter coat, his woolen muffler wrapped several times around his neck to ward off the damp air. A long, wooden sword painted a silver-gray to look like metal fit snugly in the sheath attached to his belt.

His mother had only told him this morning that they would be making a journey to Devonshire to have Christmas with the Copley family. "We will be escorted by a friend of your Uncle Andy's, the Marquis of Wetherby. I expect his lordship at any time, so you must rise and be ready.

Rupert could not believe his good fortune. Ever since that day in London when the marquis had come to the nursery and played with him, Rupert had thought him quite splendid. Now he would have the chance to be with his lordship every day and learn how to be like him. Rupert had dressed quickly and gone outside to await Lord Wetherby.

Millicent stood below. "Rupert, you must come down now and have some breakfast."

"I cannot, Momma. His lordship may arrive any minute."

"But you only had—" Millicent shrugged and pulled a cherry tart from inside her cape. "Here, take this at least."

"Thank you," Rupert said, reaching for the confection. "Do you think he will be riding a big white charger, Momma?"

"I should hope not," Millicent said. "It would be very difficult for a horse, no matter how big, to carry our trunks on his back."

Rupert snorted. "You know I did not mean that. I am certain he will bring a grand carriage for you. That is one of the rules," he said, stuffing the tart into his mouth and staring back down the road.

Millicent sighed. "Your head seems to be filled exorbitantly with rules and codes this morning, young man." Taking one more anxious look toward the village, she turned back to the house.

She had just reached for the door when Rupert let out a yell. "Momma, he's coming!"

Millicent's hand froze in the air. The temptation to look overcame her and she turned to see a black speck on the horizon growing larger and larger as it sped through the village toward them. Mesmerized, she watched as the maniac holding the ribbons turned the four berserk beasts just in time to skim neatly between the two brick pillars. "It's Lord Wetherby," she gasped. "The man is mad!

From his precarious perch, Rupert waved his sword above his head and urged them onward.

Millicent covered her mouth to keep from crying out, and rushed into the house.

Rupert leaped from his perch and ran after the carriage. Before the groom could descend from the rumble seat, the gentleman dressed in fine boots, several capes, and a tall beaver hat had already thrown the reins to the coachman and jumped down from the high seat. Rupert recognized him immediately. No nobler a man had he ever seen, and in that instant he knew that his dream was about to come true. Lord Wetherby was the man he wanted for a father. Convincing his mother might take a little longer. He was compelled to rush forward, but now that he was a sophisticated six-year-old, he drew himself up as tall as he could and refrained from throwing himself in an unmanly fashion into the marquis's arms.

Wetherby looked with amusement at the boy sporting a red mustache. "Master Rupert, is it not?"

Rupert made a sweeping bow, nearly clipping Wetherby's knees with his sword. "Yes, my lord. Master Rupert Copley at your service."

Wetherby watched half the crimson mustache disappear with a quick lick of the tongue. "What is that?" asked the marquis, trying to keep his attention on the stick in Rupert's hand.

"My sword. A good warrior must always be prepared."

"Ah, true, true. That is a magnificent weapon."

Rupert bent forward and whispered, "It is not really steel."

"Well, it had me fooled," Wetherby said.

Rupert beamed. "Really, your lordship? Our stablehand Devlin made it for me. See, he even carved a design and my initials in the handle."

" 'Pon my word," Wetherby said warmly. "That is indeed a remarkable feat." Then inexplicably, his tone changed, and he said almost sternly, "But, I am here for another reason—to take you to your uncle's. When do you think your mother can be ready?"

"Oh, Momma had everything packed last night."

A look of disbelief spread over Wetherby's face.

"She has been wondering what was taking *you* so long," Rupert said smugly, giving the marquis a sideways glance.

As soon as Millicent was inside the house, she pulled off her coat and handed it to the maid. "Hurry, Sukie! His lordship is coming. Find Beetles and tell him I shall receive the marquis in the parlor."

No matter how one looked at it—from the gray skies above to the gray of her thoughts—the day didn't look promising. Sidestepping the two trunks set in the middle of the hallway, Millicent entered the small sitting room off the entrance hall. A tremor shot through her and she reminded herself for the tenth time that morning of her resolve to remain calm when the marquis arrived. Pulling her shawl up over her head and shoulders, she seated herself in a shadowy corner away from the fireplace, and waited for Lord Wetherby.

The marquis was ushered into the entrance hall by a shaft of wheat in a dark suit. "I am Beetles, my lord. Mrs. Copley says to show you into the parlor."

After the brisk air of the out-of-doors, the heat of the room threatened to smother him. Wetherby squinted. It was so blasted dark, he could barely make out the woman who rose to greet him. Nonetheless, he smiled broadly and put forth his best manners. "Mrs. Copley?"

A shawl covered most of her head and he had to strain to hear her.

"Lord Wetherby?"

He detected a slight movement away from him. She seemed much shyer than he remembered. "Thank you for being so punctual, madam. If we are to stick to schedule, 'tis imperative that we leave as soon as possible." It was all he could think of to say.

"I did not know you had a set agenda, my lord. You should have said," Millicent spoke louder than she meant. "Surely there is time for you to take a little refreshment—coffee, perhaps? Mrs. Woodstock has made some of her delicious cherry tarts and scones with whipped cream."

She looked up at him, and for a second he caught a glimpse of her eyes—gray—plain gray. " 'Twill not be necessary . . ." he started to say more, but got no further before a serving girl clothed in a rich aroma of bakery goods and spices carried in a heavy tray. She placed it on the table in front of the fireplace, and without being told, poured two cups of steaming coffee.

Wetherby had not eaten much that morning, and his mouth began to water as he succumbed to the tempting smell. "Well, perhaps . . . while your luggage is being loaded." As she came out of the shadows, he thought he detected a smile. However, it was hard to tell, for she pulled her shawl tighter around her face. The skies forecast a bitter day, and he hoped she wasn't of such a delicate nature that the long journey ahead would prove to be too hard for her—or a burden to him.

In truth, Millicent was roasting. She could never persuade Beetles that it was not necessary to keep the rooms so hot when her mother wasn't there. She pulled out a handkerchief and patted her forehead. "Please be seated, my lord."

Wetherby took the chair on the other side of the table, farthest from the fireplace, and helped himself to a scone. "If you will have your butler tell my men where you have your things, they can help get the carriage loaded."

"That is considerate of you, my lord. Beetles is getting too old to do any heavy lifting." Millicent turned and spoke to Sukie. "Tell him to show Lord Wetherby's men the two trunks in the front hall."

Wetherby reached for a biscuit. "Where are your other bags?"

"Those are all we have, my lord."

Surely he'd heard incorrectly. None of the women of his acquaintance could possibly take a trip without half a dozen pieces. Niggled by a bit of conscience, Wetherby thought of his own three trunks that he'd had Jespers reduce to two jam-packed ones when he found he'd have more passengers. In addition, there were his three servants' valises and several boxes of gifts he'd purchased for his various hosts. "Certainly that is not all you plan to take—?"

"The quickness of our journey was unexpected, Lord Wetherby. I did not even have time to purchase Christmas gifts for my brother-in-law's family." She hesitated a minute. "I had hoped that perhaps we would have time to do some shopping in the towns we pass through."

The anxiety in her voice prompted him to reply, "Oh, yes . . . yes, we can do that. I do apologize for the abruptness of my note, but what I meant was where are your other wardrobe trunks?"

"There are no others—unless you mean Rupert's and my portmanteaux. But they are small enough to fit under our seats. You did say that we will be staying a few nights at inns, did you not?"

On the pretext of hearing her better, Wetherby leaned closer to try to gain a better look at Mrs. Copley. "What about your lady's maid? Does she not have a valise?" It was obvious to him that she dipped her head purposely to avoid his scrutiny.

"I would not think of taking Sukie away from her family during the holidays. After midday feast, all our servants are allowed the rest of the day with their kin."

Wetherby couldn't think of a less pleasant way to spend a holiday.

"Christmas is a time to celebrate with family, is it not, my lord?"

It had not been so for the marquis for more years than he could remember. His mother had died four years before, but she'd been in ill health for a long time before that. She'd spent a great deal of time in the solitude of Orchid Hill or taking the waters at Tunbridge Wells, seeking relief. Wetherby had been quite fond of his mother really, but he was away at school most of those years and seldom saw her.

Wetherby felt it better that he change the subject. "You do not plan on taking a maid?"

He thought he heard Mrs. Copley chuckle—a delightful sound that rose from deep inside her. "I am used to doing for myself, my lord."

Wetherby couldn't imagine getting along without the ministrations of Jespers. "The boy does have a nurse—or a governess."

"No, I saw no reason to employ one," she replied.

Wetherby frowned. He'd been led to believe that Copley provided generously for the boy's care and talked often of sending his nephew to Eton. Surely the baron would want to be made aware if his nephew was being allowed to run unsupervised without any instruction. If the baron's sister-in-law was neglecting the boy's education and spending his allowance frivolously, wasn't it Wetherby's duty to his friend to look into the matter? She wished to go shopping. He'd watch her closely and observe how she spent her money.

Millicent rose. "Now if you will excuse me, my lord, as soon as I get my wraps I shall be ready to leave."

"Oh, yes, of course." Wetherby sprang to his feet, showering his legs with crumbs, but Millicent was already out the door.

Wetherby brushed off his buckskins and helped himself to another cherry tart. Now that he knew where Master Rupert's mustache came from, he carefully wiped his mouth with his napkin to avoid suffering the same sort of adornment on his chin. Assured that his face was clean, he left the room.

When he next saw Millicent, she clutched an embroidered bag much larger than an ordinary reticule. She wore a brown wool pelisse and a bonnet with a thick veil which covered most of her face. He offered his hand to help her up the coach step, but the instant she placed her gloved hand in his, she withdrew it and entered the coach under her own power.

Wetherby wondered what it was he'd said or done to get him started on the wrong foot with the shy widow. Perhaps he'd stared a little too long, trying to see through the veil. He raised his hand and spoke in an aside to Rupert. "I'm afraid I offended your mother in some way. I did not mean to embarrass her."

Rupert's eyes twinkled. "Sometimes I get confused too, your lordship. The Code does say that ladies are frail creatures, but Momma keeps insisting she is not helpless."

"No, I can see that," said Wetherby, a bit puzzled by what the boy meant by *The Code.* "But we men never know for sure about women, do we?" he finished with a wink.

"No, sir. We do not." Rupert giggled and tried to reciprocate, but he'd never winked before and he feared he did a very poor job of it.

Jespers, coming close behind, took one look at the sword dangling from Master Rupert's belt, and insisted on climbing into the rumble seat with George.

Inside the coach, Millicent kept her head down until she heard the carriage door click. "Is he gone?" she whispered.

Rupert removed his sword and carefully placed it beside him on the seat. "Yes, Momma."

"Good," Millicent said, with a deep sigh of relief, leaning back against the squabs.

Rupert glanced over at his mother. "What were you searching for on the floor?"

Millicent felt the heat rise to her face. "One never knows when one will find a lucky penny," she prevaricated.

"That is a capital idea," Rupert said, looking at the floor of the carriage, then back up at his mother. "Oh, you are bamming me, aren't you Momma?"

Millicent's ready laughter turned to alarm as she saw her son press a finger to his left lid and contort his face. "Whatever are you doing, Rupert? Did you get something in your eye?"

"I'm winking."

"For heaven's sake! Wherever did you learn such a thing?" Millicent held up her hand to silence him. "No, don't tell me. I have a very good idea." She would not allow Rupert to be led astray by that vagabond. Whether or not her brother-in-law thought he could trust his own life to Lord Wetherby was his own business, but she knew that when it came to the safety of her son, the rogue would bear watching.

Three

As Lord Wetherby prepared to mount the driver's box, he heard a burst of laughter. What an extraordinary woman. One moment she acted like a frightened rabbit, the next her gaiety hinted of an altogether different nature.

In one fluid motion, he leaped up to the high seat. "I shall handle the ribbons, John," he said. As the coachman relinquished the reins, the marquis called down for the tall, gangly Devlin to release the bridle of the lead horse, and at the same time, he glanced back to make sure all was clear. Beetles, three women and two other men stood in front of the pleasant country manor, waving. He never remembered his father's servants seeing his family off when any of them left their various estates. Although all the Huxleys weren't going to be home for Christmas, the front door was framed with pine boughs and sprigs of holly. It looked very much like a part of a holiday pageant, and for some reason, instead of producing a smile, the thought made him sad—and he didn't know why.

Wetherby cracked his whip. The bays sprang forward, catapulting the carriage down the driveway.

They rode for three hours before stopping at a small country inn to eat lunch and to rest the horses. Millicent and Rupert climbed back into the coach, and instead of closing the door behind them, Lord Wetherby asked, "May I join you? We will be traveling together for the next two weeks, and as yet, we have had little time to get to know one another."

Rupert let out a chirp and quickly pointed to the seat next to his mother. "My sword takes up so much room I wouldn't want you to be uncomfortable, my lord," he said innocently.

Wetherby removed his hat and stood humbly awaiting Millicent's invitation. To his amazement and with some annoyance, the woman hadn't uttered one word since they'd left Cross-in-Hand. Now, she merely nodded and edged over as far as she could away from him. He settled himself on the seat and motioned for George to close the door. With a wink at Rupert, the marquis faced Millicent; but that puzzling lady seemed to have found something of greater interest to view out the small window. He wondered what there could be about him that prompted her to turn to the window every time he addressed her. Wetherby was used to women encouraging his interest, and now he found himself at a loss as to how to address a female who gave him the back of her head. He chose to ignore her snub altogether. "While we ride, I can acquaint you with our itinerary," he said, with utmost smoothness.

However, regardless of his mother's cold reception, Rupert couldn't hide his enthusiasm at having the marquis join them. "We thought you got lost this morning," he said, inching as far forward as he could without falling into the marquis's lap.

Wetherby was not accustomed to being in such tight quarters with children. He sat back and folded his arms across his chest. "I *did not* get lost," he said defensively.

"That is all quite all right, my lord," Rupert said. "Most people watch for the windmill." Then making a careful study of the marquis's posture, he inched back against the squabs and crossed his arms.

Wetherby caught the mimicry. Eyes twinkling, he relaxed. "Yes, I saw it. 'Tis a good landmark."

"Well, next time you come to visit us, you will know what to look for."

Mrs. Copley suddenly gained her tongue. "Rupert! You

must not talk to his lordship in such a straightforward manner."

Wetherby jumped, but it seemed that her tone startled him more than it did her son. However, Rupert looked over at him so apologetically that Wetherby felt obliged to rescue the boy from further tongue-lashing. "I realize there was little time to explain at the manor—to tell you that I received an invitation to the Teagardners' in Haslemere. You may have met them at your brother-in-law's in London." He was glad to see that that diverted her attention.

Millicent clasped her hands together and faced him. "Oh, dear. Were the Teagardners expecting you tonight? Andersen . . . that is, Lord Copley, led me to believe that you would be taking a straight route to Devonshire, and it would not be out of your way to fetch us. If I'd known it would be an inconvenience, I would not have . . ." She didn't finish.

Once Rupert saw that his mother was now off on another tack, he settled back and stretched his legs the length of the seat, knocking his sword into Wetherby's knees and stopping his mother's apology in midsentence.

Wetherby heard the quick intake of breath from behind the veil. Without losing his smile or taking his eyes away from Millicent, he quickly handed Rupert his weapon. "My dear lady, let us hear no more on the subject," he said smoothly. "Believe me when I say that it has not been an inconvenience, but my pleasure, to serve you."

Rupert's eyes gleamed their approval. "That is Number Five of the Code, is it not?"

Feeling at a complete loss as to the codes the boy kept referring to, Wetherby didn't know how to react, so he simply nodded. Presently, Rupert became absorbed in watching the snowflakes that began falling outside, and soon had his nose pressed to the window.

Wetherby tried to maneuver in such a way as not to crowd Mrs. Copley, but he couldn't escape his leg pressing against hers in the tightly packed coach. Even with the thick robe covering her, he felt her quiver at his touch—as if any contact with him could prove dangerous. The poor little mouse wouldn't even be a mouthful for his appetite. He gave her what he hoped was his most reassuring smile, but how could he guess her reaction behind that demmed silly piece of gauze? "Have no fear, madam. I sent a message ahead from Orchid Hill informing the Teagardners that you and your son will be accompanying me. In fact, I received several other invitations to stop over at friends' on my way to Devonshire."

He had to lean toward her to make out her soft reply. "Oh, I am sorry if we have caused you to miss out on anything."

"But you have not. I sent word to them also. All the houses have adequate facilities and are used to entertaining many guests. We will be stopping at the Maudlins' in Hampshire. They have two daughters who have already been presented at court. Lady Maudlin has arranged a holiday ball. I also received an invitation further on in Somerset from my friend Sir Jonathan Bridges, a congenial old bachelor who loves company. His sister lives year round at their ancestral home, and he is spending the holidays with her there. Everyone has promised parties aplenty. Fear not, you will not have a dull moment."

Again Wetherby was met with silence, yet he sensed she was watching him, so he doubled his effort to bring her out. "Tonight, however, since we cannot reach Haslemere before dark, we will probably stay over near Horsham. It is a pleasant market town with a variety of stores."

Originally the marquis had planned to go directly from Orchid Hill to the post road at Guildford, which would have taken him south to Haslemere. Now, because of this unexpected and inconvenient detour to Cross-in-Hand, he'd have to cut across Sussex through tiny hamlets and narrow country lanes, most of them muddy traps at this time of year.

Not a word came from behind the veil.

Wetherby's smile froze on his face. What did she have to be so prickly about? It was he who'd been thrown a whole day off schedule, not the other way around. Yet he was the one trying his damnedest to be pleasant about the situation. "You mentioned wanting to purchase some Christmas presents, and I thought since we do not have to make such an early start tomorrow as we did this morning, perchance you would like to take a look in some of the shops before we continue."

She clapped her hands so quickly, she nearly startled him off the seat. "Oh, that will be delightful!

Wetherby was just congratulating himself for having finally seduced some positive reaction from his reluctant traveling companion when the coach lurched, tilted dangerously to one side, and came to an abrupt stop, throwing all three passengers into a tangle of arms and legs on the floor.

Rupert quickly clambered back up on the seat and started jumping up and down on his knees. "Oh, that was a jolly good spill, was it not, my lord?"

Wetherby clasped Millicent's shoulders and raised her gently to a sitting position. Her bonnet sat sadly askew, and as one might do for a child, Wetherby reached over and put it straight again. The veil hung tattered and torn down one side of her face. It was a pleasant face, he thought: young, gray eyes wide, lips half parted. More like that of a girl fresh out of the schoolroom who had never been kissed. Wetherby removed his hands. What was he thinking of? The woman was mother to a six-year-old boy.

"Are you all right?" he asked her, just as Jespers opened the door.

Millicent nodded. She made a few futile attempts to drag the veil back over her face, before she shifted her gaze to her hands in her lap.

"I'm glad," he said, watching with a surge of male pride as the color crept into her cheeks. She would be such an easy conquest, he thought. What a pity Lord Copley had appointed him her protector. If their circumstances had been different and she were more adventurous, their journey could have proved most interesting. With a shrug, Wetherby turned to answer his valet's anxious enquiries. "We are all fine, Jespers. Is anyone hurt?"

"It does not seem so, my lord. The coachman says we hit a pothole. He's checking the wheels. The groom says the horses are all right."

"Thank God for that," Wetherby exclaimed. Stepping from the vehicle, he took a closer look at his servant. "Jespers, your face is blue and your nose as red as a beacon. When we get under way again, I want you inside."

The valet looked apprehensively at the boy, who was climbing out of the coach with sword in hand.

By now they had attracted a number of fellow travelers: farmers, a tinker, and one of the local gentry on horseback, all asking if they could help.

While Wetherby was assuring the crowd that nothing was seriously wrong, he glanced sideways to see Rupert, his sword withdrawn and at the ready, walking stoically beside him.

The coachman approached him. "There seems to be no damage to the vehicle, yir lordship."

"But you have a bad bruise on your face, John."

"Nothing worse than I've had b'fore."

"Nonetheless, it looks a nasty blow. You climb back up with George. Jespers will be riding inside. I can handle the ribbons alone."

The coachman chuckled. "Seems ye have a partner a'ready."

Wetherby looked up to see Rupert sitting in the driver's box, then back at the unmoving Jespers, whose eyes were riveted on the interior of the carriage.

Wetherby walked back to where he knew Mrs. Copley could see him, and called over his shoulder, "Master Rupert, perhaps your mother will permit you to help me drive the coach."

Rupert shrieked, "Oh, Momma! May I?"

Wetherby gave Millicent one of his most trustworthy smiles, and raised his eyebrows. From the disapproving look she gave him, she obviously did not share the same opinion of his abilities to tend to her son. However, she had finally nodded her assent. Jespers quickly climbed in. With one last glance at Millicent, Wetherby closed the door. He hoped she wasn't going to be so missish the entire trip.

Wetherby swung himself up and took his seat beside the wide-eyed boy. A snowflake settled gently on the end of Rupert's turned-up nose, melting almost instantly. "What did she say?"

"She gave her permission."

"Oh, jolly good!"

Wetherby reached over and wrapped Rupert's muffler one more time around his neck. "It might be a good idea to sheath your sword."

Rupert eyed the long stick. "But what if we are attacked?"

"I don't believe we need to worry about that in broad daylight. Besides, I don't see how you can possibly hold such a formidable weapon and handle the ribbons at the same time."

Rupert looked at the reins in the marquis's gloved hands. "Me?" he said, then quickly plunged his sword into its sheath. "You are right, my lord."

Wetherby signaled for his groom to release the horses.

"You are going to teach me how to drive neck or nothing?"

The marquis chuckled. "That I am," he said good-naturedly, placing his hands over Rupert's. Now that he had the loquacious child out from under the wing of his protective mother, he'd surely be able to glean some helpful information from him. A sliver of guilt ate at Wetherby. He wasn't used to the feeling, but he was determined that it was his duty to find out what the widow was doing with all the blunt Lord Copley was sending her.

Rupert wriggled as close to the marquis as their thick clothes and his sword permitted.

Wetherby grinned down at him. "I'll have you tooling along with the best of them in no time at all."

"Just like you, my lord?"

Wetherby threw back his head and laughed. "Of course, just like me."

As the horses sprang into action, Rupert reveled in the feel of the strong, hard body next to his. The marquis's hands, completely encompassing his, were both strong and gentle. Rupert savored the brisk wind, the clippity-clop-clop of the horses' hooves, and the closeness of Lord Wetherby. He wanted very much to lean his head against the great coat and savor the moment, but that of course wouldn't be in keeping with his new grown-up situation, and he sat boldly upright once again.

The only thing he truly wished for was that his mother could be with them. He wondered why she'd been so quiet since they'd left Cross-in-Hand. She didn't seem to take too well to Lord Wetherby. It wasn't at all like her. She liked everyone. Maybe she was just bored, all shut up in the coach. Momma loved excitement. She was very good really with the ribbons, and had even won a race driving their donkey cart against Mr. Brussels's old cob and wagon. Next time they stopped he would mention it to the marquis, and maybe he'd ask her to sit in the box with them.

The snow fell faster. Rupert opened his mouth and let the moist flakes tickle his outstretched tongue. He heard a deep chuckle from above and, embarrassed, snapped his mouth shut.

"I haven't done that in a long time," Lord Wetherby said.

Embarrassed to think the marquis would think his game a childish one, Rupert looked up, not quite knowing how to respond.

The marquis was letting the snowflakes fall on his own tongue, then, eyes sparkling, asked. "Did you ever get your tongue stuck on an icicle?" He didn't wait for an answer before going on, "I did once. Learned my lesson fast."

Rupert laughed. "Me, too." Oh, he had to make his mother see how much fun his lordship was!

* * *

Inside the coach, Millicent raised her hands to her bonnet. *Your brains must have gone begging for you to let Rupert go off with that madman,* she chastised herself. Her veil hung in shreds. It didn't much matter. Lord Wetherby hadn't recognized her nor did he remember kissing her in the garden in London. She would have seen it in his eyes if he had. She should have been relieved, but she wasn't. Disappointment was more what she felt.

A shiver of apprehension ran through Millicent, and she clasped her hands in her lap to keep them from shaking. When Lord Wetherby had asked her if she were all right, she had only nodded, because she'd not been able to say anything with him being so close. He'd studied her with those dark, shadowed eyes and said, "I'm glad," as if he really meant it. Oh, she could see that the marquis was a dangerous and wicked man.

Millicent looked up as if she could see right through the roof of the carriage. Rupert was right when he told her, "Soon I shall be a man and then you will not be able to keep up with me." He needed a father, a just and honorable gentleman who could watch out for him. She must stop being selfish and begin to consider marrying again.

As Millicent thought of the men who had courted her, a cloud of dismay settled around her. There was Mr. Peebles the shopkeeper, who had a squint and couldn't put two sentences together; Devinian, Squire James's son, who would inherit his family house and two hundred acres of fine farmland when his papa died but spent all his time, and much of his father's money, gambling; and Mr. Ketchup, a widower with three grown children. who was old enough to be her father. The other two men who'd asked for her hand had married long ago. She sighed. There had to be someone out there who would be up to the mark, but until she could attract such a paragon, she'd have to protect her son from scalawags like Lord Wetherby. Rupert winking! The very thought of it brought a blush to her face.

A stifled cough startled Millicent. Lord Wetherby's valet sat observing her with great interest from the opposite seat. Wrapped in her own thoughts, she'd forgotten all about him. Although his muffler was wrapped to his bulbous nose and his hat was pulled down to his ears, he still shivered uncontrollably.

"Goodness," she cried, all concern for herself evaporating, "you must take this robe." But as she gave him her fur coach rug, she noticed he favored his left hand. "Oh, my, you have hurt yourself," she said sympathetically. "Why did you not say?"

"It is only a slight twist, madam," Jespers mumbled through the thick layers of wool. He watched her warily as she leaned over and tucked the rug in and around his legs.

Millicent gave him a sympathetic look. "Nonsense. Nothing is just *slight* if it hurts. Let me see it," she said firmly.

The servant obeyed, holding out his arm like a child to his mother.

Millicent peeled back the edge of his glove and pressed the flesh gently.

Screwing up his face, Jespers made quite a pitiful sight.

"You have sprained your wrist." Millicent reached into the space between her and the side of the seat, pulling out a large linen bag. She extracted a piece of cloth and tore it into strips. "I shall bind it up." As soon as she'd wrapped his wrist, Millicent pulled his glove over the bandage and placed his hand carefully on the coach rug with a little pat.

"There now," she said, "doesn't that feel much better?"

Adoration shown in the valet's eyes. "Yes, madam," he said, relaxing with a sigh. Five minutes later, Jespers was snoring.

Millicent melted back into the squabs and once more looked out the window, seeing nothing. What a pickle! She didn't even know how to attract a man. That was her failing. She didn't know how to flirt. There had been no one to teach her, least of all her mother. Her parents were all that were kind and giving, but they'd grown up as neighbors and melded into marriage as if it were the most natural thing in the world. False pretense was foreign to their nature.

She had just celebrated her sixteenth birthday when she'd met the humorous, outgoing Captain Bertram Copley at a seaside picnic. Their courtship was short, and with the war hanging over them like a dark cloud, her parents had permitted them to marry. A year later, Rupert was born, and Bertie dead, killed in battle.

Four years later, Millicent had embarked with the greatest of expectations on her first trip to London to meet her new sister-in-law's family. Bertie's brother, Andersen, Lord Copley, had married the daughter of a country squire like herself. Not only was Sarah Greenwood friendly and generous, but Millicent's and Sarah's fathers found that they were both related through the dowager Countess of Dankleish, who had been a Huxley. It was at the countess's mansion near Kingston-on-Thames that Millicent had stumbled into the arms of Lord Wetherby. Oh, the humiliation of it. It only emphasized the fact that she didn't know how to go about in polite society. The strain had been more than she could bear, and it was with a great deal of relief that she had returned to her father's house in Cross-in-Hand with her son.

Atop the carriage, Wetherby found that Rupert didn't need much prompting to divulge his life history the way he saw it. "My grandfather is mayor of Cross-in-Hand," Rupert said proudly. "Momma says that is a very important job—nearly as important as fighting in the war. Momma said you are a marquis and will be a duke someday and could not go to war because you are an only son."

So she had been discussing him with Rupert. Wetherby remained silent and let the boy run on.

Rupert nodded knowingly. "I suppose you have been studying awfully hard to be a duke."

Wetherby circumvented what he considered a sticky subject by digging for more of the information he wanted. "My school days are long behind me and of little import. But tell me about your lessons. Your mother said she does not feel it necessary to hire a governess for you?"

"Hah! I am too old for a governess. I am six years old, and being tutored to go to Eton. Momma pays Mr. Tipple to teach us. He fought in the war like Papa, only he didn't die—he just lost his legs."

"She hired a crippled soldier to instruct you?"

"Momma says he isn't crippled in his head and that is what is important."

"I stand corrected," Wetherby said, hoping he'd not said something to disrupt the boy's discourse. "I did not mean that he was not capable." But it sounded to Wetherby as though she'd just brought the man in off the streets. Why hadn't she engaged a tutor from one of the fine preparatory institutions?

Rupert didn't seem to notice the marquis's reticence. "Grandpapa had a schoolroom made in the back of the stables, so that Mr. Tipple doesn't have to go up and down stairs. He has a chair with wheels on it. We take turns pushing him."

"Who are *we?*"

"Momma and me . . . and the others."

"Ah, children of the local gentry?"

"No, Sir Alden's sons live in the big manor on the hill and have their own tutor. Jason Hibbit already goes to Harrow. Then there are the Collings. They have only daughters and their own governess until they go away to some school for girls in London. But there is the curate's son Robert and his sister Penny." Rupert stopped a minute, obviously running the names over in his mind. "Billie Bee is the blacksmith's son and Momma thinks she just about persuaded his father to let his daughter come, too. Then there are Christina and Angie Strawberry who come on their days off from working in the big house on the hill, and the four Dowser boys when their father can spare them from the farm. Pokie and Beenie are our stableboys. Momma says they have no excuse for missing school." Rupert laughed at that. "Of course there is Sukie . . . Momma insisted she at least had to learn to write her name."

Wetherby was not quite sure he'd heard right. "But that is unheard of—servants being taught to read and write?"

"Momma says it is just as important for girls to be educated, too."

"I mean . . . how can a farmer pay for four sons? How can serving girls afford tuition?"

"Momma pays Mr. Tipple. She says that Uncle Andy gives her lots and lots of money. More than we can ever use, and when we can do good for others, it is selfish of us to keep it all for ourselves."

Good God! Wetherby thought. He'd wondered why her wardrobe was meager enough to go into one trunk. Copley would be fit to be tied to find out that the monies he was sending for his nephew's comfort were going to servants and a crofter's sons. Wetherby felt little relief in finding out that she was not using her allowance selfishly, but rather irresponsibly. Foolish woman. Her naivete wouldn't be appreciated by the local gentry either when they found their servants demanding better wages and fewer work hours.

Wetherby could see that Mrs. Copley needed someone who could manage her affairs and keep her from squandering her son's allowance on ill-conceived schemes and misdirected charities. That was what Wetherby decided he would tell the baron as soon as he saw him. And he would also urge Lord Copley to find his sister-in-law a husband as soon as possible.

Four

That same afternoon in London, Lady Caroline Cavendish, beautiful beyond reason and quite accustomed to having her own way, was just rising from her bed. "How dare Wetherby treat me that way? I could not sleep another minute for thinking about it."

Suzette looked at her employer and shook her head. "It is no wonder, *mademoiselle,* after the way you rebuffed his lordship. But I do not see why you persist to let it bother you after your father ordered you not to see him."

Throwing her arms wide, Caroline flounced back onto her pillows, spreading her golden curls in an arc around her head. "That is because Papa needs a son-in-law who is deep in the pockets to pay his bills. He says the marquis does not have the ready, yet I do not see that it stops him from acquiring anything that pleases him."

Caroline curled a lock of her long hair around her finger. The only child of the Earl of Favor, she was quite aware that she couldn't go on forever unmarried. Although her father had told her that he didn't consider the Marquis of Wetherby eligible for her hand on his small allowance, she couldn't keep from being on the lookout for the jackanapes.

The effect of the earl's edict only served to make the marquis appear more attractive. Yet all her attempts to entice the stubborn man were getting nowhere. When she hinted that she'd be staying in London over the holidays, Lord Wetherby had had gall to tell her, "I'm sorry, my dear, you will have to find someone else to entertain you. I shan't be here."

Caroline jumped off the bed and began to pace the room. "I overheard him accept an invitation to the Teagardners' while I was dining at Grillon's. Then at Lady Sefton's I heard Lady Maudlin say that Wetherby was going to spend a couple of days at their country house in Hampshire on his way to Lord Copley's. They have two daughters they wish to marry off, but the eldest, Prethoria, is quite certain that he is coming especially because of her. Silly girl! Knowing Wetherby, he will dally there a few days and be off. I heard he'd received enough invitations to set him up for a month, but I know he has to be at Roxwealde Castle by Christmas. It is for certain that with all his charm he will not have to stay at many inns along the way." She turned to Suzette. "Have you found out if he has left London yet?"

The petite woman held out her mistress's robe and waited for her to shrug into it. *"Oui.* He has gone back to his estate in Kent."

Caroline tapped her chin with her finger. "Then he must be leaving from there. Have you found out any more information on what his itinerary will be for the trip?"

Suzette tied the sash around her mistress's slender waist. "I have, *mademoiselle.* Your chambermaid Jesse has a sister in Lord Wetherby's residence here in town, and she has told her of all the invitations his lordship has received for the holidays. Your coachman likes the cook's daughter, and he told her that the marquis's men spoke in the mews of their route. I can find out exactly where his lordship plans to stay."

Caroline looked at her companion with a new appreciation. "You are a great asset, Suzette."

Suzette held her head proudly. "Your father was kind to me. He gave me employment when I had no means."

Caroline gave a very unladylike snort. She knew her father had hired the girl because she was cheap. But for a fraction of a second, Caroline wondered about the war in France

which had caused those like Suzette to lose all their wealth
and position—but it was only a passing thought. The little
dark-haired woman was French, and such an occurrence
would never happen to someone like herself. After all,
Caroline was British. Besides, there were more important
matters that concerned her now, such as the exciting game
of recapturing the attention of the Marquis of Wetherby. A
little shiver of anticipation ran through her.

"Suzette, make me a list of all the homes Lord Wetherby
will be visiting during the holidays."

"Oui, mademoiselle."

"And I want my trunks brought down from the attic."

"Oui, mademoiselle. Is there anything more?"

Caroline sat down at her dainty escritoire. "I went to
boarding school with Prethoria Maudlin. She came to
Cavendish Hall in Gloucester last year; now it is her turn to
entertain me." Caroline riffled through her supply of station-
ery, selected a few sheets, crumpled most and threw them
to the floor. "As soon as you make up the list, fetch me some
fresh paper. I have several letters to write."

While she waited, Lady Caroline began to devise her plan.
The marquis could not escape her forever.

Half an hour before sunset, Wetherby turned over the reins
to his coachman and spoke to Rupert. "I don't want your
mother blaming me if you catch your death."

Rupert snorted.

Wetherby was not used to small boys, so it took awhile
before he finally realized that more than a suggestion was
needed to get Rupert back in the carriage. However, he had
a feeling that an outright order might start a rebellion.

Rupert looked at him slyly. "I should not wish you to
catch your death either, my lord. If you promise to come
with me, I shall ride inside."

"Checkmate!"

Rubert grinned smugly.

Wetherby, glad that he'd been able to resolve the situation without bloodshed, boarded the coach.

Now they approached the outskirts of the market town of Horsham. "It is not large by any means, Mrs. Copley, but I think you will find the Pig and Goose a quite exceptional inn," Wetherby said as they pulled into the courtyard. He had still not managed to further engage the widow in any meaningful conversation; yet that didn't stop him from maintaining an amiable facade. "I have stayed here often and found the accommodations comfortable and the food excellent."

Anticipation of things to come made Wetherby smile as he looked out the carriage window at the familiar two-story stone building. He always received a warm reception at the Pig and Goose, and unless the proprietor Ben Feverfew had managed to marry off his obliging redheaded daughter since his last visit, Wetherby would expect as much tonight. The detour may have been well worth the inconvenience.

Wetherby was not disappointed. Just as their party entered the common room, Clara Feverfew came from one of the private parlors with a tray full of dishes. Her flaming hair couldn't stay hidden under the mobcap, nor could her well-rounded charms be disguised by any number of aprons. He sent her a message with his eyes, but he was sorry to see she missed it, because she was glaring at Mrs. Copley.

"Oh, I say, she *is* very pretty, is she not, my lord?" a voice piped from somewhere under his left elbow.

Guiltily, Wetherby jerked his gaze away from Clara and looked down at the boy standing beside him. He was beginning to feel as though he was growing a second skin.

"Rupert, where are your manners?" Millicent spoke sternly.

Rupert tried to look repentant.

Caught off guard, the marquis winced. The woman's eyes were like a hawk's. She stood, lips pursed, looking at her son—but somehow Wetherby felt that her censure was meant for him.

A beefy man with long sideburns hustled toward them. "Lord Wetherby. How good to see you, milord."

"Feverfew." Wetherby inclined his head, and without missing a beat, orchestrated a well-ordered arrival. "George, have the lads set the night bags down at the foot of the stairs until I register. Jespers, see that they are directed to the proper rooms." Only then did he turn to the big man bobbing his head up and down in front of him. "I would like a room for my charges, Mrs. Copley and Master Rupert. I am seeing them safely to her brother-in-law's, Lord Copley, in Devonshire, for the holidays." He said this louder than was necessary, but unfortunately he saw that Clara had already disappeared into the kitchen. He was sure he could straighten out any misconceptions the hoyden had about his and the widow's relationship later. Aloud, he said, "I will have my usual."

The proprietor rubbed his knobby hands together. "Anything your lordship wishes. A room for the lady and the boy is available now, but there will be a little delay while your accommodations are made ready." Which meant someone was already in the rooms and would be told to move.

Wetherby could have easily said that he'd take other facilities, but the rear apartment was much more to his liking—and—convenient to the back stairwell which he liked to use to come and go as he pleased. There were decided advantages in having a title. "We will want a private dining room and one of your wife's delicious meals as soon as possible. We are quite famished."

"Oh, yes indeed, I am quite famished, too," Rupert echoed.

Wetherby quickly remembered his manners. "Mrs. Copley, forgive me. You surely want to refresh yourself after the long journey." He gestured toward the stairs, where a serving girl stood waiting to take them up to their room.

He thought the widow was about to say something to him, but instead, she addressed her son, "Come, Rupert."

Wetherby watched them go, then handed his hat and coat to Jespers and entered the parlor. "Have wine sent in. I can wait in here while my room is being readied." Wetherby settled onto a chair in front of the hearth and stretched his legs toward the fire, letting his mind drift off pleasantly to the evening's entertainment he anticipated for himself after he'd done his duty and seen mother and son off to their room after supper. Let no one ever say that the Marquis of Wetherby lacked *savoir faire*. He chuckled. Mrs. Copley would surely disapprove of what he planned for the evening. Strangely, her pursed lips came to mind instead of Clara's full red ones, and he wondered what it would be like to kiss them.

Millicent entered the bedroom behind the serving girl. The marquis had no scruples whatsoever. He couldn't even stop his rakish ways when he was among strangers. She'd much rather have been running about the countryside with Rupert, instead of being cooped up in that coach all day. He probably thought no one saw the unconscionable way he'd looked at that innocent young girl belowstairs. What a racket. Was no one safe from the Marquis of Wetherby? Apparently not.

As soon as their portmanteaux were placed on a stand and Millicent was shown the trundle under the high bed, the serving girl curtsied and prepared to leave.

Millicent threw her a smile. "Thank you, dear. I shall speak to Mr. Feverfew about how kind you have been. The bed looks lovely—not a wrinkle—and you arranged the towels in such a pretty pattern on the rack."

The girl looked at her, unbelieving "Oh, ma'am, no one ever notices the little things I do."

Millicent glanced around the small and pleasant room.

"Well, they should. 'Tis plain you took great effort to make things tidy for your guests."

"If you wish for anything else, ma'am, you just ask for Sally," the girl said breathlessly. Then bobbing a deep curtsy, she closed the door behind her.

Rupert had already pulled off his hat and scarf and shrugged out of his coat. "Can we hurry, Momma? Lord Wetherby will be waiting for us. I am going to ask if he will play a game of chess with me after we have eaten."

If she'd had her choice, she would have had supper sent up to their room. Well, one more hour with his lordship couldn't be that bad, and she was starving. The aroma of roasting meat and freshly baked bread wafted up from below. Millicent removed her bonnet and tugged her mobcap into place in front of the mirror. Since the knave obviously had no recollection of their encounter in London—an encounter which had haunted her for a year and a half—she had no further reason to hide her face from him. "I think we shall eat supper and come right back to our room," she said a little peevishly.

Rupert's pleading eyes held no sway over his mother.

"Don't you want to find a present for your Uncle Andy?"

"Oh, yes, Momma. And something for Aunt Sarah and Percy, too."

Millicent smiled lovingly at her son. That seemed to give him another train of thought to pursue. "So if we want to be up early to go shopping tomorrow morning, we shall get to bed as soon as possible."

Which is what they did. But Rupert had never been in an inn overnight before, and after they had said their prayers and his mother had fallen asleep, he lay on the trundle listening to the somewhat raucous voices echoing up from below, mostly male, he noticed. How did men act and what did they talk about when they were away from the ladies? How was he ever to find out if he didn't have a father to tell him?

He would keep a close watch on the marquis to find out how to go about it.

Unhappily, Rupert's plans for his mother and Lord Wetherby were not going as well as he wished. They had barely spoken to each other at supper. The marquis was too formal when he was around her—his manner quite different than it had been when the two of them had been tooling across the countryside atop the carriage—and his mother wasn't any fun at all. Then after they'd eaten, Momma had whisked him upstairs before he'd had a chance to ask the marquis to play a game of chess. His lordship was doomed to spend a lonely evening speaking to strangers. It wasn't fair.

Rupert tossed restlessly, running all sorts of schemes around in his mind. Sleep had totally flown out the window. Curiosity, restlessness, and temptation had taken their place. He must see if he could find the marquis.

Wide awake now, Rupert slipped out of bed and dressed. He thrust his sword into its sheath and opened the door as quietly as he could. Stealthily, he crossed to the end of the corridor and pressed his nose through the bannisters. Most of the ruckus was coming from the taproom at the end of the commons area. Rupert quivered. He knew he dared not descend those stairs, for he'd surely be sent packing right back up again. He had to find another way down where he could watch the goings-on and still remain unobserved.

Rupert heard a door open and close nearby. He held his breath and flattened himself against the wall. The sound of footsteps led away from him and soon faded. Cautiously, he followed the sounds to a back stairwell. He had forgotten there would be servants' stairs which would lead to the kitchen and rear courtyard.

He crept down the steps to a black hallway. The rattle of pots and pans and muffled voices came from the right. Not quite sure which doors led to what, he opened one. A lantern hung on the wall bathing shelves stacked full of sacks and containers with a pale yellow light. He had just concluded that he'd have to go to the length of the hallway to find the taproom, when he heard a squeal—high-pitched and excited—a woman in distress! Rupert swallowed hard. He'd never rescued a woman before, and he was sadly in doubt as to how one went about it. However, he'd read enough daring tales about chivalrous knights to know that the faint of heart never won fair maidens. There was no one that he could see to call to for help. Rupert was on his own.

Again the cry came, louder this time, and very near. Rupert ran to a heavy wooden door that was slightly ajar, and pressed his ear to the crack. He heard shuffling noises and knew there was a struggle within, but now the lady's cries were muffled and he feared for her life. A shiver ran down Rupert's spine and sweat dampened his brow, but he was a stout lad. Drawing out his sword, he bravely threw his shoulder against the door and heaved it open. "On guard!" he called out into the shadows.

To his astonishment, the marquis rose up before him, a maiden swooning in his arms. "My lord!" Rupert cried in relief. "Thank goodness you are here. I see you have saved the fair lady already."

"What the deuce!" If Wetherby could have disappeared through the floor, he would have. Clara raised herself quickly from where she lay back in the marquis's arms, and stared mesmerized at the small person who stood before them waving a wooden stick in the air.

"Are you all right, my lady?" his voice piped. "Did you see who her assailant was, my lord?"

Wetherby shook his head in disbelief.

Rupert turned concerned eyes back to Clara, who now stood stuffing her hair back under her mobcap. "I hope you were not frightened too badly, my lady. Do you know who the knave was? He must be punished."

Wetherby, striving to regain his composure, said, "I think he has been punished enough, Master Rupert. Now, what are you doing belowstairs?" He looked uneasily over the boy's shoulder, as if looking for someone. "Where is your mother?"

Rupert shifted from foot to foot. "She is asleep, my lord."

"And you sneaked out. That was naughty, was it not?"

"Yes, my lord. But just think what would have happened to the pretty maiden if we had not come along when we did." Rupert cast a shy glance up at Clara, then bowed. "May I escort you back to the kitchen, my lady?"

Clara, her eyes still glistening, her lips full and pouting, brushed down her skirt. "I think I hear my father calling me," she said, and with a toss of her head, marched out the door.

Wetherby sighed. "I think it is time you returned to your room, also."

Rupert watched Clara go, then sheathing his sword, turned bright eyes on Wetherby. "I think I shall have to tell Momma about your brave exploit, my lord."

Wetherby took the boy's free hand and led him out into the corridor. "I don't think that a wise idea at all, Master Rupert."

"But tonight you combined both Codes Four and Five. That is quite remarkable, my lord."

Wetherby frowned. Whatever the devil this code business was, he wasn't about to ask the boy now, or he'd never get him to bed. "A deed bragged about loses its value. Besides, if you tell your mother about me, she will know that you disobeyed her."

Rupert hung his head. "I broke Number Three, didn't I? I shall have to put an X in my journal, and I have not had to put a bad mark in for ever so long. Mr. Tipple said it was quite remarkable that I had done so well for four straight weeks." He blinked back the moisture welling up in his eyes. "I'm sorry if I am a disappointment to you, my lord."

As a tear spilled over and ran down Rupert's cheek, an unfamiliar surge of tenderness tugged at the marquis's heart, and he grabbed wildly for an antidote. "If I combined Four and Five, as you said I did, then you must have done also. Surely that means something." Wetherby crossed his fingers that it worked.

"Oh, do you think so, my lord?" Rupert perked up hopefully. "Yes, I must have done."

"Ah," said Wetherby, more in relief for himself than for Rupert. "So I should think that Four and Five combined would cancel out your one minor infraction of Three." He had no idea of what they were talking about, but he prayed it worked.

The frown on Rupert's forehead disappeared instantly. "Oh, you must know if it is so, my lord."

On the contrary, Wetherby was beginning to think that he knew nothing—especially about little boys. The fact that he'd been one himself at one time didn't help him at all. However, they were now at Rupert's bedroom. He saw the boy inside, and quietly closed the door behind him.

God! How could one small boy wreak such havoc in so short a time? Wetherby decided he had two choices: he could go downstairs to join those in the taproom, or he could go to his own room. He chose the latter. The evening was already in shambles, and for some reason his desire to go after Clara had left him.

The next morning, a light sprinkling of snow powdered the ground. After a warm meal in the private dining room, the three set out to explore the shops. Wetherby called for his carriage, but Mrs. Copley, with a surprising show of willfulness, stuffed her hands inside her muff and insisted she wanted to walk into town. "It is such a short distance, my lord."

Finally, they reached a compromise. They would go into town by foot, but the coach would drive in later to carry them back to the inn.

The marquis took his fine walking stick, and Rupert his

sword. Wetherby was beginning to think that the child would look undressed without it.

Holiday decorations appeared everywhere. Wreaths decorated the shop doors and evergreens framed the shop windows. Bells tinkled when the shop doors opened, much to Rupert's delight. Confectioners' shops were especially set up to tempt small boys, and Wetherby insisted on stopping in nearly every one to buy some sort of goodie or another.

Rupert discovered a little tea shop where a nativity scene made of bakery goods and confection was featured in the middle of the shop window—they specialized in Christmas biscuits shaped like camels and stars. Wetherby insisted they buy a box to take to the Teagardners, and of course bought a sack for Rupert.

Millicent finally protested. "You will spoil him, your lordship."

He saw her nose wrinkle, and he suspected she was trying not to smile. "I doubt that," Wetherby laughed. "He seems a sensible boy." In truth, Wetherby hadn't had so much fun in a long time. His sister's children were so rotten that they merely asked what else he had for them once they'd opened all their gifts. Before he thought, he found himself calling, "Happy Holidays" to the proprietor as they left the shop.

But it was the young widow who captured Wetherby's attention. He heard her laughter and turned to see the two of them running from window to window, pointing at some gimcrack or another. Wetherby had a hard time keeping up with them. It was as though they had forgotten he was with them, and a sense of being left out unsettled him.

At one time when Wetherby had caught up with Millicent, Rupert had completely disappeared from view. They found him peering down an alleyway at a passel of urchins who were rummaging through a trash barrel. He collected Rupert and was about to give the boy a scold for running off, when Millicent disappeared. After a few minutes of frantic searching, Wetherby found her coming out of the same alleyway, closing up her reticule.

"The children said their mother is ill and they had no food," she said, as if that explained the matter.

"Good God, Mrs. Copley! You must not go about without an escort," Wetherby scolded.

She looked at him as if he belonged in Bedlam. "In Cross-in-Hand I go everywhere by myself."

He wasn't sure his meaning was getting to her. "But you must not do so where you are a stranger in a strange town. You never know who means to do you harm."

"Who in the world would want to harm *me?*"

Wetherby looked at her upturned face and couldn't answer that either.

His lordship's scrutiny unsettled Millicent, and she quickly changed the subject. "We only have a little time and I must buy gifts for the Teagardners. You say they have twin sons, my lord? How old are they?"

Wetherby looked blank. Her eyes twinkled. Why had he thought her eyes plain? They were like soft gray clouds with flecks of gold in them.

"When were they married?"

"The twins? They are only infants."

Millicent put her hand over her mouth and for a second he suspected she was trying not to laugh. "I mean . . . when were Mr. and Mrs. Teagardner married."

Wetherby gave a crooked grin and concentrated on the answer. "Just before pheasant-hunting, if I remember correctly . . . two seasons back."

Her laughter came softly from inside her. "That sounds just like a man. I calculate then that the children must be under two years of age."

Wetherby had the uneasy feeling that she was making fun of him. He had thought his to be a very logical answer.

Millicent selected two rubber balls, one red, and one blue.

Later, she purchased a pair of gloves for Mrs. Teagardner and a silk scarf for the woman's husband.

Wetherby didn't know why he bought Mrs. Copley the expensive cashmere shawl. Perhaps it was because it reminded him of the purplish-pink fragrant orchids his mother used to raise at Orchid Hill, their clove-scented fragrance filling the air each June and July. Perhaps it was because he saw her admiring it and he wanted her to have something prettier than that plain brown coat she wore. When she was attracted to a display of ribbons, he quickly paid the clerk and tucked it under his arm, handing it to her when they arrived on the street.

"Oh, my lord, you should not have." She held it to her face and looked at him for just a second, questioning. The color, he noted, brought out the pink in her cheeks.

Wetherby realized it was the first time he'd bought a gift for a lady without expecting anything in return—unless it was to have one more of those few and fleeting smiles. She didn't disappoint him.

He coughed. " 'Tis time we get back to the inn for a bite to eat before we go." Wetherby said. "It should not take us more than two or three hours to reach Haslemere."

Rupert frowned. Wetherby put it to the child's reluctance to leave the shops, but by the time they returned to the inn, he knew something was definitely bothering the boy, but he couldn't figure out what it could be. Perhaps his mother had been right, and he'd eaten too many sweets. Yet the boy ate a hearty lunch without complaint.

But now there was no time to find out, since John had the coach ready. For some unexplainable reason, Wetherby found himself selecting to ride inside, as did Jespers, who was showing a great deal of attentiveness to Mrs. Wetherby, and beat the marquis in assisting her up the step. So all four crowded in together and set off for the Teagardners'.

One look at her son's Friday face, and Millicent didn't beat around the bush. "Is something wrong, Rupert?"

The boy wriggled on the seat and gave the marquis a pleading look. "No, nothing, Momma."

"It is not like you to be tired. We went to bed so early last
night you should have had a good night's sleep. Well then,
it will be off to bed early for us both tonight. We have had
a busy day."

Wetherby was still concerned about Rupert, but glad that
at least Mrs. Copley had seemed more kindly disposed toward him since he had given her the shawl. She sat now with
it draped across her shoulders. For a moment when she
turned to the window, he saw her hold the soft fabric to her
cheek. While she was absorbed in the sights outside the
coach, Wetherby leaned toward Rupert and said confidentially, "I want you to know that if there is anything that you
need talk to me about—man to man—I shall always be glad
to hear you out."

Rupert forced a smile as his gaze flicked to his mother.
He told himself that he must set aside his own concerns for
the moment and rejoice in the new developments between
her and his lordship. The look Momma had cast in the marquis's direction when he had presented her with the colorful
shawl gave Rupert hope that his lordship was gaining some
favor in her eyes. To Rupert's way of thinking, if the marquis
was too modest to brag about his feats of honor, it was up
to him to make his mother realize how brave his lordship
was. That thought renewed his spirits completely, and Rupert
decided then and there that he must reveal to her what he'd
seen with his own eyes. Then she would realize how brave
his lordship was and what a perfect father he would be.

"Momma, I must tell you how Lord Wetherby rescued the
pretty, red-haired maid at the inn last night."

Five

Millicent's eyebrows shot up to her hairline.

Rupert was happy he'd gained his mother's attention so quickly. Before he lost it again, he breathlessly recounted the entire tale from the attack on Miss Clara by an unknown assailant to finding Lord Wetherby with the swooning girl in his arms. Oh, he could see that his mother was impressed by the way her eyes widened and her mouth popped open without a word coming out. Thus encouraged, Rupert proceeded to describe in greater detail everything he had seen the marquis do the night before. If he embellished the story a bit, he felt himself justified, for he wanted to paint his lordship in the most dazzling light possible. "Don't you think Lord Wetherby is a very bold and daring man, Momma?"

Rupert hadn't meant to embarrass his lordship, whose face was now a brilliant shade of red, but it was well worth the effort to see his mother absolutely speechless. Even Jespers seemed moved by the tale, for he was shaking all over.

Rupert sat back quite satisfied. His plan to make his mother take notice of his lordship's many outstanding attributes was working perfectly. If he received a scolding for having left their bedroom without Momma's permission, then so be it.

Millicent didn't know what to think. Rupert had been with her in their room all night. He must have had a terrible dream. Oh, she hoped so. What other explanation was there for it?

The marquis had been so kind to them all morning. Then there was the unexpected gift of the shawl. Or was it all a ploy to cover up his tryst? She'd found out firsthand in London that he had a penchant for kissing the ladies. But how could Rupert become privy to the rogue's assignation? Millicent chewed on her lower lip. No matter how much she wanted to laugh at her son's silly story, deep down she feared there could be some truth in it

As Rupert's tale turned exceptionally graphic, Lord Wetherby's presence became all the more evident to Millicent. His maleness filled the small coach, triggering feelings she'd long forgotten. Pictures flashed across her memory. She saw a young couple running through the meadow hand in hand, falling into the high grasses, lying in each other's arms. Heaven help her! Her thoughts were becoming those of a wanton woman, and she was too ashamed to look at him for fear he could read her thoughts.

For the next three hours, an uneasy silence engulfed three of the four occupants in the coach—until late in the afternoon, when they entered the great woods of Haslemere. Wetherby supposed it to be not more than four o'clock; yet under the dense umbrella of ancient pollards, it was already night.

Rupert, with his face to the window and his sword in his hand, seemed oblivious to any strain. "Oh, Momma, do you suppose we shall see any dragons?"

"I imagine they are out there, dear, but I doubt if they will let themselves be known to us."

Wetherby was glad to see a smile finally grace Mrs. Copley's face as she and her son became caught up in the make-believe world of their own. She seemed to have accepted her son's story of Clara's rescue as nothing more than a figment of a child's overactive imagination. At least, he hoped so.

The Teagardners' large manor house stood in a clearing on the lower slope of the high Black Down. It was impressive more in its size than for its architectural splendor. There were deer prints in the thin dusting of snow along the carriageway,

and though it was winter, there seemed no evidence that formal gardens existed even in summertime.

They were greeted at the front door by John Teagardner himself. "Welcome, welcome," he shouted, as if they were a mile
away instead of only a few feet. "So this is Mrs. Copley. Glad
to see you again, ma'am—Wetherby. Bangs, take their wraps."
A short, stout fellow in livery stepped forward, followed by a
sliver of impeccability dressed in black who detached himself
from the shadows and came to stand beside Teagardner. "Popper here will see you to the library—Mrs. Teagardner doesn't
want to mess up the sitting room." He didn't explain that statement any further, but fell into step beside Rupert. "You must
be young Master Copley. My, my, how you've grown. This way,
everyone. Mrs. Teagardner is waiting."

Millicent, Wetherby, and Rupert dutifully paraded behind
Popper and their host down the hallway and through the double doors off to the left. A shambles greeted them. The floor
was strewn with torn papers and toys. A huge log blazed invitingly in the deep fireplace. Plump Mrs. Teagardner struggled up from where she sat on the floor, stepped over one
crawling baby, then another, and greeted her guests. "My, oh,
my, you must be Millie," she said, holding out her arms to
Millicent.

"Mrs. Teagardner," Millicent said, the corners of her
mouth turning up.

"Jane. Just plain Jane, dear. Wetherby," she said, "do come
in. Just be careful you don't trip over anything. And this must
be Master Rupert. Go over and play with the children, dear.
Oh, I didn't mean you, Rupert. I meant Mr. Teagardner. Now
let us all sit down here somewhere—" She bustled around
putting pillows back on the sofas and sweeping a cloth rabbit
off onto the floor. "John insists on having the children with
us as often as we can. He says they are more fun to watch
than a kennelful of puppies. Of course, we knew you'd want
to see them right off."

The two roly-poly babies crawled over to the marquis,

clutched the tops of his boots with sticky hands, and proceeded to pull themselves up.

"Ain't they something?" Teagardner crowed. "Only nine months old and already trying to walk."

No matter how ambivalent her feelings were toward Lord Wetherby, Millicent's sense of compassion came to the fore. Taking pity on his plight, she extricated one pair of sticky hands from the marquis's formerly spotless trousers. The instant she picked up one infant, the other plopped down and howled. Rupert dug out one of the rubber balls from his mother's satchel and rolled it to the child. The crying stopped.

Considerably relieved, Wetherby dragged a chair as far away from the hazard area as possible, and was about to sit down when a commotion erupted outside in the hall.

The doors flew open and a whirlwind in deep blue velvet sailed into the room. Her blond mane, curled and coifed, and her trim-waisted figure, bespoke the daughter of a peer. "Ernest, darling," she said, extending both gloved hands to Lord Wetherby, "what an unexpected surprise!" Before he could react, she stood on tiptoe and kissed his cheek.

Millicent rose quickly, the baby still in her arms.

Teagardner laughed heartily. "Oh, forgot to tell you, Lady Caroline arrived only this afternoon too. Ain't that a coincidence?"

Rupert jumped to his feet, eyes wide with wonder. In that instant, he knew he had fallen in love.

Wetherby eyed Caroline warily. He didn't miss her familiarity with his first name, and he could see that the Teagardners and Mrs. Copley didn't miss it either. Disentangling himself from her arms, he bowed formally. "It is indeed a surprise to find you here, Lady Caroline. May I present Mrs. Copley. You may have met in London some time ago."

Rupert rounded to Wetherby's side, and studied his lordship's every move with great intensity.

Caroline narrowed her eyes and assessed Millicent. "I'm

afraid I didn't have the pleasure," she said, casting a look of suspicion at the marquis.

Wetherby didn't think Caroline would acknowledge a country girl like Millicent even if she *had* met her. "I have been asked to escort Mrs. Copley and her son to Roxwealde Castle for the holidays."

"Andersen's sister-in-law?" Caroline looked in horror at the child chewing on the corner of Millicent's shawl and pulled her scarf tighter about her shoulders, as if to save her own clothes from a similar fate. "I didn't think she was your type, Wetherby," she said only loud enough for the marquis to hear.

Millicent thought Lady Caroline one of the loveliest women she'd ever seen. She couldn't blame Lord Wetherby for being enchanted by her. She tried her best to curtsy, but soon found it an impossible feat while holding a wiggly child in her arms. "My lady," she said breathlessly.

"Charmed," Caroline said, never once lowering her chin from its exalted state. "What a lovely shawl, my dear—"

Millicent placed the baby on the floor. "You are most gracious to mention it, Lady Caroline. Lord Wetherby gave it to me."

Caroline stepped back and studied Millicent. "Really? I hate to tell you, but it is all wrong—totally inappropriate for that drab-colored suit."

Millicent looked longingly at Caroline's fine attire. "I agree with you wholeheartedly, my lady."

The chit's concurrence threw Caroline off balance and completely cancelled the clever barb she'd had on the tip of her tongue.

Millicent leaned closer and said confidentially, "I am afraid from the dark looks he is casting my way that Lord Wetherby thinks the same as you. He probably feels his stature lowered considerably, having to escort such a country goose as I."

A sudden surge of feminine rage ran through Caroline. "How dare he?" she found herself saying. "No matter how high in the instep Wetherby considers himself, he has no right to insult a woman."

"Oh, please do not mistake what I meant," Millicent said. "I am quite aware that I never acquired the high state of polish such as you possess. In Cross-in-Hand, I am afraid I never thought beyond dressing modestly."

"Good heavens! You come from Sussex." Caroline said it in such a way, that it seemed a statement that explained everything.

Millicent became thoughtful. "But now that I think of it, his lordship did buy me the shawl yesterday and asked me to wear it right away. I had not thought until now that he may have been embarrassed to be seen with me."

Caroline huffed. "What business has that bounder to be passing judgment on what a woman should wear? Men meddle too much in affairs they have no business meddling in." She looked harder at Millicent. "However, the fact that I am a woman makes it perfectly proper for me to give you a few suggestions along those lines, my dear."

"Oh, my lady, you are too kind."

Caroline was about to agree when Teagardner called for her attention. "Here, here, Lady Caroline, you haven't met Master Rupert yet."

Rupert tried desperately to imitate the marquis's graceful bow, but he was unable to move.

"Rupert!" Millicent said. "Remember your manners!"

His mother's words broke the spell. Rupert fell to his knees at Caroline's satin-slippered feet, and bowed his head. He wanted to tell the lovely lady that he would be her servant forever, but his tongue remained glued to the roof of his mouth.

Caroline stared down at the curly blond head, and for once in her life, she couldn't think of a word to say, either. She never cared for children nor particularly wanted to be near them, and here was one paying her the homage she expected of all men. She could think of nothing else to do but pat him on the head.

Lightning from heaven had struck Rupert twice in as many minutes: once when his vision of the perfect woman glided into the room; and now when she had given him her blessing, anointing his head with her touch.

"How sweet," Caroline cooed, looking smugly at Wetherby. "Some gentlemen know how to treat a lady."

Rupert scrambled to his feet and ran to stand by the marquis. "She is an angel, is she not, my lord?"

Wetherby put his hand on the boy's shoulder and gave it a squeeze. He didn't want to disillusion one so young. The lad would soon learn the truth about women like Caroline—probably the hard way—as was the wont of most of her suitors.

"Well, now," Mrs. Teagardner said, "here is Nurse Picking and Nina to fetch the boys." A friendly-faced, angular woman and a young serving girl stood in the doorway. "Rupert, dear, go with Miss Picking. Your things have already been taken to the nursery."

The exaltation that had lit Rupert's face for the last few minutes was extinguished with those few words. No one except Wetherby noted the change, the drooping shoulders and downcast eyes, as the boy obediently followed the two women and the twins out of the room.

Mrs. Teagardner had already turned to Millicent. "I have given you a room in the west wing next to Lady Caroline's apartment, dear. I do hope you don't mind that yours is smaller, but she had her companion with her and quite a number of trunks to accommodate. Lord Wetherby said you were not able to bring your abigail with you, so I have assigned Mercy to help you in any way that you wish. She is a cheery girl and most obliging."

"I am sure she will do just fine," Millicent said.

"The girl should be in your room now unpacking your things," Mrs. Teagardner said. "Popper is in the hall and will point you in the right direction. I am sure Lady Caroline will not mind showing you your room when she goes up. Wetherby," she said, turning to the marquis, "your valet has already had your things taken into the east wing. That is to the right. Now, if everyone will excuse me, I must see the cook about the pudding. Dinner will be at seven o'clock."

Caroline sniffed and walked off ahead of Millicent, up two flights of stairs to the landing of the second floor. Two large potted plants stood sentinel at the corners of the stairway that led to the third floor. The two women continued down the hallway to the left, and when they reached the third door, Caroline pointed elegantly with a wave of her hand, then proceeded on, still not saying a word.

"Thank you," Millicent called after her.

After the abrupt dismissal, it was with some surprise when two hours later Millicent opened to a knock to find Lady Caroline standing outside her room, dressed to the eyes in silvery-gray silk and lace, her hair trimmed with green ribbons that matched her emerald necklace. "May I come in?" she asked, sweeping in without waiting to be invited. Her gaze took in the pile of clothes on the bed. "You are not ready yet?"

Millicent patted the bun at the back of her head and looked sadly at the two frocks, a dark green with a bluish tint, and a brown that was lighter than her traveling costume. "I sent Mercy down to iron my blue muslin. I could not make up my mind which one to wear."

Caroline threw up her hands. She'd never seen anyone of supposedly good breeding who knew less about fashion. "These are terrible," she said, picking up the dresses, then dropping them into a jumble on the bed.

"I know," Millicent said, in desperation. "I would give anything to be as modish as you, but I am afraid I am a hopeless case."

Caroline agreed, of course, and could not pass up the temptation to show the little country chit how right she was in her assessment. She opened the clothes press and looked inside. "You must have something with more possibilities."

Millicent peered over Caroline's shoulder as if she hoped to see a miracle happen, and a beautiful frock of magnificent hue would appear which Caroline had somehow overlooked.

At that moment, Mercy entered the room carrying the blue gown.

Caroline snapped it out of the maid's hands and viewed it from every angle. "It will have to do," she sighed with resignation.

As soon as Mercy had buttoned up the back of her frock, Millicent began to cover her hair with her mobcap.

"Oh, for heaven's sake!" Caroline cried, throwing her hands into the air. "You do not plan to wear that dustmop on your head."

"I don't have anything other," Millicent sighed.

"Where is that shawl Wetherby bought you?"

Millicent hurried to get it, and handed it to Caroline.

"Stand still while I figure out what I should do with you." Now caught up in the opportunity to show her superior expertise as a lady of high fashion, Caroline draped the soft cloth over Millicent's head, then drew the corner up and over one shoulder. "Do you have a pin of some sort?"

Millicent pointed to a small box atop the dressing table.

Caroline opened it and rummaged through the modest collection of necklaces and eardrops. "These are useless. You, gel," she said to Mercy, "go next door and tell Mademoiselle Suzette to fetch my jewelry box."

"Oh, my lady, I cannot possibly expect you to lend me any of your fine jewels," Millicent lamented.

"Nonsense, I can do as I please," Caroline said, opening the door for Suzette and telling her to place the chest on the table. She withdrew several pieces before making her selection, a delicate gold and multi-jeweled clasp that she used to pin the shawl on Millicent's shoulder. "There, that will have to do. It gives you a little color, and since we will be sitting down, the lower part of your frock will be of little import. Now show me the fan you plan to take."

"I left it at home," Millicent said. "I did not think I would need it visiting my brother-in-law."

"It? Surely you have more than one."

Millicent blushed. "A fan is only needed in the country to keep cool in the summer or to swat flies."

"Heaven forbid!" Caroline expounded impatiently. The young widow presented her with a challenge she'd never contemplated—and Caroline was ready for a fresh challenge— one which would give her an excuse to be near Wetherby. "You are nothing but a lump of clay ready for molding," she said, starting for the door. "But . . . a bit of advice before I go. Don't look straight into people's eyes—it confuses them."

"It does?"

"It does—especially if it is a man. Flutter your lids and glance up through your lashes—like this." Caroline illustrated.

Millicent tried.

"You look like someone who has a speck of dust in her eyes. Don't you know how to flirt?"

Millicent sighed and confessed, "No. I fear it is one of several of my shortcomings. The marquis said that we will be attending a party at the Maudlins' Hampshire estate in a few days, and I would give anything to learn how to go about it. I watched you at the Countess of Dankleish's in London— just the way you twirled your fan was magnificent. It seemed almost as if it spoke a language all its own."

Caroline bathed in Millicent's adulation. "It does." she said solicitously. "Tonight before we retire, we shall have a little coze and I can show you some movements. Perhaps I can find a fan to loan you. I always bring one for every ensemble."

"You are so kind, Lady Caroline."

Caroline shook her head. The gel had no idea how to play the game, but she seemed biddable enough, and it might prove amusing to teach her some of the tricks of *le beau monde.* Caroline preened in front of the cheval mirror. "I see that helping you has unraveled a couple of my curls. I must go back to my room to have Suzette recomb them. I shall see you at dinner, Mrs. Copley."

"But it is nearly seven o'clock now," Millicent said.

"A lady is never prompt," Caroline said, sweeping out the door.

Nonetheless, Millicent proceeded toward the head of the stairs and had just reached the end of the corridor when a small figure jumped out at her from behind a potted plant. "Rupert!" She no sooner got the words out of her mouth than she saw Lord Wetherby approaching them from the east wing. She lowered her voice to speak to her son. "Whatever are you doing here? And why are you dressed in your Sunday clothes?"

"Momma, I don't want to eat in a nursery with babies."

"Where do you plan to eat, then?"

The marquis was now upon them. "What is this I hear? You are expected to eat in the nursery? A fine young man of your education and maturity? Unthinkable!"

Rupert threw him a grateful look.

By now Caroline had joined the party. She raised her eyebrows at the sight of the child.

Millicent saw no alternative but to tell the truth. "The blame must be laid at my feet, I am afraid, my lord. Rupert is allowed to eat with his grandparents and me at home. He has done so since he was four years old."

"Oh, I say," came the jolly voice of their host from the floor below. "Is everyone hungry?"

Wetherby saw the stricken look in the boy's eyes. "We shall see what we can do," he whispered, placing his hand on Rupert's shoulder and guiding him down the stairs toward their host.

"I say, Teagardner, don't you think that Master Rupert here is a fine young lad—on the brink of manhood?"

The big man took out his quizzing glass and bent over to observe Rupert better. "By Jove! Indeed he is."

Lady Caroline followed close behind. She fluttered her

fan, then snapped it shut. "Really, Wetherby, I never knew you to take to children."

Millicent watched carefully, and even though she held no fan, she tried to move her hand in rhythm with Caroline's. She sadly concluded that she did a poor job of it.

Wetherby caught the strange movements out of the corner of his eye, but kept his downward path until they stood on the next landing. "Don't you think a lad of his stature should eat with the adults?"

Rupert glanced hopefully back and forth at the two men.

Teagardner bounced his several chins up and down. "I can think of no reason why he should not. Popper, see that another place is set at the table. That will please Mrs. Teagardner, y'know. She was just saying 'twas a pity we were short one man to make an even number. Much obliged to you, Master Rupert, if you would join us."

They had all now reached the hall below, and Popper announced that dinner was ready to be served.

Wetherby bowed to Mrs. Teagardner and as he offered her his arm, spoke again. "Teagardner, you cannot expect a guest to take his own mother into dinner, now can you? I am sure that Master Rupert would make an excellent escort for her ladyship."

"Oh, right, your lordship," the big man boomed, extending his arm to Millicent. "D'you mind, Lady Caroline?"

Caroline did not miss the comradery in Wetherby's eyes as he winked at Rupert. She'd been told that there comes a time when a man begins to think about starting his own nursery. The thought of getting into bed with the marquis did not bother Caroline one bit. If being sweet to the boy was what it took to bring Wetherby to heel, she would play the game. She bathed Rupert in a brilliant smile and curtsied. "Master Rupert, I shall be honored to have you escort me to dinner."

Rupert held out his arm the way he'd seen Lord Wetherby do. The moment Lady Caroline placed her hand on his, he

was sure he'd evaporate into thin air, but when he saw that
he hadn't, he raised his head high and proudly walked his
princess into the dining room.

Six

Dinner went quite well, considering. The Teagardners were excellent hosts. Mrs. Teagardner never let the conversation lag, and Mr. Teagardner made sure the footmen kept the plates full and the wine flowing. Rupert was even allowed a small amount of watered-down claret.

Millicent tried to engrave on her mind every inflection of Lady Caroline's voice and every graceful movement of her hands, so that she could repeat them later.

Rupert, seated to the left of Mrs. Teagardner and beside Lady Caroline, did his best to keep his nose above the table and not spill any food onto his lap. Occasionally, when he cast a glance in the direction of his mother, a shadow came over his eyes, but he quickly recovered and basked in the glory of the lovely lady beside him.

Lord Wetherby was alternately amused by his hostess's chatter, suspicious of Caroline's overzealous interest in the boy, and fascinated by the strange twists and turns of Mrs. Copley's wrists. Rupert's odd mood swings confused him, but he put it down to the child's excitement at being permitted to eat with the adults.

Finally satisfied that all their guests were thoroughly stuffed, Mrs. Teagardner led the ladies into the drawing room. When the gentlemen joined them after their port and cigars, they declared it a delightful but exhausting day and all said their good-nights. John Teagardner, however, begged the marquis to come see his collection of butterflies in the library before retiring.

Rupert delayed as long as possible after Lady Caroline had left, hoping to be included, but when he saw that he wasn't, he reluctantly followed his mother.

Millicent was not fooled by Rupert's attempts to prolong the journey to the second-floor landing. The pale yellow light of the candles cast flickering shadows up and down the hallways. "There is nothing for it," his mother said. "You must return to the nursery for the night."

"Why can I not stay with you, Momma?"

His request presented a quandary for Millicent. If Lady Caroline came to her room for a coze, she couldn't have a six-year-old listening in on her lessons in flirting.

"I don't want to sleep with babies, Momma."

"Of course, you don't," came a deep voice behind them. "No man wants to sleep with babies."

Millicent jumped. She hadn't heard the marquis come up the stairs behind them, but she was too much out of countenance with her problem to be startled. "And where do you propose for him to sleep, my lord? In the corridor? My room is too small," she prevaricated.

"Hmm," Wetherby stalled. The wine had mellowed his brain and loosened his tongue more than he had thought. Now he was in the pot. "Meant to tell you how lovely you looked tonight, ma'am." He did think the shawl wrapped around her face gave her something of an ethereal look—like the Virgin Mary in the nativity scene at St. Vincent's. No, that really was not what he was thinking. He managed a weak smile. "There is a spare room across from mine. I don't think the Teagardners will mind if he stays there."

"Oh, Momma, please?"

Millicent had an uneasy feeling that whatever she decided was going to lead to trouble somehow, but she knew Rupert would be very unhappy if he had to go to the nursery. Besides, she was certain that one night near Lord Wetherby couldn't erase all that she had taught her son over the last six years.

"Well . . ."

Rupert gave a whoop. "Oh, thank you, Momma." Then, remembering his manners, he bowed to the marquis. "Thank you, my lord."

"But, Rupert," Millicent said, "you don't have your night-clothes. I would hate for you to upset Miss Picking. Do you think you can get your clothes without waking the babies?"

"Oh, yes, Momma," Rupert cried, running to the corner of the stairway. He pulled out his portmanteau and his sword from behind the potted plant where he'd hidden them, and hurried back, smiling smugly.

Millicent fisted him on the arm. "You," she said, giving him a kiss on the cheek. "You knew just what I would say."

Rupert popped her back. "Fooled you that time," he chortled, turning and running toward the east-wing corridor. "Good night, Momma."

"Just for one night, Rupert," she called after him.

"Yes, Momma," his voice echoed back from somewhere far away.

Wetherby saw the byplay and grinned. "The little devil!"

Her laughter caught him off guard. "Yes, he is sometimes." The smile was still on her face as she turned to look up at him. "Good night, my lord."

Wetherby raised one eyebrow. "I believe you forgot something, Mrs. Copley," he said. And without so much as a by-your-leave, he cupped her face in his hands and kissed her on the cheek. "Good night," he said.

He smelled of wine and slightly of tobacco, and Millicent heard him chuckling as he walked away from her. Her hands went to her face. My goodness, whatever had he meant by that? Lord Wetherby's inclination to kiss came at the oddest and most unexpected times, she thought, as she scurried to her room.

* * *

Wetherby caught up to Rupert halfway down the corridor. God! Fine escort he was turning out to be. He'd wanted to take Mrs. Copley in his arms and kiss her thoroughly. He was totally reprehensible, he thought with a grin. It had to be the candlelight and the wine.

"My chambers are here," he said to Rupert, opening the door and calling inside. "Jespers, Master Rupert will be staying in the room across the hall tonight. Would you fetch him a pitcher of water and some towels." That done, the marquis walked into the room opposite and lit the candle on the table beside the bed. It was a pleasant room with a sizeable bed, a single window, and the usual table, chair, and chest of drawers—but it was very cold. Wetherby changed his mind. "Come back to my room, and while you are getting ready for bed, I shall have Jespers start a fire for you."

That seemed like a good idea to Rupert, and he picked up his portmanteau and sword and followed Lord Wetherby back across the hallway. The marquis's room was much bigger—and warm. Jespers came out of a connecting door, carrying a towel. "The housekeeper will have gone to bed by now, your lordship. I shall give Master Rupert one of your linens and go down to the kitchen to get the water."

Wetherby gave him instructions to set a fire, and sent him on his way.

It didn't take long for Rupert to divest himself of his clothes and pull on his nightshirt. Meanwhile, Wetherby had shrugged out of his coat and vest and donned a dressing robe. He was standing in front of the blazing grate when Rupert came out from behind the screen washed and pink-cheeked from his efforts. For the first time, Wetherby saw the resemblance to his mother. The boy stood politely, waiting.

"Would you like to sit by the hearth until Jespers has a fire going in your room?" Wetherby asked, indicating one of the chairs that were placed opposite each other.

Rupert climbed into one of the highbacks, clasped his hands in his lap and turned an expectant smile on the marquis.

Wetherby cleared his throat. What did one say to a six-year-old when one wasn't trying to pry for information? "I thought your mother looked quite lovely in her new shawl tonight at dinner." The frown that had bothered Wetherby in the coach and at dinner reappeared, and he was at a loss as to the reason. "Does it bother you that I bought your mother a gift?"

"Oh, no, my lord," Rupert said, wriggling uncomfortably. "It is just that . . . It is just that when you bought the pretty shawl, I was reminded that I had no Christmas present for Momma. I saved my pennies all year, but we had to leave so quickly there was no time for me to buy her a present. Then in Horsham this morning, I was going to give some money to the poor children in the alleyway, until I realized that if I did I would not have enough left to buy Momma something. Was that selfish of me, my lord?"

So that was what had been bothering the lad. Wetherby thought back to the incident. He remembered ringing a peal over Rupert's head for going into an alley full of beggars, but until now he'd not put any significance on seeing Mrs. Copley coming out of that same alley, closing her reticule. The impossible woman had given the ragamuffins some of her own blunt. This Wetherby couldn't understand. "No, I do not think it at all selfish," he said to Rupert. "You say you have not bought your mother a present yet. Do you have something in mind?"

"I was thinking of buying her a bow and arrows—she bought me a nice set last year—but when I saw how much she liked your gift, I began to think that perhaps she would like something different."

Wetherby had a hard time trying to conceal his smile. "When we leave here day after tomorrow, we will be going through a rather large town with many fine shops. Would you like for me to help you select something more . . . more appropriate for your mother?"

"Oh, would you, my lord?" A glimmer of hope shined in the boy's eyes. "I think you get a good mark for that." Rupert turned thoughtful for a moment. "Does that come under Code Number Three or Five, do you think?"

"What is this *code* you keep speaking of?"

Rupert turned a knowing look at Wetherby. "You know, the Code of Chivalry—like the stories you told me in London."

Wetherby looked at him with amazement. "You remembered those?"

"Oh, yes, and Mr. Tipple read to us a lot about knights of old and how brave and noble they were. Wait!" he said, jumping down from the chair and going to the table where he'd placed his portmanteau. He opened it and pulled out an oblong, leather-bound journal. He returned to the hearth and placed the open book on the marquis's knees. "Mr. Tipple said that each night I should review what I have done during the day. He told me to put a star for the good things and an *X* for the bad."

Wetherby ran down the list: One, Faithfulness. Two, Loyalty. Three, Respect. Four, Valor. Five, Ladies. Before he could query further, Rupert had turned several pages.

"See, my lord, I have even started a column for *you*."

Wetherby's gaze became riveted on the first mark. "What is this star for?"

"That is when you insisted John Coachman ride up back because he banged his head."

Wetherby didn't know that the boy had noticed.

Rupert continued, "This one is for when you picked Momma up off the floor of the coach." He pointed to two stars beside *Number Five*. "This, of course, is when you rescued Miss Clara. I thought that deserved two stars, don't you?"

Wetherby winced. His life had been on stage and he hadn't been aware of it. What else had the boy seen? He supposed he'd be sorry for his next question, but he asked anyway. "What are these *X*'s for?"

Rupert blushed. "That is when you took the Lord's name

in vain. I'm not quite sure if that belongs on *One* or *Two.* You have quite a few of those, my lord," he said apologetically.

An uneasiness ran through Wetherby's conscience, and he flipped back to Rupert's page. "I see you put similar marks beside the same numbers, Faithfulness and Loyalty."

Rupert sighed. "I said *the word,* too. I thought if you said it, it must be a way of praying, but . . ."

"But, your mother did not take it that way," Wetherby finished.

Rupert looked sheepish. "Momma said it was swearing, and I was not to do it again."

Wetherby raked his fingers through his hair. "My God! That is my . . . goodness," he changed quickly. *'Tis more than enough that I must chaperone the unpredictable Mrs. Copley and her eagle-eyed son, but am I to be monitored for everything I say or do for the entire next two weeks, as well?* "Those sound like your mother's rules, not a warrior's."

"Oh, Momma would be a splendid knight, my lord—if she were not a woman. Women are frail creatures to be protected, are they not? That is rule Number Five." Rupert paused a moment to reflect. "Momma says that my father was the bravest of soldiers. She said he looked so handsome in his uniform. Did you know my father?"

"I did—and your mother was right. I never met a more valiant officer."

Rupert smiled proudly, and Wetherby wondered what it must be like to be so worshiped by wife and son. Captain Copley had been a fortunate man.

Wetherby closed the book and attempted to change the subject. "I wonder where Jespers is? You should be able to go back to your room as soon as he has a fire going." Saying this, Wetherby looked expectantly at the door, but when his usually prompt valet did not appear, he sighed and said, "Is there anything else you would like to do?"

"I haven't said my prayers yet. Momma always listens to them."

"Oh, yes—of course," Wetherby answered. He couldn't remember the last time he'd done any praying—unless it was at the gaming wheel.

Rupert looked across the room. "My bed at home is not as high as yours."

Wetherby didn't know what was expected of him, so he remained sitting where he was.

"If it is all right with you, I will kneel here," Rupert said.

"Oh, yes. I suppose that will do."

Rupert knelt down in front of the marquis and steepled his hands against his legs. His prayers were lengthy, and included all of his family and seemingly everyone in the entire town of Cross-in-Hand. Wetherby even found himself included. "I am sorry if his lordship forgets *Your* rules now and then, God, but Momma says he will be a duke someday, and I suppose that is a great burden to undertake—so if *You* want, I shall be most happy to remind him when they occasionally slip his mind." Finally winding down, he said, "I will hear your prayers now if you wish, my lord." Truthfully, Rupert wanted very badly to hear what a man prayed about.

Wetherby was obliged to say something, so he mumbled a few unintelligible words, adding some *"Bless my's,"* and hoped his attempts passed muster.

"A man does not use as many words as a woman, does he, my lord?"

Jespers appeared at that moment and saved his master's supplications from further scrutiny. "I have fetched a pitcher of water and built a fire in Master Rupert's room, your lordship."

Wetherby felt Rupert's hands tremble against his legs. He didn't know why he did so, but he reached down and took one of the boy's hands in his. Rising, he walked Rupert to the adjoining dressing room. "Would you like to sleep in here tonight?" he asked.

"But isn't this where Jespers sleeps?"

"I do not think Jespers will mind staying in the room across the hall."

The subject of their conversation raised his eyebrows but said nothing. Quietly collecting his nightshirt and a few other articles, the servant started toward the door.

On seeing the embarrassed look in Rupert's eyes, Wetherby leaned over and made an aside behind his hand. "Besides, Jespers snores abysmally. I hope you do not snore."

"Oh, no, your lordship. Not so as anyone has complained," he whispered back.

"Good, good, then we shall make good sleeping companions, you and I."

While Rupert and Lord Wetherby contemplated the heavy burdens of chivalrous behavior, Millicent was in her room receiving lessons in the importance of artifice and deception.

In a chair across from her, Lady Caroline studied her protégée. "You say that you have been invited to a country party at Sir Gifford Maudlin's in Hampshire?"

Millicent nodded.

Caroline made a grand sweep of the room with her arm. "Then let us imagine that a gentleman of the first stare has arrived at the ball. His piercing eyes take in every woman in the room. They settle on you for just a second. Now keep your fan in your left hand—that means you have some desire to make his address . . ."

Millicent giggled. "Why don't I just ask a friend to introduce us?"

Caroline raised her gaze to the ceiling. "No, no, no!" she scolded. "He must come to you, you ninny. Intrigue. Mystery. That is what attracts a man to a woman. Though I truthfully can say I doubt that you will ever be able to attract anybody of any consequence."

Millicent sighed. "I am afraid I am not too intriguing."

"Listen to me. Take your fan and let it rest on your right cheek."

Millicent did.

"That means, *Yes*."

"*Yes*, what?"

Caroline sighed in resignation. She knew full well that her charity toward the young widow was doomed to failure. "That is what you want the gentleman to ask. He will seek you out just to satisfy his curiosity." She sat back a moment and laughed.

"What is so funny?"

"I was just thinking about a party two years ago where three young bucks all started in my direction at the same time from three different places in the ballroom. They collided in the middle of the floor and knocked each other over."

"Oh, you must have some fascinating stories to recount," Millicent said, laying her fan in her lap.

Caroline leaned forward and spoke confidently. "Well, I have had my share of admirers."

"Do tell me all about them."

The genuine interest in Millicent's eyes was an impelling temptation for Caroline to set aside her original plans of making a flirt of the young widow—especially now that she'd admitted to herself that it was a lost cause anyway. So for the next two hours she regaled Millicent with stories of all the broken hearts she'd left behind over the last three years. However, the one thing Caroline didn't tell her was that she was readying the final battle plans for her one last conquest, the Marquis of Wetherby. "It is too bad that I must leave tomorrow, or I would have given you more instructions," she said, preparing to exit the room. "Just remember to be mysterious."

"I shall try," Millicent said, realizing for the first time why she'd only attracted such dull fellows of late. "Thank you for the fan."

"Think nothing of it," Caroline said. "I did not like it anyway. The lace is unraveling and the colors are too dull."

* * *

Wetherby went riding the next morning. To his surprise and some annoyance, he found Lady Caroline up and ready to accompany him.

"Good morning, Ernest."

"You are looking lovely as usual," Wetherby said. He had to admit that Caroline was the picture of pulchritude, the pink of the *ton.* She wore a scarlet riding outfit with a black velvet bonnet, its sweeping brim and scarlet plumes an appropriate setting for her yellow hair. But the whole picture didn't attract him as it once had.

"We might as well go together, since we seem to be the only ones of a sporting nature."

Caroline was right on that account. John Teagardner, with his expanding girth, had told the marquis that he himself found carriages much more to his liking; but he admonished Wetherby to select from his stables any mount that he wished.

Although Rupert had been reluctant to sleep in the nursery the night before, he'd been agreeable to Wetherby's suggestion that he go entertain the twins after breakfast.

"Just like you did for me in London when I was little," Rupert said, remembering.

"Exactly. Except that I think amusing two children instead of one will earn you another star, Master Rupert," Wetherby called out, watching the boy skip up the stairs.

Wetherby was now without companionship for a morning ride, for he supposed Mrs. Copley would stay abed late. He rather missed seeing her this morning. He'd wanted to explore a path through the dense forest, but Caroline had had other ideas, and had set her horse on a tamer trail, skirting much of the medieval part of the woods. It made little difference to him, so he followed. He looked back and saw her groom riding behind at a discrete distance.

"Knowing how particular you are about what is under you,

I am surprised you did not bring one of your own horses, my lord."

Wetherby studied Caroline through heavy lids. "I shall ignore your barb, Caro. There was no way of knowing what weather we would encounter this time of year on a cross-country trek. I wasn't going to take the chance of one of my fine racers stepping into a mud hole and breaking a leg. Besides, most of the estates I am visiting have plenty of cattle, and Lord Copley has assured me that now that he has regained his fortune, his stables are well-stocked also."

"I have other invitations, too."

"Then you will be off after breakfast?" he asked hopefully.

"Actually, I plan to leave after we have our noon meal."

They were now on an open road, and without having to say anything, they let their horses break into a gallop. Wetherby had to admit, Caroline was an excellent horsewoman. "Don't you think we should turn around now?" he asked.

"Oh, they don't expect us back 'til later," she said, nonchalantly taking the next path.

Suspicion made Wetherby turn in his saddle. He hadn't really been paying attention to the road behind them, and now he saw that they were being followed by a donkey cart, as well as the groom.

Caroline smiled. "Mrs. Teagardner gave me the direction to their hunting lodge. She said they pay an old forester to keep a fire going all winter in case anyone wants to use it. I asked Cook to pack us a picnic basket. I hope you don't mind."

"You know I don't like your maneuvering, Caro."

She threw a pretty pout. "You have to be hungry, darling. Surely you will not say *no* to Bolognese sausages, chicken pie, and slices of lamb . . ." her voice trailed off. "I do believe that besides some of her finest breads, Cook has included some cheeses, fruits, and nuts, and of course wine."

Wetherby could hear his stomach rumbling. "Stop! I beg for mercy."

"I knew you would not be difficult."

He held up his hands in surrender. "Does a starving man have much choice?"

Caroline reined up in front of a wooden structure, more cottage than lodge. Smoke curled from the chimney. "It looks as if we were expected."

By the time they arrived back at the manor later that afternoon, Caroline's coach was at the front entrance awaiting her. She didn't bother to change her clothes, but after making her *adieus* to the Teagardners, she boarded with her companion and set off. John remained outside to see them off.

The picnic lunch hadn't been as unpleasant as Wetherby had anticipated. Lady Caroline was in fine fettle: charming, witty, very beautiful, and not at all pushy. The two servants sat at a discreet distance in another corner of the room, eating. If Wetherby didn't know her better, he'd have thought Caroline to be an unselfish and caring person. The cottage had been warm and comfortable and they'd stayed much longer than he'd planned. However, now that they were back at the manor house and Caroline was gone, he looked for his charges. "Where is Mrs. Copley?"

"Why I have no idea, my lord," Mrs. Teagardner said. "Lady Caroline asked that a picnic lunch be packed, and I gave her directions to our hunting lodge. She mentioned that Mrs. Copley said something about going into the forest. I took for granted that she was with you."

Apprehension filled Wetherby. "Call Master Rupert. He went up to the nursery to play with the twins."

"He was there early this morning, but Nurse Picking said his mother came to fetch him soon after. The maid told me that Master Rupert was talking nonstop about dragons the whole time."

"Good God!" Wetherby said. "It will be dark in a couple of hours."

"What is the matter?" Teagardner asked, coming into the room.

"Oh, my dear," said his wife, "Millicent and Rupert have come up missing."

Seven

"Surely she must be close about," Mrs. Teagardner said. as she instructed Bangs to assemble all the servants. "We shall ask everyone if they have seen them."

Since Miss Picking's midmorning sighting, no one had.

The stablemaster reported as soon as he came in, "All the cattle taken by his lordship's party are back in the stables, including the donkey cart."

"Then that means they are on foot," Wetherby said.

"Oh, my goodness, no one would go far afoot in this weather." Mrs. Teagardner protested.

Wetherby found himself becoming more and more ill-at-ease. "It is better we spread out in different directions. I know they did not go the west road or we would have seen them."

"Yes, yes, right you are," Teagardner blustered, waving his arms about in great circles. The serving maids flew to search the kitchen gardens and around the manor house. The stable-boys said they'd check the outbuildings, and the older men fanned out into the woods surrounding the park.

Mr. Teagardner called to Popper to bring his coat and hat. "I shall take the phaeton and cover the lanes in and about the immediate area. Surely Mrs. Copley and Master Rupert are on one of the paths and have just wandered farther than they realized."

"There is always the forest," Wetherby said, not wanting to think that a possibility. But Miss Picking's mention of dragons was Wetherby's only clue. Rupert had been so positive that he'd find a dragon in the forest. Therefore, Wetherby reasoned, that is exactly where Rupert and his easily persuaded mother would have gone.

The denseness of the ancient monarchs was so forbidding that even Wetherby would hesitate under normal conditions to go in alone. However, he had no choice. So while Teagardner was having a team of bays hitched to his family carriage, Wetherby singled out a broad-backed farm horse, much like the medieval destriers ridden by armored knights. Such a mount could better traverse the rugged hillsides, and, God forbid—carry an injured or unconscious person out.

"If we don't find them by dark," Teagardner said, "I'll have word sent to the authorities in Haslemere first thing tomorrow and request a search party."

Half an hour later, Wetherby came upon them by chance in a glen. All traces of snow had disappeared, leaving a musty ground cover of mud and rotting leaves. First, he heard a voice—a very loud voice. The violent pounding and cracking sounds that followed brought to mind a wild beast crashing through the forest. Hurriedly, he dismounted. Leaving his horse tied to a tree, he crouched low and ran toward the ruckus. From where he hid, he could see only Mrs. Copley teetering atop an outcropping of rock, her hand clutched to her breast, obviously in great distress. Wetherby was about to spring into action to save her from a nasty fall when from the foot of the rock he heard Rupert's voice, calling out encouragement. "Fear not, fair damsel, I shall slay the dragon and set thee free."

Not quite believing what he heard, Wetherby parted the branches of the bush and leaned closer. He heard the *whack* and saw a dead branch thud to the ground. He glimpsed an incensed Rupert, arms uplifted, sword in hand. The boy was shouting his words as if he were reciting verse.

"The valiant knight's sword cut a wide arc in the air. The blade came down, hitting its mark, Crack! The demon beast

fell to the ground. Triumphantly, the warrior looked up at the pretty damsel quivering precariously on the tall rock, trying to keep her footing. Thee need fear no more, my lady, he cried. I have saved thee!"

Rupert bowed.

Millicent splayed her hands across her chest. "That you have, my brave knight. Surely I would have been devoured by the beast if you had not rescued me."

Wetherby, caught up in the fanciful sights and sounds unfolding before him, nearly became oblivious to the danger of his being discovered.

Rupert placed his foot solidly on the dead branch he'd whacked from the tree. " 'Tis a pity, Momma, that there are no more dragons to slay."

Millicent laughed heartily. "Thank goodness for that!"

"Well, I do not feel that way," Rupert complained. He wiped the leaves and bark from his sword. "*Women are frail things to be protected,*" he said. "*They are cherished and honored, to be watched from afar and never handled roughly.*"

"Ahah," Wetherby said, under his breath. "Number Five of the Code, if I remember correctly."

"Oh, posh!" Millicent said. "At the moment I don't want to be watched from afar, young man. Give me your hand; this rock is slippery."

"Of course, fair lady," Rupert said, sheathing his sword and clambering up the short slope to help his mother.

Wetherby was tempted to step forward, but if he did, Mrs. Copley would know he'd been spying on them. He didn't want to add eavesdropping to her list of his failings. Besides, Rupert seemed to have things firmly in control.

Millicent accepted her son's hand and stepped carefully off the rock.

"I think it vastly unfair that the knights of old did not leave at least a few dragons to slay, don't you, Momma?"

Millicent set her bonnet straight and brushed off the few

leaves that had clung to her pelisse. "I believe we have enough dragons to face in this life without adding to the lot." Suddenly, she looked up through the canopy of trees. "My goodness! Wherever did the time go? If we do not hurry, dear, we shall be caught in the dark."

Wetherby had already backed off to where he had the horse tethered. He mounted and waited until he heard them approaching before making himself known. He hoped it would appear that he'd run into them accidently. "What a surprise, Mrs. Copley. I was myself just on my way back to the manor." He thought he saw relief in her eyes.

"May I offer you a ride? I am sure you are exhausted after being out all day," he said.

She eyed him warily. "I don't believe so, my lord."

"The animal is nothing to be afraid of—"

"Oh, I did not mean—" She got no further.

The marquis leaned down and in one movement, slipped his arm around her waist and swooped her up onto his lap.

Millicent gasped.

He put his face down close to hers and spoke for her ears only. "Madam, I do not have time for missish vapors. The horse is perfectly safe."

Millicent snorted.

Rupert stood with his head straining back, eyes transfixed, staring up at the marquis.

Wetherby reached down his hand to him. "Well, Master Rupert, what say you?"

Rupert grabbed the gloved hand. "Oh, I should like that above anything, your lordship."

"Well, at least one of you is agreeable," Wetherby quipped, swinging the boy up behind him.

Millicent wanted to glare at him, but the rim of her bonnet, already smashed beyond repair, wouldn't permit her to do so. Besides, any movement was nigh impossible, the way his arm held her prisoner against his body.

"We had best hurry. 'Twill soon be dark as Hades, and I

do not particularly look forward to spending the night with you in this medieval jungle. The temperatures will most likely plunge to freezing."

Millicent attempted to thrust an elbow into his stomach, not that it did much good, taking into consideration their thick apparel.

Wetherby chortled, picturing her standing on top of the rock. Actually, it might be quite enjoyable holding Mrs. Copley all night. Yes, the little widow was showing far more pluck than he had first thought her capable of. "I believe the Teagardners will be waiting for us."

Millicent held onto her hat. "Lady Caroline bid me good-bye last night. She said she was leaving early today, and I need not get up to see her off. Did she?"

So Caroline had schemed to keep Mrs. Copley from attending their picnic. "Yes, she has gone."

"I shall miss her," Millicent said.

Wetherby felt that the woman *missed* the point altogether. "Yes, Lady Caroline has a way of leaving an empty void whenever she departs," he said.

"She is so gracious—and generous. And I think she likes you, my lord."

Wetherby smiled in amusement. "You don't say. I had not noticed."

"Men of your ilk probably wouldn't."

Wetherby wasn't quite sure what she meant by that, but under the circumstances, he felt it might be too dangerous to ask. Instead he pulled her even closer. That shut her up.

Rupert squeezed his arms tighter around the marquis. "Oh, this is jolly, your lordship. Can't we go faster?"

"Hang on," Wetherby warned, and with a shout of laughter, he urged the horse into a gallop.

The moment they burst out of the forest, the wind whipped their faces and the rain fell, but they arrived back at the manor house just before dark. Rupert heralded it all as a great adventure, but what surprised the marquis the most was that not once did Mrs. Copley scream or cry. In fact, if his ears hadn't been filled with the capricious howling of wind and rain, he'd have said that he'd heard her laughing.

They stayed another day with the Teagardners. Wetherby wrestled with his conscience. He was trying his best to take on the responsibilities delegated to him by the baron, but he was beginning to question his abilities—and his patience—at being guardian to two free spirits such as Mrs. Copley and her six-year-old boy. His experience with widows had been much differently directed, and as for children, the only ones he knew were his nieces and nephews. He gave them presents, and then they were hustled off to the nursery.

That evening when the men joined the ladies after dinner in the library, Mrs. Teagardner excused herself to go check on the twins, and her husband hauled Rupert over to a particular shelf of books. Wetherby grabbed the opportunity to approach Millicent. She sat by herself in a corner of the room making those crazy gyrations with her wrists that he'd seen before. "Mrs. Copley . . ." he began.

The minute she saw him, her face turned red, and she quickly clasped her hands in her lap.

Her reaction momentarily threw him off balance, but he recovered himself nicely and continued, "Andersen, Lord Copley, has entrusted you to my care. You don't seem to realize the start you gave us when you disappeared for hours. In the future, you are not to go anywhere unless you are accompanied by me or one of my men." He thought his request a reasonable one, but Mrs. Copley obviously didn't agree.

"That is ridiculous!" she quipped. "Why, in Cross-in-Hand . . ."

Wetherby gave her his best scowl. "While you are under my care, madam, you will obey me. Is that understood?"

He was afraid she was going to come back with another

argument when he discovered Rupert dancing up and down at his elbow.

"Oh, your lordship," he said breathlessly, "you must come see the book about King William's knights that Mr. Teagardner has found. Perhaps we can read it before we go to bed. Momma, may I stay with Lord Wetherby tonight? Please?"

Wetherby kept his gaze on the boy. "That is a splendid idea, Rupert. I should like that." Then, grasping at straws, he bowed to Millicent. "Excuse me. I believe Teagardner is signaling me." With a grin, Wetherby made his escape before Mrs. Copley could ring a peal over his head.

Millicent pursed her lips, but Rupert paid no heed. "It is only one more night. Please, Momma. Let me stay with Lord Wetherby."

She shrugged. The man was impossible. but her son was even more persistent. "Oh, all right. But just tonight."

"Thank you, Momma," he cried. running back across the room toward where the two men stood talking.

Millicent wrung her hands. What was she thinking of? Her problem was that she could never say *no* to Rupert. She watched her son become engaged in a deep discussion with Lord Wetherby. Curiosity engulfed her. Of course, she certainly wasn't interested in the marquis, but as a mother, she just wanted to know what he talked about to her son when they were alone. She'd questioned Rupert to find out. Rupert told her about Jespers letting him have his room and how he and Lord Wetherby had said their prayers together. She couldn't picture the marquis talking to God. Well, after tonight, she would be the one to hear her son's prayers and tuck him into bed.

"Momma is ever so much fun," Rupert said, later that night as he got into his nightshirt.

Wetherby tried to hide his amusement. Although he'd witnessed the whole episode, he encouraged Rupert to recollect the entire dragon fight.

"But it would be so much more jolly if we had someone to play the dragon. Grandpapa says his lumbago hurts too much to hop around—and what good is a dragon that cannot huff and puff and rear up on his hind feet?" He looked at Wetherby hopefully. Rupert sighed. Lord Wetherby didn't seem overly eager to volunteer for that part, so he brought out his journal and they contemplated which marks they deserved.

Wetherby put his arm around Rupert's shoulders. "Indeed you displayed *Valor* and *Respect,* however . . ." Wetherby said, looking into the two big brown eyes and clearing his throat. "There is one matter—of *Loyalty.*"

"I didn't swear," Rupert said.

"No, no, I didn't mean that. There is also a matter of loyalty to your country, your king, and your liege lord. Your uncle has appointed me your guardian. You and your mother went out without my permission. I have spoken to her about this omission already. But I am afraid we shall have to put an *X* down in your journal." The destitute look in Rupert's eyes made Wetherby melt a bit, but he knew that if he was to have any peace during the remainder of their journey, he had to be adamant. "Just a small *x,*" he said, marking an almost invisible letter on the page. "Have I made myself clear?"

Rupert nodded solemnly.

"Well then," Wetherby said, with a bit more joviality, "I do believe it has been an exceptionally good day, and that we both deserve several stars."

"Except for one thing, my lord," Rupert said.

Wetherby raised his eyebrows. "And what is that?"

"I think Momma would like you a bit better if you did not tell her what to do."

"I disagree," Wetherby said. "Consider Number Five. Aren't women frail things to be protected?"

Rupert chewed on his lip. That part of the Code still puzzled him. However, the marquis was an older man and knew all about ladies, so he must be right.

"Now, it is time to say good night," the marquis said.

Rupert knelt at the marquis's feet and listened, then mumbled his own prayers the way his lordship did.

Wetherby winced. He'd have to do better next time, or Rupert's mother would have his hide.

The following day, the weather became Wetherby's ally in that it was so disagreeable that no one was able to go outside, and Millicent couldn't have disobeyed his order even if she'd wanted to.

They spent their time engaging in games of cards, playing with the twins, or just making pleasant conversation. Although it was a far cry from what he'd pictured his holiday to be, Wetherby was surprised to find that he was enjoying himself. Millicent and Mrs. Teagardner played with the twins, and though he couldn't bring himself to play the part of the dragon, he afforded he saw nothing unmanly about John Teagardner down on the floor with the children, roaring about in a most ferocious way.

"To Basingstoke," Wetherby called up to John Coachman just before entering his carriage the next morning. Settling himself beside Jespers, he explained to Millicent, "Not only is it on the wide mail-coach road going west toward Sir Gifford Maudlin's Hampshire country seat, but it is a growing town that should afford you a larger range in shops. As the cloth industry is increasing, it is spilling over into the rural towns surrounding greater London."

It had not escaped Wetherby's notice that Mrs. Copley was wearing the purple-pink shawl that he'd given her. Although it gave her some color, it unfortunately still had to cover the same homely brown suit she'd worn each day of their travels.

He found himself wanting to buy her something prettier. Perhaps a deep purple traveling suit with gold trimming. Or something in a silver-gray to match her eyes. After all, Wetherby did consider himself somewhat of a connoisseur of women's frocks. He'd paid enough to clothe his ladybirds over the years—and he always insisted on getting his money's worth from the modistes he engaged.

As soon as Wetherby had obtained rooms at the Hantsworthy Arms outside Basingstoke, he had John Coachman carry them into town.

The holiday spirit was evident everywhere. Sprigs of holly decorated market stalls, bells jingled on horses' harnesses, and happy moods brightened the faces of shoppers carrying armloads of packages tied with red ribbons. Fashionably bonneted ladies getting out of coaches to enter the milliners or drapers called "Happy Holidays" to each other, and men in high beavers tipped their hats as they entered the coffee or tobacco shops.

When they reached the center of town, Wetherby had his coachman drop them off near an apothocary's shop. "Pick us up around half six, John." They could explore to their hearts' content, and still have time enough to return to the inn for supper.

Wetherby found that there were two separate areas of shops they wished to see, and as soon as they had browsed through the bookstalls and market area, they had to proceed past a poorer section of old brick residences that had turned into rentals for the spreading population of factory workers. They also found a greater number of beggars on the streets than they'd seen previously on their journey: homeless soldiers in worn army uniforms, legs or arms missing, eyes bandaged; ragged adults and hungry-eyed children huddled around firepots in garbage-strewn alleys.

Millicent, eyes wide, pulled her shawl tighter around her shoulders. "How terrible," she said.

Wetherby took her arm to hurry her on. "I am sorry you

have to see this, but it is just a little farther to the shops I wish to show you."

"I did not mean . . ." she started.

Just then three little urchins, wrapped to their frostbitten noses in rags, spilled out of an alleyway. "Please mister," said a tiny, brown-haired snippet, "can you spare a ha'penny for some bread?" Behind them stood a woman with a baby in her arms, shivering in her thin tattered coat.

Millicent started to open her reticule. "What is your name, darling?"

"Betsy Collins, m'lady."

Wetherby didn't hesitate to step in front of Millicent and dig into his pocket. "Here, buy a whole loaf," he said, placing a coin in the small hand.

The child chirped, "Thankee!" and handed the money to her mother.

"God bless, ye, sir," the woman said.

"That was kind of you, your lordship," Rupert said, gazing up with admiration.

Thankfully, it was only a short time until they burst onto a street lined with brightly decorated shops. Wetherby glanced at Millicent. He wished he could bring back a smile to her face as readily as he had to her son's, and he spent several minutes pointing to the holiday windows, a man with a monkey that held a cup, and a group of children singing carols on a street corner. Wetherby was glad to see Millicent's eyes brighten. He said in an aside to Rupert. "I shall keep a sharp lookout for a trinket for your mother."

"What are you two whispering about?" Millicent asked.

Rupert, his eyes dancing, put his finger to his lips.

Wetherby looked sheepish.

"His lordship was just asking me if we would like some hot chocolate and a jelly roll, Momma." Rupert said smugly.

Wetherby innocently glanced up and down the street. "Why, yes, that is exactly what I was saying."

Millicent tried unsuccessfully to hide her smile. "That would be very welcome. It is turning quite chilly."

"We just passed a very nice tea and confection shop called Grandmother Willowby's," Rupert said helpfully.

"Then Grandmother Willowby's it is," Wetherby said.

They spent the rest of the afternoon shopping, but no matter how diligently he searched, Rupert couldn't make a decision on a present for his mother. They had now made a complete circle of the town and were almost back to their starting point, when Lord Wetherby leaned over and spoke to Rupert. "Do you want to go back to the little jewelry store and look at the eardrops we were shown when we were in before? I think your mother would like them."

Rupert nodded.

Wetherby had noted that the proprietor's wife had the connecting shop, one that sold fabrics and laces made by the local women. He turned to Millicent.

"Would you like to revisit the little sundry shop on the corner? I saw you looking at some of the lace earlier."

While Millicent was occupied in looking at handkerchiefs, Wetherby and Rupert stole into the jewelers. They viewed the small display, but Rupert couldn't make up his mind.

"You aren't sure," Wetherby said.

For a few minutes, Rupert seemed preoccupied with watching something outside in the street. Then, looking once more at the eardrops, shook his head. "They aren't special enough."

Wetherby put his arm around the boy's shoulders. "Then we shan't take them. Never fear, we will be stopping in other villages. Now let us collect your mother and go back to the inn for a good supper." But when he looked for Millicent, she was nowhere to be seen. "Damnation!" he spouted. "Where the devil did she go?"

"I saw her go back in the direction of where all those poor people were huddled around the fire in the alley."

"Good God! That foolish woman!" Wetherby bellowed, grabbing Rupert and heading into the crowds billowing from the factories. He was too angry—and frightened—to worry about all the *X*'s he would be getting in Rupert's journal that night. "That is too rough an area for a lady to be walking alone. She could be . . ." He stopped midsentence. He didn't want to frighten Rupert with his own unsettling thoughts.

Eight

Millicent was coming toward them when he saw her. Unhurt. She smiled when she spied him, and he wanted to run up and take her in his arms. But all he could say was, "Hell, woman! I ordered you not to go off alone."

Her eyes widened and her smile disappeared. It was then that he noticed she wasn't wearing the shawl he'd given her. "They stole your wrap. You are fortunate nothing worse happened. As soon as I get you away from here, I shall notify the authorities."

She grabbed his arm. "Oh, don't! It wasn't stolen. I gave it away."

Wetherby stared at her. "You did what?"

"I gave it to Mrs. Collins. I could not bear to think of her having such a threadbare coat. She told me her husband was injured in a factory accident, and they have been put out on the street."

Wetherby looked over her shoulder at the wretched woman bending over the open fire, wearing a cashmere shawl worth a king's ransom. He gritted his teeth and said, "I suppose you gave her some money, too?"

"I didn't have much, only enough to feed the children for a few days."

Wetherby shook his head in disbelief as he watched Rupert pull out his little drawstring bag. "Wait," he said, reaching into his own pocket. "Put your purse away and take this to the woman. It should be enough to get them lodgings for a while." He watched Rupert trot off, smiling. Wetherby knew good and well the blunt he was giving them should find the family a room and food for at least three months. Perhaps by then her husband would be well enough to go back to work.

They didn't speak again until they were in the coach going back to the Hantsworthy Arms. He should have been pleased that Millicent was once again looking on him with favor, but his own disposition was in a hole. Why the shawl? Did she think so little of him that she could so easily throw away the present he'd given her?

Rupert seemed to hold the same question in his mind, but he wasn't as reticent in seeking the answer.

"Why did you give away your pretty shawl, Momma?"

Wetherby folded his arms across his chest and waited to hear what Millicent had to say to that. Of course, she couldn't know how much the shawl was worth. But he thought she could give him some credit for his generosity.

"What sacrifice is it to give something you can well afford to give, my lord?" Millicent said. "Remember, Rupert. A gift has more value if you give something you hold dear to your heart."

Something you hold dear to your heart. Wetherby pondered that for a moment. She'd meant his shawl; but then if it meant so much to her, how could she have given it away? He didn't understand at all.

Tomorrow they'd be at Maudlin's estate. Three days of parties. That should keep Mrs. Copley well enough occupied so he could enjoy himself.

The next day they arrived at Maudlin Manor. It was a grand house. Sir Gifford was only a baronet, but his was an old and distinguished family of great worth, and he'd married wealth as well. They were ushered into the drawing room to meet Lady Maudlin and her two smiling and rather good-looking daughters, Miss Prethoria Maudlin and Miss Angelina. Their eyes were all for the marquis.

"I am sorry Sir Gifford is not here to greet you, my lord," Lady Maudlin simpered, all the while watching Wetherby's reaction to her daughters. "We expect him and young Harry back from London by tomorrow."

Millicent had just curtsied to her hostess when Rupert squealed, "Momma! Momma! Lady Caroline is here. Isn't that stupendous?"

"What a pleasant surprise," Millicent exclaimed sincerely as she turned to see Caroline entering the room.

"My, oh, my!" Caroline gushed, acknowledging Millicent only slightly. She curtsied, and held out a gloved hand to Wetherby. "We do seem to turn up at the same places, don't we, my lord? It must be fate."

Wetherby took her fingers and gave her a crooked smile. "If you say so, Lady Caroline. You seem to have more inside information on those matters than I do."

Caroline looked with annoyance at the child dancing attendance in front of her. Then catching Wetherby's solicitous demeanor toward the boy, she extended her hand to him. "Master Rupert."

Rupert tucked his sword out of the way and took her hand in his, bowing exactly as he'd seen Lord Wetherby do—only deeper and longer. Her fingers smelled of dark flowers and exciting adventures, and he was reluctant to let them slip from his grasp. Once more, Rupert entered the gates of heaven.

Wetherby watched him and chuckled.

Caroline narrowed her eyes. Perhaps being nice to the boy would serve a purpose after all. She honored Rupert with a brilliant smile.

Guests continued to arrive. All of Maudlin Manor was in preparation for the Christmas Ball, to be held the following evening. Millicent got up to the nursery only briefly to see that Rupert was settled.

"Lord Wetherby has forgotten me altogether," Rupert commiserated.

"Now, darling, you know that his lordship did not expect to have to take us on his holiday, so we must try not to be a nuisance to him—or he may drop us by the wayside altogether," Millicent said, with a twinkle in her eye.

"Oh, Momma, do you think so?"

Millicent laughed. "Of course not, silly. A true gentleman always carries out his obligations."

Rupert glanced sideways at his mother, grinning. "You are bamming me again, Momma."

Millicent knew Rupert was unhappy. There were no children at Maudlin House, and he had been installed in the old nursery on the third floor with only the housekeeper's elderly sister, Mrs. Peesbody, to watch after him. "Think on the bright side, dear. We will only be here two more days, then off again to your Uncle Andy's."

"Then I shall pretend I am being held prisoner by a wicked sorcerer and he has appointed a wicked witch to guard me."

Millicent looked over at the old woman in black bombazine who was sitting in a rocking chair by the window, knitting. "Rupert, that is not kind of you. Mrs. Peesbody is probably just as uncomfortable having to stay up here with you as you are with her."

Rupert shuffled his feet.

"Perhaps if you try, you can find something you have in common."

Rupert looked doubtful.

"You be pleasant, now," she said, before she shut the door behind her.

That evening, Sir Gifford returned in time for dinner with his one and only heir. Mr. Harry Maudlin, a well-proportioned young man of three and twenty years, soft-spoken, with quick blue eyes.

There were twenty-four guests at the dinner table. Ascot Delphinny, a bright young man dressed in the latest of fashion, accompanied the Maudlins back from London. Sir Richard, another Oxford man, had driven over with his mother. It was obvious to all that Lady Maudlin was making certain that there would be no shortage of dancing partners for the ladies at her ball.

Millicent soon realized that most of the guests were already acquainted and the conversation flowed freely among them. She wore her dark blue gown with a single strand of pearls, her hair pulled back and simply tied with a matching ribbon. She found herself seated far from both Lady Caroline and Lord Wetherby, the only two people she really knew. Therefore, she mainly listened, smiled, and observed the elegant crowd, admiring their fashionable clothes and their unabashed ability to flirt so freely.

Strangely, Wetherby noted that Caroline's attention was directed more toward Millicent than toward him, and he wondered at her motive. Her pursuit of him was obvious, and it was no secret that Lady Maudlin's purpose in inviting him to the party was to meet her daughters. Yet Caroline seemed to show no great concern over having Prethoria or Angelina throw themselves at him. Caroline's interest in anyone of her own sex was usually to size up her competition—however, that was not the half-lidded study she directed at the little widow. Wetherby found his suspicions growing.

It was to Millicent's great surprise, also, when she answered a knock later that night to find Lady Caroline standing for the second time in only a few days outside her bedroom door.

"May I come in?" she asked, sailing past Millicent and seating herself elegantly in a dainty chair.

Millicent didn't hesitate to welcome her visitor. "With all

those people, I have not had a chance to tell you how happy I was to see you."

Caroline rearranged the folds of her gown over her knees. "That is not why I am here. Why did you wear that terrible blue dress again?"

Millicent seated herself across from Caroline. "You said it looked better on me than my green or brown ones."

"But that evening I draped it with that lovely shawl that you said Wetherby had given you. Why did you not wear that?"

Millicent looked down at her hands. "I don't have it anymore."

"You cannot mean that he took it away from you? Wetherby may be a scoundrel, but he'd never take back a gift."

"Oh, he did not. I gave it away to a poor woman who had no warm wrap." When Millicent had finished telling Caroline the whole story, she was met with silence for one whole minute.

Then Caroline jumped up and pulled Millicent out of her chair. "Mrs. Copley," she said, "I can see that someone needs to take you in hand. What pray tell do you plan to wear to the ball tomorrow night?"

Millicent hunted for an answer, for it was a question she'd asked herself several times. "I did not think that I would be going to any fashionable parties. It was just to be a family affair at my brother-in-law's. Perhaps it would be better if I did not attend. Lady Maudlin really did not expect me."

Caroline walked around Millicent, studying her. "Nonsense! The party would not be the same without you."

"I fail to see why any festivities would be at a disadvantage with me not being there."

Caroline really wasn't listening. "We are of about the same height. Your waist is not as tiny as mine, but the styles are high-waisted anyway. I am sure I can find something in my wardrobe that would suit you."

"You would do that for me?"

"There are always a few frocks I never cared for much, and you might as well have one."

"You are just being modest, my lady. You are indeed one of the most generous persons I have ever met."

Caroline smiled and nodded. "Be that as it may, we must now think about your hair." She frowned. "Well, I shall send Suzette in tomorrow to see if she can do anything with it. I hope that you have been practicing how to flirt."

"Oh, I have," Millicent said. "Every day."

"Then you are ready."

Millicent didn't get near enough to Caroline to speak to her all the next day. The overnight guests were arriving by droves. She met nearly everybody, but they all seemed in such a hurry that they had no time to chat. The servants and handymen were putting the last-minute finishes on the decorations in the ballroom. The musicians arrived and began practicing, while the grand dining room was being readied for the dinner to be served to forty-eight special guests.

Later in the day, Millicent went to visit Rupert. It had started snowing and she had thought that he might like to take a walk outside, but to her surprise she found him happily playing chess with Mrs. Peesbody. "She has the most monstrous stories about the French Revolution, Momma. She told me how the poor people knitted names secretly into their sweaters and things. She is even showing me how to knit."

Relieved that Rupert was content, Millicent returned to her bedroom, where she found three pretty dresses laid out on her bed. She tried on all of them, each one lovelier than the next, and finally decided on a bright green with apricot trim.

True to her word, Caroline not only sent Suzette to set her hair, but came herself to supervise. Two maids followed, one with a box of cosmetics, the other with a jewelry box.

"Now," Caroline said, "I have picked young Maudlin to be your first victim. He is the perfect specimen for you to practice what I have taught you. Harry is also a good catch on the marriage mart, deep in the pockets and not difficult to look at."

Millicent tried to think of a last-minute excuse not to go at all. "But I am four and twenty with a six-year-old son."

"Posh! It only proves you can breed—all the better for a family who has only one son. Shows them you can produce the next heir."

Millicent flushed. "Why don't you take him?"

"Being the daughter of an earl puts me far above a mere baronet. Besides my sights are set much higher than yours can ever be. But you, my dear, are well enough connected, given your tie to the Countess of Dankleish and being the sister-in-law of a baron, to make it a good match."

"I would not want to marry a man I did not love."

"You have other considerations now that you have a son. He needs a father."

Millicent had to agree. She must think of Rupert.

Caroline clipped on the emerald eardrops and stepped back to survey her creation. "Now you look quite presentable."

Millicent was almost afraid to look at herself in the cheval mirror. "Oh, do you really think so?"

"Remember what I have taught you and you will have Harry eating out of your hand in no time. I have arranged to have him escort you to dinner."

"You haven't! However did you manage that?"

"My dear, never ask another woman how she maneuvers."

"Oh, I am sorry."

"Think nothing of it," Caroline said with a flip of her pretty head. She then turned her protégée around to face her reflection.

Millicent gasped, her fingers clasping the delicate jewelry that adorned her neck. "My goodness! Will you look at me." She laughed. "Oh, my lady, I shall never be as clever as you."

Caroline straightened one of the folds in Millicent's gown. "Of course not. But if you do as I say, you will come off well enough. Now don't forget to bring your fan," she flung back, sailing out the door.

Millicent obediently picked up the fan, and after shyly taking one more peek at her reflection, descended to the drawing room where all the guests were assembled.

Wetherby had barely caught a glimpse of Millicent all day. He'd gone riding in the morning with friends, and he could scarcely be rude to his hostess, who kept putting one or the other of her daughters in his path wherever he ventured. But his luck took a turn for the better when he ran into an old acquaintance, Lord Bently—a middle-aged widower and country gentleman who was lonely but well enough off, his children all out on their own. "The perfect match," Wetherby said to himself. "The perfect match for Mrs. Copley." *What better news could he take to Copley than that his sister-in-law had received an offer from a distinguished gentleman before she arrived in Devonshire?*

However, he was not quite prepared for what he saw when Millicent entered the drawing room. In her green gown, she appeared to be a spring flower, her cheeks pink and petal-soft . . . her lips . . . ? He decided the idea that came most readily to mind was not a proper one, so he commanded his attention to travel upward. Her eyes looked like those of a mischievous child peeking into forbidden territory—even her hair piled atop her head only made her seem younger than she was. "Bently is way too old for her," Wetherby said to himself. "Definitely so." But he had already made the arrangements. He saw his lordship making his way toward her, and there was nothing he could do to stop him now.

"Mrs. Copley?" The words came from behind her.

Millicent whirled and found herself face-to-face with a pleasant-looking gentleman. "Lord Bently!"

"I did not mean to startle you, my dear lady, but I am flattered to find you remembered my name."

Millicent blushed and fanned herself—and it wasn't even warm out. "Of course I remember you, my lord. I did not mean to jump. It was just that . . ." *Oh, dear, she couldn't tell him she was expecting someone else.*

Lord Bently made a leg and bent over her hand. "Lord Wetherby has been so kind as to obtain permission for me to escort you into dinner."

"But I thought . . ." Millicent began, only to find Harry Maudlin standing at her elbow. She became so flustered that she dropped her fan.

Both men dove to retrieve it, and the resulting *thud* told Millicent that their heads had collided.

Millicent's hand flew to her mouth. "Oh, my goodness. How clumsy of me. I've made you hurt yourselves."

Both men quickly denied any great damage, and only glared at one another.

Lady Caroline seemed to appear from nowhere, picked up the fan, and handed it to Millicent. "I am sorry, Lord Bently, but Lady Maudlin has appointed Harry to be Mrs. Copley's partner for dinner."

Confusion showed in Bently's eyes, but he bowed once again. "Then, I do hope you will save a dance for me this evening, Mrs. Copley."

Millicent took a deep breath and collected herself. "Why of course I shall, Lord Bently. Are you sure you are all right?" she said, touching his forehead. "I am afraid you are going to have a nasty bruise there. Do you want me to get you a cold press?"

Lord Bently grasped her hand in both of his, his eyes aglaze with adoration. "A dance will be all that I need to set me aright, kind lady. I shall be looking forward to it," he said, bowing off.

Caroline gave Millicent a knowing look and took her leave.

"Ow!" moaned Harry, holding his head with a most pained expression on his face.

"Mr. Maudlin!" Millicent exclaimed, looking quite guilty.

"I did not mean to neglect you. It is just that Lord Bently is such a much older man than you, and I felt I must tend to his injury first. Someone as young and strong as you can suffer an injury much better than an older man, can you not?"

Harry quit moaning immediately. "Of course, Mrs. Copley," he said, extending his arm to her. "A mere bump on the head is nothing to a round of fisticuffs at Gentleman Jackson's in London."

Millicent switched her fan into her left hand to take his arm and fell into step with the others entering the dining room. "My, you must be very brave to stand up to a strong opponent. Tell me all about it."

He glanced at the fan in her left hand and leaned closer, a gleam in his eye. "You did drop your fan for me then."

Millicent blinked. What was it Lady Caroline had said about dropping one's fan? *Oh, my goodness, I do believe it means a lady wants to be friends.* But what was it about carrying it in her left hand? Did it mean she wanted him more—or less? Millicent blushed. From the look in Mr. Maudlin's eyes, she'd given him an invitation to be familiar. But it was too late now to tell him differently, because he had her right hand imprisoned in the crook of his arm.

The ball commenced and to her surprise, Millicent found herself dancing every dance. She watched in amazement as the other ladies twisted and turned their fans so easily, raised and lowered their lashes, laughed in funny little birdlike trills, and still didn't make one mistake in their dance steps. She tried her hardest, but she feared she was doing everything poorly. She liked to look into people's eyes when she spoke to them. She poked her own face when she unfurled her fan, and even banged Sir Gifford in the nose with it. She was afraid Lady Caroline would be very disappointed in her. But regardless of her *faux pas,* both Mr. Maudlin and Lord Bently had asked her to stand up for two dances, and when she declined a third with Mr. Maudlin, he said, "Then permit me to find you a seat where we can talk."

Millicent was suddenly aware of her tired feet and laughed. "I would like that above all else." She found herself in a tiny little alcove with statues at the entrance and green ferns that made it look like a garden. "How lovely," she said, chattering on about her mother's indoor plants, until she suddenly became aware that Mr. Maudlin was saying nothing. *Oh, dear, she thought, Lady Caroline said men don't like women who jabber.* Millicent tapped her mouth with the handle of her fan to remind herself not to talk so much.

Mr. Maudlin moved quickly. "Oh, my dear Mrs. Copley, I had not hoped—" Harry began, drawing her into his arms and kissing her fervently.

"Mr. Maudlin, please," Millicent gasped, pushing with all her might against his chest.

"But you . . . your fan . . ." he stammered.

Millicent looked down at Caroline's fan, crushed all out of shape. What had she done? "I did not mean—" she started.

"Of course, you did not mean we should do it *here.* My passion for you made me forget all propriety. Forgive me, please, dear lady," he begged.

Her hair had come loose and was falling over her eyes. Mr. Maudlin made an attempt to push the curls back into place, which only wrought more havoc. With a final shove, Millicent broke free. Humiliation turned her cheeks scarlet. Holding up her fan to hide her face, Millicent rushed from the alcove across the ballroom. All she wanted to do was get to her room before anyone saw her disarray, but she nearly tripped over young Ascot Delphinny, then ran into Sir Richard. Mumbling her apologies, she rushed into the hallway and headed toward the stairs.

Lord Wetherby was just finishing a country set with Miss Angelina when he saw Millicent streak past with three young men trailing her. "What the devil?" he spouted, taking out after them. It was outside of enough that she had come dressed like a coquette, but then she'd had to get young Harry Maudlin and Lord Bently scrapping over her at dinner. Now it looked as if a three-way fight was about to begin. He pushed past the trio and caught up with her on the stairs.

A curl covered one eye, and from the blush on her face and the swollen lips, Wetherby surmised that Mrs. Copley had just been kissed. Rage surged through him and he rounded on the three young bucks following her. His scowl soon sent them packing.

Millicent gave him a look that put him in the same category as her admirers, then turned and flounced up to the next floor landing.

Wetherby followed her. "Well, what did you think would happen after the outrageous way you have been flirting all evening?" He expected her to defend herself. Instead the tears began to flow down her cheeks, and to his surprise, he found his arms around her and her cheek against his chest. She didn't make a sound, but he could tell that she was crying. He stood for a moment not knowing what to do—an unheard-of circumstance for him when handling a female.

"Oh, I have made a mess of everything. I don't know how to flirt," she sobbed, giving him a good bang on the chest with her fist. "That is, I don't do a very good job of it, do I? Lady Caroline will be so disappointed with me."

"Caroline?" He should have known she'd have something to do with this. Wetherby held Millicent away from him and grappled for his handkerchief, which he handed to her. "Mrs. Copley," he said, "you were running through the room holding your fan in front of your face with your right hand."

Millicent looked at him blankly. "I didn't want anybody to recognize me, I was so ashamed."

Wetherby threw up his hands. "You were inviting every man you passed to follow you."

"I was?"

"You were."

The tears started again. "Oh, dear, what am I to do? Everyone will think me a fallen woman."

Wetherby had no choice but to fold her in his arms again.

Nine

Wetherby held her away from him. "I should have kept an eye on you, but that is beside the point. Someone took advantage of you and I want to know who it was."

She looked him straight in the eyes. "I am not going to tell."

And Wetherby knew she wouldn't. "Then the first thing I want you to do is go to your room and fix your hair. I shall wait for you here. Then I will escort you down to the ballroom."

Millicent clasped her hands to her bosom. "I cannot go back down there!"

"You must. You cannot act the coward."

But that was exactly what she was, for she was wishing that he had been the one to have kissed her. "If I go back with you, they will think . . ."

Wetherby crooked an eyebrow. "They will think that you have just gone up to the retiring room to refresh yourself."

"No, my lord. With a reputation like yours, if I come back after such an interval, they will think that you are the one who has compromised me."

A knife struck the marquis in the stomach. He knew she was right. He watched her walk away from him, then returned to the ballroom by himself.

* * *

After her fiasco of the previous night, Millicent wanted to avoid having to face anyone in the household. Many of the guests were departing today, and she felt that she would not be missed. She rose late and had lunch with Rupert in the nursery, then took him outside for some fresh air. A thick layer of damp snow covered the ground, so they entertained themselves by walking in their own footsteps in and among the great trees that circled the gardens.

Now, Rupert patted out a large snowball and sent it flying toward a large oak—a satisfactory target for a while, but not for long. He scooped up another fistful and molded it carefully to just the right size. Eyeing his mother, who moved about the edge of the gravel path several feet away, he took aim and let go. The resulting squeal was quite satisfactory.

"You scamp!" she yelled, scooping up her own clump of snow. Her retaliating missile missed her retreating son—but her second one didn't, and caught him squarely between his shoulders.

Rupert yelped and hurried down a gravel path, his sword slapping against his leg with every step.

"You cannot get away from me," she called after him.

"Yes, I can."

Rupert ran around the side of the manor house and dove behind a thick tangle of rhododendron bushes to hide. He grabbed up a handful of snow and lay in wait for his mother to appear. But he'd no sooner settled himself than Lord Wetherby's familiar voice broke the silence on the other side of the hedge.

"Ah, my dear Miss Maudlin, you cannot ask me to decide which of all you lovely ladies was the most charming last night. Even Solomon was not as wise as that."

Several giggles accompanied his statement.

Rupert hunkered down and peeked under the bushes. If he was not mistaken, he spied not two skirts, but four surrounding the marquis's distinguishable fine leather boots that were coming his way. How was he ever to get Lord Wetherby to notice his mother when she was out in the woods and he was here with so many other women who demanded his attention?

Rupert rose, aimed, and fired. The snowball that he'd at first intended for his mother flew straight to its mark, and the resulting exclamation brought a smile of satisfaction to Rupert's face.

"What the deuce?" shouted Wetherby, as his high beaver hat flew off his head. Stooping to pick it up, he zeroed-in his gaze on the high bushes behind him. "Wait here, ladies. I believe I know where the culprit hides."

Rupert knew he was doomed, and was debating whether or not to make a run for it, when he heard a scream. Miss Maudlin's bonnet fell to one side of her head, and another snowball ripped through the air from the opposite side of the garden and hit Lord Wetherby full in the rear.

Rupert broke for the woods at the same time that he saw his mother speeding away along the outer edge of the formal gardens.

Coming to a stop under a stand of elms, Millicent raised her hands to her chest and gasped for air.

But Wetherby caught her.

Her blood had been pounding so loudly in her ears that she'd not heard his lordship's footsteps closing in behind her. From the stern look on his face, there was no telling what mayhem he intended, when a snowball smacked him in the side of the face.

Millicent fully expected a thrashing, but the eyes under the forbidding brows were laughing. "I surrender," he called out to his invisible foe.

Rupert came out of the trees, his sword raised, demanding, "Unhand that fair maiden, sir."

Before Wetherby released Millicent, he bent and whispered, "I really was quite bored to death with those schoolgirl misses, but I shall let Rupert think he rescued you. For no telling what your punishment would have been if he had not appeared when he had." He gave her a smile that she knew had probably been attracting women since he was in leading strings. A shiver of apprehension ran through Millicent. Oh, Lord Wetherby was indeed a dangerous man, for even she was becoming susceptible to his charms.

"Now," he said, wiping the snow from his face, "I believe we should be getting back to the manor house. It is, after all, our last evening at the Maudlins'."

Rupert sheathed his sword. "I hope you don't take offense, my lord."

"Oh, no . . . no, not at all. You did what you had to do to save the fair maiden. You have perfect aim."

Rupert let out a sigh of relief. "Momma, too. She can throw straighter than Jeremy Spitberry."

"Is that a fact?" Wetherby said, not missing the blush in her cheeks as he gave Millicent a sideways glance. "Well, Rupert, for your part in this afternoon's adventure, I believe you deserve a double star, for you rescued me as well as your mother." When he saw the question posed in Rupert's eyes, he laughed. "Some day you will understand what I mean."

The snow melted overnight, leaving no trace of its promised beauty. Jespers insisted he would ride up back with George, for the beginning of the journey, at least.

"We will have to travel most of the next two days to reach Tiverton," Wetherby announced as they climbed into their carriage the next morning.

His lordship was observing Millicent through shadowed eyes, and she had the horrible feeling that she was blushing. "We are not going straight on to Roxwealde Castle, my lord?"

There was a new sparkle in Mrs. Copley's eyes, and Wetherby prided himself to think that he might be the cause. He leaned back against the squabs with a sense of self-satisfaction. By the flirtatious looks the Maudlin sisters had been casting his way, he'd say that he'd had a successful trip so far to have captured three hearts in seven days. "Sir Jonathan Bridges and his sister live just beyond Tiverton and have invited us to stay over. From there it is only one day's journey to Roxwealde Castle."

"Oh, dear," Millicent said, "I still have presents to buy."

Wetherby tried to reassure her. "Tiverton is a wealthy wool town and has some fine shops."

Rupert eyed him intently.

Wetherby caught his thoughts and winked. "But if we see any interesting places along the way, we will stop," he said.

Rupert winked back, and felt quite pleased with his performance until he saw the look of disapproval on his mother's face.

Millicent glowered at Wetherby, and he was obliged to find something of great interest to study outside the window.

They visited two little villages that day. Millicent bought a little knitted cap for her nephew Percy, but Rupert found nothing of interest. "What if I cannot find a present for Momma, my lord?" he asked with a note of concern in his voice.

"We will find something, don't worry."

Wetherby tried to pass the time away by flirting with Mrs. Copley, but she seemed to have had enough of flirting. Maybe she wasn't as taken with him as he thought, and he began to fear that she was going to fall back into her habit of silence. For some reason the thought frightened him. Perhaps it was only to get her to smile, or to see her eyes light up, or wrinkle her nose the way she did when she was trying not to laugh—but he made a face at Rupert.

Rupert let out a *whoop* and proceeded to push up his nose and stick out his tongue.

Millicent turned horrified eyes first at her son, then at Wetherby.

The marquis found himself completely engrossed in the game. My God! He hadn't made faces for twenty years. Ignoring Millicent's glare. he pulled down his eyes and blew out his cheeks. "Nurse Jane used to hate that one," he said cheerfully.

Millicent felt the smile coming, in spite of the fact that she was using all her powers to stop it.

"See, Momma, his lordship can do it better than you."

The mirth rolled up from somewhere deep inside her, and Millicent broke into uncontrollable laughter. It wasn't until she realized that he was staring at her that she stiffened and tried to gain some semblance of dignity. But the tears kept coming.

Wetherby handed her his handkerchief.

Millicent dared a look at him. "Who was Nurse Jane?"

"She took care of my sister and me when we were at Orchid Hill." He saw the question on Millicent's face. "That was my mother's estate near Tunbridge Wells. The one I stay in most often now."

Millicent sat back and looked at him as if she really cared. No one had ever shown any interest in his upbringing before.

"Why there? The Lance family seat in Leicestershire is considered one of the most beautiful houses in England, and you must have accommodations in London."

"And an estate with twelve hundred acres in Kent, and many others which I cannot recall—" Wetherby added.

"Then why Orchid Hill?"

"It is mine. My mother left it to me when she died four years ago. My father bought the house for her when they were first married, because of its nearness to Tunbridge Wells. She found great solace in the waters and spent much of her last few years there. It was a small house, as houses go, and only a few dozen acres."

"That is a pretty name—Orchid Hill."

"Mother did not know of the orchids at first. She would bring my sister and me down with her when my father was in London. He hated the place. *Nothing to do,* as he put it. But Mother loved all the outdoors. One day while she was out walking, she came into a small gorge that was nearly hidden by the surrounding forest. There she discovered a surprisingly large array of rare orchids thriving on the chalk hillsides. She renamed the estate Orchid Hill."

Millicent's manner was now completely devoid of shyness. "It must be lovely to see in the spring."

"At one time, the conservatory attached to the house was filled with her orchids. I am afraid that it has been sadly neglected since she died."

Millicent looked into space as if she were viewing a picture. "What a pity. It must have been a sight to see."

Wetherby focused his gaze on Mrs. Copley. "Yes, it was."

They stayed the night in a crowded inn along the high road, and set out early the next morning. Wetherby insisted that Jespers ride inside with them now. It had started to snow sometime in the night, and it didn't look as if it were going to melt this time. The atmosphere was becoming much more Christmaslike wherever they went. They stopped at two towns to look in the shops, but Rupert found nothing for his mother.

It wasn't until the afternoon of the second day that Rupert saw the gift he was looking for. He tugged on Wetherby's arm to get his attention. It was a small shop called the Piddle-Dee-Dee, with mostly antique dishes and pottery strewn about the window. A dark oil painting was propped against the side, and in the corner was a china statue of a man and a woman in a court dress, embracing. "That's it," he said, pulling the marquis down to his level.

Wetherby thought a statue of two lovers an odd choice for a boy to make. "Are you sure you don't want to get her some jewelry?"

"No, no! That is the perfect gift for my Momma. It will remind her of Papa."

Wetherby swallowed hard. "If you are sure, I will see what I can do to distract your mother, and you can go in and have a closer look at it."

Rupert's eyes sparkled. "We'll fool her."

"By Jove! Right you are," Wetherby said, walking on up to Millicent. Jespers stood quietly behind. The marquis was glad he'd thought to have his valet come shopping with them. It took two to keep an eye on Mrs. Copley and her son, and Jespers seemed quite eager to accompany the young widow.

While they were talking, Rupert slipped into the shop. The clerk, however, didn't take kindly to a small boy wandering about his store, and Rupert was being led to the door by his ear when his lordship walked in.

"I am the Marquis of Wetherby," he said, much louder than was necessary, "and this young man is my charge."

"My lord," the clerk stuttered, giving Wetherby a frightened look before skittering off to the back of the shop. Barely a minute later, he returned with a skinny little man who was trying to tuck in his shirt, rake the few strands of hair over his bald head, and adjust his spectacles all at the same time.

"Your lordship," the man said. "How honored we are to have you in our store. Brixell's the name. Adam Brixell. Dealer in fine antiques."

Wetherby was actually surprised to see the fine quality of merchandise the man had. "We are interested in the china statue in the window."

Mr. Brixell hurried over to fetch the figurine, and handed it to Wetherby. "It is a fine piece, my lord. From the collection of a local squire who is needing to gain a little money."

To the shopkeeper's horror, Wetherby held the piece out to Rupert, who ran his finger over the delicate figures.

"Actually, it is Mr. Copley here who has the blunt and wishes to make the purchase," Wetherby said.

The shopkeeper looked from Rupert to the statue and swallowed hard. "And how much is Mr. Copley willing to pay?"

Rupert quickly pulled out his purse and began to dig out his coins, one by one. "I saved my allowance all year," he said proudly, as the little pile began to grow.

Mr. Brixell began to sputter.

Rupert looked startled. "Wait, I have a few more coins," he said anxiously.

Wetherby had the horrible feeling that if he didn't act swiftly, the little boy's heart would be devastated. "Mr. Brixell, I saw a snuff box over here that interests me very much. While Mr. Copley is getting his money, would you please show it to me?"

Five minutes later, they returned to an anxious Rupert, who showed them twelve neat stacks of coins.

"Now Mr. Brixell will count it and see if it is enough," Wetherby said, sticking a small package in his pocket.

Mr. Brixell's disposition had mellowed remarkably in the last few minutes, and he very carefully picked up and called out each coin.

"Is it the right amount?" Rupert asked, a worried look on his face.

"Well, not exactly," Mr. Brixell began. "Actually, I owe you two pence back."

Rupert let out such a sigh of relief that Wetherby was afraid he'd blow Mr. Brixell away.

"It is very delicate, you know," Wetherby said, frowning at the statue.

"I shall take very good care of it, your lordship," Rupert assured him.

"I can have it wrapped," Mr. Brixell said. "I shall see to it personally. And unless it is used as a ball in a game of cricket, I do not know how it can possibly be broken." He broke into a nervous little laugh.

When Mr. Brixell returned from the back room, Wetherby took the package. They were just coming out of the store when Millicent and Jespers came toward them. "I hope we were not too long. It was rather difficult finding the sort of biscuits you wanted, your lordship."

Wetherby winked at Rupert. "No, Mrs. Copley. You have not kept us waiting at all."

They had not traveled as far as Wetherby had wished that

day. They had, of course, taken longer to shop than he'd
planned, but he was glad that Rupert had found a gift for his
mother. Wetherby had instructed John Coachman to leave
the post road when they came to Chard and cut cross-country
to Tiverton, but now he began to doubt the wisdom of that
choice. The snow was slowing them down much more than
he had anticipated. It really didn't matter all that much. He
wasn't obligated to stop at Sir Jonathan's; he'd just said he
would if he happened that way. They could go straightaway
to Roxwealde Castle if he wished.

That night they found a comfortable inn, but because of
the inclement weather, it was already filling up with the travelers who were trying to get in out of the snow. When Millicent wasn't looking, Wetherby slipped the wrapped statue
to Rupert, who lovingly placed it in his portmanteau before
he took it up to his room.

When Millicent and Rupert came down for supper, they
found Wetherby already there.

"We were lucky to have gotten a private dining room," he
said, pulling out a chair for Millicent. "From the ruckus out
front, I would say that a lot of travelers will be sleeping on
the floor tonight. I sent Jespers off to have something to eat."
He turned to Rupert. "Everything go all right?"

Rupert nodded happily.

Millicent had been watching the signals passing back and
forth between the two of them. She worried that the marquis
was exhibiting far too much influence over her son, especially
when Rupert wouldn't divulge what they had been whispering
about all afternoon. Yesterday in the coach—the way Lord
Wetherby spoke of his mother and her orchids—almost made
him seem human—not at all a rake. It was hard to believe that
he'd been a little boy at one time, making faces and playing
jokes on his nurse. For a few brief moments, she'd looked
back with him. She saw he remembered too, and she didn't
think all the memories were bad. Heaven knows, she hadn't
laughed so hard in a long time—not since—not that way. His

maleness filled the room even now. How skillful he was in seducing without making any effort. Oh, dear, she thought, she was undeniably becoming attracted to Lord Wetherby.

The noise in the outer room was becoming more and more discordant, and, it seemed, was now even louder right outside their private room.

The resonance of the voice seemed distinctly familiar. All three pairs of eyes turned as the door crashed open and Lady Caroline threw herself into the room.

"My dears, you cannot imagine the terrible experience I have just had. It is a miracle that I am alive!"

Wetherby rose from his chair. For once even he was so jarred by her tone of voice that he forgot to ask her what she was doing there. "What has happened, Caro?"

Caroline threw herself into his arms. "It was devastating, my darling. My coach overturned on that dratted road out there."

Wetherby raised his eyebrows. Even Caroline's gentility slipped now and then into cant.

Millicent didn't seem to notice. "Was anyone hurt, my lady?"

"Only my pride," she said. "Oh, yes, my coachman has perhaps broken his leg, and one of the grooms was knocked unconscious. But Suzette is all right." Almost as an afterthought, she asked, "Where is Suzette?"

"I am here, *mademoiselle*," the maid said, standing in the doorway.

Millicent immediately went to the woman, and taking her by the hand, led her to a chair and made her sit down.

Wetherby's mouth quirked into a half grin. Now that he looked closer, Caroline seemed as devastatingly beautiful as ever, and quite healthy, when it came right down to it. He called to a servant to fetch Jespers. "I shall get my coat and go see to the matter immediately, Caroline. Where is your carriage?"

"They got us uprighted and dragged the miserable contraption here. Something about a crooked wheel or something." Caroline pulled out a handkerchief and dabbed her eyes. "You aren't going to leave me, are you, Ernest?"

"Millicent will stay here with you," Wetherby said, with a certain suspicion beginning to creep into his voice. "I shall see that there is a room prepared for you and your maid."

Rupert, who until now had remained silent, picked up a glass of wine from the serving table and offered it to Caroline. "Here, my lady, perhaps this will refresh you."

Caroline glanced toward the door, saw that the marquis was nowhere in sight, and sighed. She'd heard the disbelief in his voice. "I am beginning to think you are the only true gentleman here, Master Rupert."

Rupert fell to his knees. "I shall be your humble servant forever, my lady."

"Well, it looks as if you may be the only one. Is there any food left? I'm starved."

"I shall call for more," Millicent said. "Isn't it a wonderful coincidence that you have stopped at the same inn? Are you going to visit someone near here?"

"As a matter of fact, I am due at Karkingham Hall just past Wellington, day after tomorrow." Caroline omitted to say how many miles *past* the town. "Lady Karkingham shall be terribly disappointed if I do not arrive. She is planning a large party for me," Caroline said. "But that, of course, would probably be out of the way to take me with you."

"I don't know why we couldn't. Now that his lordship says it is unlikely we shall be going to Tiverton, I'm sure we can adjust."

Rupert jumped up. "It would be jolly fun if she could go with us, wouldn't it, Momma?"

When it came to helping someone, it took no time at all for Millicent to make a decision. "Why, yes, it would. I shall speak to Lord Wetherby. He cannot possibly have any objection."

Ten

An hour later, Lady Caroline and her maid were settled in a room. Rupert had gone upstairs with Jespers, and Wetherby had just come in from speaking to the local apothecary about the injured coachman. His broken leg had been set, and the groom had sustained a slight concussion. Both were resting comfortably in rooms over the stables. A wheelwright was to come out in the morning to inspect the carriage. Millicent was still in the private dining room, eagerly waiting to inform the marquis of their plans.

Wetherby stared at her as if she had just come down from the attic. "Good God, madam! Where do you suggest we put her? On the roof?" *What was it about the woman that drove him to profanity?* He was glad Rupert was not around, or he'd have another *X* in his journal. "The carriage is crowded now with four of us inside, and our luggage fills the top. I have never known Caroline to travel with anything less than half a dozen trunks."

Millicent was beginning to realize what an obstinate man the marquis was. "But Lady Caroline says she must be at her friend's house in Wellington by day after tomorrow, or she will miss a party. She enjoys them so much. Surely it won't be much out of the way if we carry her with us. She says it is only about seven miles from here."

Wetherby ran his fingers through his hair. "Have you seen

the snow outside? Of course you haven't. We may not get
out ourselves tomorrow."

"Oh, dear, we are behind a day now, but surely if we are
not going to Sir Jonathan's in Tiverton we can just as easily
go by way of Wellington. Rupert is so afraid he will be late
for Christmas Day at his Uncle Andy's." She could see that
the marquis was not in an accommodating mood, even when
she explained things to him logically.

Wetherby attempted to be reasonable. "We will stay here
one more night and see what the morrow brings. I shall send
a messenger ahead to Copley to let him know that we may
be delayed. After all, the holiday season runs on for twelve
days. One day more or less will make little difference. We
must make the best of it."

"I suppose so, but it will be difficult to explain to a six-
year-old. It has been a most unordinary trip for him."

"Madam, nothing has been ordinary about this dem . . .
this unusual holiday, for you or for me." He smiled in spite
of himself. Rupert would be proud that he'd managed to by-
pass a swear word.

Later that night in their room, Millicent sat with her hands
folded in her lap, straining to hear Rupert's prayers. "Speak
up, dear, I can't hear you."

"His lordship doesn't have anyone to say his prayers with
tonight, Momma."

Millicent couldn't imagine that bothering the marquis too
much. "Well, you say yours, so you can get to bed."

Rupert mumbled a little louder.

"Do you have a toothache, dear?"

"That is the way Lord Wetherby says them."

"His lordship said his prayers with you?"

"Well, yes, but I couldn't hear him very well."

"Well, no wonder if he mumbled."

"I asked Lord Wetherby about that."

"What did he say?"

"Lord Wetherby said he was sure God hears our prayers whether we say them out loud or to ourselves. He said that maybe we would be more honest if no one else heard them."

"Well, perhaps he is right, but I think God likes little boys to be very clear."

"I wish you wouldn't call me a little boy, Momma. Lord Wetherby treats me like a grown-up."

Long after Rupert had fallen asleep, Millicent lay in her bed trying to picture Lord Wetherby saying his prayers. It was difficult to do. She felt that the marquis was exhibiting far too much influence over her son, especially when Rupert wouldn't divulge what the two of them had been whispering about so much lately. What terrible things could he be teaching her son? Millicent pondered everything Rupert had told her tonight. Perhaps she'd have to start from the beginning to rethink her opinions about the man. Was he a sinner but a little bit of a saint, or was he a saint but a little bit of a sinner? No matter how much she agonized over the gossip she'd heard about him, she found that she was becoming undeniably attracted to the man.

They awakened the next morning to another six inches of snow. Wetherby sent a messenger on to Roxwealde Castle to inform the baron of their possible delay.

They passed the day entertaining themselves with reading, games of chess and cards, and staring morosely out the window, wishing the weather would clear.

The wheelwright said Caroline's coach would need some minor repairs that would take another two days to complete. She was still hinting for a ride to Wellington, but Wetherby had made it clear that they didn't have room. She'd just have to miss her party and wait until her coach was fixed. He still thought it odd that she had turned up at two of the same residences as he had—and now this inn in a way-out corner of Somerset.

The following morning brought no better news. They were having breakfast when the proprietor told them that a traveler arriving at the inn had warned him that the storm of the previous night had made many of the roads impassable.

"We will have to stay another day, then," Wetherby said. "I shall have John Coachman return the carriage and cattle back to the stables."

Rupert was becoming visibly upset. "But, if we don't leave now, we will miss Christmas Day with Uncle Andy, Momma."

Seeing the disappointment in Rupert's eyes was too much for Millicent. "I agree with my son, my lord. We must go on. The horses have been resting for two days. Surely if we are careful they can make it to the higher road."

Wetherby knew he was defeated. Thank God Caroline had stayed abed and he didn't have to contend with her also. "All right," he said. "Can you be ready and out front in half an hour?"

"Yes, my lord," Rupert said, jumping down from his chair. "Thank you, my lord." He raced for the door and just as he reached it, ran headlong into Lady Caroline.

After separating herself from a most apologetic little boy, she said, "I saw your coach in the courtyard, Wetherby. Were you planning on leaving without me?"

"Caroline," Wetherby said, rising. "I have told you we have no room."

"You are always telling me what a great whip you are, why don't you take the ribbons? After all, it is only seven miles to Wellington. My carriage will be ready to travel tomorrow. My driver is in no condition to handle four horses. If I sacrifice my maid, and you your valet, your coachman can drive it up tomorrow with the rest of my servants and their luggage. I know that the Karkinghams will think nothing of putting you up for a night or two. A marquis is always welcome, don't you find?"

Millicent clapped her hands. "That would be the perfect solution. Then you will not have to miss your party and we will be so much nearer to Roxwealde."

Caroline, Millicent, and Rupert all looked at him expectantly.

Wetherby accepted defeat. "All right, Caro, you may come." He turned to Millicent. "You had better go to your room and get your wraps. I had the trunks put on earlier, taking the chance that we would go."

As soon as mother and son left, Wetherby rounded on Caroline. "I have agreed that you may come, but I see no reason for putting my servants out. You will ride inside with Mrs. Copley and Rupert. My valet is not strong enough to take the cold and will ride with you. I will be up front with my driver, for it may take two of us to handle the horses. You will have to make do with one trunk. That can be squeezed into the rumble seat with my groom. That is my last word on the matter. We have already wasted ten minutes in this discussion. If you are not ready, we leave without you. Is that clear?"

Caroline smiled smugly. "You promise you will be off in twenty minutes, my lord?"

An uneasy feeling shredded through Wetherby, but he wasn't going to back down. "You now have less than twenty minutes, my lady."

"Actually, I am ready," she said. "When I saw your coach outside, I had my things carried on."

Wetherby's eyes narrowed. He should have wondered at her heightened color, her pink cheeks. She'd been outside. "What do you mean, you had your things loaded?"

"I have already talked to your coachman. He said he would take care of my man and bring him along tomorrow. My groom is still weak and cannot possibly handle the ribbons." She started out the door. "I am afraid my trunks are already strapped down and there is no room in the rumble seat for anyone. If you don't want your valet to sit up front with you,

he will have to come with the others in my carriage."
Caroline sailed out the door. "I only have to fetch my coat
and bonnet, and I will be ready."

She was gone before he found his voice. By the time Wetherby got to the coach, all three of his passengers were inside
surrounded by bags and packages. Caroline held a large
leather case on her lap. The rumble seat was full, and there
was even a large trunk up on the high driver's seat.

"Isn't this jolly?" Rupert said.

Caroline smiled. "Don't look so down in the mouth, Wetherby, it is only a short distance." She wouldn't tell him how
many miles outside of Wellington the Karkinghams lived
until they got to the town.

Wetherby slammed shut the coach door and climbed into
the driver's seat. He told John he planned to follow their
scheduled route as if he was going to Tiverton, then the inn-
keeper directed him, "After about four miles, turn north onto
Catscow Lane to catch the road to Wellington."

With a curse that would surely give him at least five *X*'s
in Rupert's book, he cracked the whip over the horses' heads
and off they went.

The snow kept falling, eventually rising to such heights
alongside the hedgerows that it was difficult for Wetherby
to make out the signposts at the cross lanes. Finally, he
stopped the horses and went back to the carriage. "I shall
need Rupert's eyes to help me find Catscow Lane," he said.

"Yes, your lordship," Rupert cried.

"Impossible," said his mother.

"Madam, I need your son—we all need him."

Rupert eyed his mother intently.

Millicent was acutely afraid that she was losing control
over her son. "All right, but you be sure you wrap your muffler tightly around your neck, dear."

"Oh, Momma."

Caroline pouted. "Can't we stop at an inn and get something to eat. Wetherby? I am starving."

"You should have thought of that before you suggested this insane escapade," Wetherby snapped.

"Well, you don't have to be so touchy," Caroline huffed.

Wetherby shut the door with a bang and marched back to the front of the coach.

Rupert was too happy at being allowed up top with his lordship to give any deep thought to his mother's finickiness. "Women worry a lot, don't they?"

"Hmph," was the only answer he got until they were both seated, then the marquis pulled up a blanket from the floor. "I have a fur rug here," he said, tucking it in around Rupert's legs. "Now wrap your muffler around your neck and pull your hat down over your ears."

"We men have to take care of the fair maidens, don't we, Lord Wetherby?"

"Right," he said, slapping the horses with the reins. Actually, Wetherby was frightened. He had the responsibility of two women and a child. He hadn't seen a snowstorm like this since the freeze of 1814.

They had been on the road a good three hours and Wetherby had no idea of where he was. A few lines on a sheet of paper were different than what he was now seeing. It seemed strange that not one crossroad had a sign posted. But Rupert hadn't been in his seat more than five minutes before he pointed. "I see a sign ahead," he shouted.

It sat high above the snow bank, as if someone had just planted it in the snowdrift.

"It's Catscow Lane, my lord. It points to the right."

"Right you are," Wetherby laughed. "Thank God!"

"That's praying, isn't it, my lord?"

"Yes, my boy, that's praying."

"We aren't lost anymore, are we?"

Wetherby laughed. "No, son, we aren't lost anymore." He stopped the coach and went back to inform the women. "It shan't be long before we are on the road to Wellington."

"Well, it has taken long enough for you to get there,"

Caroline complained. "You are just fortunate that Mrs. Copley and I are so patient."

Wetherby was too relieved to be upset. He guided the horses to the right. The lane was so narrow that the hedges scraped the sides of the carriage. He was just thinking that there would be no way to turn around if they met another vehicle, when the lead horse shied and reared up.

A log lay across the entire road, blocking their path. Behind it stood an imposing, blackhooded figure, a gun in his gloved hand.

His voice, deep and extremely polite, drowned out the howling wind. "Lord Wetherby, I believe? How accommodating of you to drive yourself right into my trap." With a wave of his arm, a great hulking figure appeared from the dense white fog and took hold of the lead horse.

Wetherby placed his arm protectively around Rupert. "Who are you and what do you want? If it is money, you can have all that I have with me."

"Ah, that would not suffice, I'm afraid. I am after much richer gain. You are familiar with the Christmas kidnappings, are you not?"

Wetherby sucked in his breath. "The Bandit King."

"So I hear I am called."

"You, sir, are a coward."

"Don't think you can provoke me, my lord. Mine is merely a useful profession."

"I would call it stealing."

"And I would not take a farthing from someone who has earned his money by the sweat of his own brow. I only harvest from those who have done nothing for their riches."

"Than you are no better than they," challenged Wetherby.

Rupert began to shiver.

"Ah, I don't know where you came upon such a small driver, Wetherby, but if you don't wish him to freeze, you will get back into your coach with your fellow travelers, and I will have one of my men drive you to your destination."

As if on cue, four more men appeared. Three of them, heavily coated and muffled to their eyes, began to remove the log. The other, dressed all in blue with a scarf hiding his features, stepped forward, brandishing a gun. He silently motioned for Wetherby to come down from the high seat.

"What are we going to do, my lord?" Rupert whispered.

"When you have two guns pointed at you, the wise thing is to do as they say," Wetherby said, climbing down. Before he could reach for Rupert, two of the men had his arms pinned to his sides.

"You don't mind if I bind you, my lord, and place a blindfold over your eyes. It is just a precaution."

Rupert jumped to the ground and ran to stand by the marquis. "You will have to bind me too, you scoundrel, or I will run you through." Rupert was sorry now that he'd left his sword inside the coach.

"You have a faithful vassal I see, my lord, and I agree with his suggestion. I will have to tie you both, or he will cut you free the minute I am not looking."

One of the robbers pulled Rupert's arms behind his back and had just begun to wrap a leather thong around his wrists, when the coach door flew open and Millicent jumped out. "You beast!" she screamed, running at the man and pounding him with her fists. "Let go of my son!"

The man crossed his arms over his face to protect himself.

"Hold her!" the Bandit King barked. The man wrapped his arms around Millicent from behind. If she could have bitten him, she would have.

As they struggled, Caroline stepped down daintily from the coach and threw her shawl around her face the minute she felt the cold air. She sized up the situation and faced the masked man. "What is the meaning of this, sir? How dare you accost Mrs. Copley!"

The bandit seemed taken aback for a moment. "I had not expected women to be with you, Lord Wetherby. A pity, but they will just have to come with us, I am afraid."

Caroline's voice was muffled, but she made herself clear. "I cannot come with you. I have a party to attend tomorrow night."

"You will just have to miss it, my lady. Now I order you to be silent and keep your servant under control, and no harm will come to either of you." He then went to the coach and looked inside. "I am surprised, my lord, that you would travel without any men. Quite unwise, don't you think?" He still held his gun, and he motioned again to one of the thieves. "Under these unexpected circumstances, you will all have to be bound and blindfolded. We have some distance to go before we reach our destination. There you will be my guest until I can notify the Duke of Loude that his son has been borrowed for a short time."

It seemed hours before the coach stopped. Raucous voices were heard as the horses were unharnessed and speculations were made about the contents of the baggage. Millicent was terrified, but she managed somehow to keep hold of Rupert's hands, even though they were tied behind him. They were led into a building and their blindfolds removed. It was a large, cavernous kitchen, the thick air filled with odors of food cooking, that were coming from a large iron pot that hung from a chain in the largest fireplace. Herbs and pots hung on pegs around the walls. A manor house, she decided, ancient and long neglected, by the looks of the chipped brick walls and uneven flagstones. There were three fireplaces, one large enough to walk into, and two smaller ones at opposite ends of the room. A long trestle table with several stools around it sat in the middle of the room, already set with large wooden trenchers and bottles of wine, as if someone were expected for dinner.

Upon their entrance, a tiny man with a large wooden ladle in his hand came running, the ladle dripping a path of liquid in its wake. Thin spikes of silver sprang out of his head as if he'd been electrified. He came to a skidding stop a few feet from them, his bright little shoe-button eyes surveying the entire parade with interest.

"Peen," the masked bandit said, "we have some unexpected guests for supper."

The little man nodded eagerly.

Their captor strode to the wide hearth and stood with his back to the blazing logs—a black silhouette, his mask hiding all of his face. Even the slits for his eyes didn't reveal what lay behind them.

Two of the men, both burly with unkempt beards and foul-smelling clothes, accompanied them. They shed their coats and threw them on the table.

Millicent winced.

"Tooter, untie the women and boy," the bandit ordered. "But you, my lord," he said to Wetherby, "will remain bound until you are locked in the room where you will stay until your father comes up with your ransom."

The second man, a wide grin on his face, pushed the marquis down onto a straight-backed spindle chair.

"Now, now, Boggles. That will never do." Then, tapping his chin with his riding crop, the tall man studied the women as they rubbed their wrists. "I shall have to figure out what to do with you and your maid," he said to Caroline.

When she saw that Caroline was about to repudiate him, Millicent put her hand on her arm. "Let him think I am your abigail, or he may separate us," she whispered.

Caroline turned around, motioning to the little man to help her off with her coat.

"Peen," the bandit said, and nodded for him to oblige her.

Caroline carefully removed her bonnet and patted her hair. The ringlets shown like pure gold in the reflecting light of the fire.

Rupert thought she was the most beautiful lady he had ever seen. He declared to himself right then and there that come what may, he would protect her with his life. But his thoughts were interrupted when the kidnapper walked toward her.

"Why, 'tis Lady Caroline Cavendish, I believe," he said, taking Caroline's chin in his hand, and turning her around to face him.

For one of the few times in her life, Caroline had no retort.

His voice was low, but everyone in the room heard every word. "One would think that I had captured a double prize. However, it has come to my ears that your father is unfortunately quite empty in the pockets. So, my dear lady, I must claim my reward in another way." He raised his mask and lowered his lips to hers so quickly that no one saw his face.

Wetherby growled through his gag and struggled to gain his feet. Millicent tried to free herself from Tooter's grip. And, alas, poor Rupert saw that his princess was being attacked by the villain. Oh, that he had his sword, but it had been left in the coach. However, he was a resourceful boy, and not devoid of innovation. He ran to the cavernous hearth and grabbing the end of a stick ablaze, whacked the blackguard across his backside. "Unhand the fair maiden, you knave," he yelled, brandishing his weapon.

The Bandit King dropped Caroline. Whirling about, he snatched the burning stick and hurled it across the room. It struck the far wall and fell sizzling to the stone floor.

Rupert glared, but stood his ground with shaking fists clutched at his sides.

The man in black saluted the angry boy. Even though she was not inclined to let him touch her, he took Caroline by the hand and lifted her up. "It seems, my lady, that you have a champion. I shall have to watch my back from now on."

Ignoring the disdainful look she cast his way, the bandit addressed Rupert. "Fear not, brave knight, I shan't kiss your lady again. I have far more important things to tend to. Now it is time to see Lord Wetherby to his room. In the morning, I shall decide what fate awaits my three uninvited guests."

Eleven

Tooter dropped Millicent's arm and rushed pell-mell toward the marquis. "Can we take his lordship to his cell now?"

The Bandit King put up his hand. "Words, Tooter. Watch your words. You will frighten the ladies. Remember, we have prepared nice accommodations for his lordship."

Rupert didn't like the renegade's tone of voice. "I won't let you put Lord Wetherby in a dungeon," he challenged.

Millicent pulled her son protectively to her.

The masked bandit laughed. "Boldly said, young man, but I am afraid your imagination is running to the medieval. All these old farmhouses have a spiderweb of underground cellars. I have chosen one small room. It may be a bit cold and damp, but a brazier warms at least a corner of his chamber. Under the circumstances, I doubt his lordship will be wandering about and catching a chill."

Wetherby let out a frustrated growl and with his teeth, ripped at the cloth that was twisted tightly over his mouth.

The Bandit King bowed and with a voice as soft as velvet, said, "Tooter and Boggles will now escort you to your room, my lord."

In his enthusiasm to beat Tooter to the prize, Boggles tripped over his own feet and fell onto Wetherby's lap, pinning him to the chair. Swearing a string of oaths, the bumbling fellow pushed himself off the marquis's legs, only to slip again and fall flat on the stone floor.

Tooter slapped his knees and guffawed like a donkey.

Glowering, Boggles struggled to his feet and fisted Tooter in the nose. "You noddy. A gud lick o' the chops will wipe that grin offen that bracket-face of yers."

Millicent put her hands over Rupert's ears, while the little man named Peen stood timidly, wringing his hands, oohing and ahhing behind her.

The bandit's voice cut the air like a bullet. "Boggles! Tooter! Do you want our guests to think we are barbarians?"

The two fustians sheepishly dropped their arms to their sides and shook their heads vigorously.

The Bandit King grasped Wetherby under one arm and hoisted him to an upright position. "If his lordship wishes to rise, he may."

His gag now loosened, Wetherby had a few choice words of his own, which were easily heard through the tattered cloth.

"My lord!" the Bandit King said in mock astonishment. "Where are your manners? There are ladies present."

Wetherby was a man of good height and well-muscled, yet his abductor towered a full head over him. He wanted to wish the bandit to hell, but with his hands still tied behind his back, he couldn't very well fight.

The bandit said smoothly, "I am sorry, my lord, but as you can see, my men are loyal to me, but easily provoked. I beg you to remember that fact when I am not here to see that they behave."

The two women and Rupert all glared at him.

"Surely you are not going to keep him bound and gagged," Millicent said, finally gaining her tongue.

"Never fear, Mrs. Copley. His bindings will be removed as soon as he is safely in his room." The bandit turned back to Wetherby. "I hope you don't mind the inconvenience, your lordship, but after a couple of the other young men were so foolish as to try to escape my hospitality, I am afraid it will be necessary to keep one of your ankles chained to a wooden post."

Millicent and Caroline passed sidelong glances between them.

The masked bandit seemed to read their minds. "I suggest that you do not waste your time trying to unlock his chains. Boggles keeps the key fastened to his belt at all times."

Boggles, a wide, toothless grin splitting his face, lifted up the sloppy folds of his shirt and showed them the large key which was fastened by a leather thong to his belt.

"Peen," their host called, "bring the lantern."

The little man scurried across to a table and lit a lantern, then ran back and handed it to Tooter.

The bandit grabbed a torch from a sconce on the wall, and in a few long strides, covered the distance to a brick wall on the other side of the large fireplace. "Now if you will come this way, Lord Wetherby, we will escort you to your chambers." Holding the torch high, he removed a brick that revealed a metal ring. One quick pull, and a door swung outward. He bowed. "I hope you find your accommodations to your liking, my lord. They may not be quite what you would expect at Grillon's, but there are many in this kingdom who would call themselves fortunate to have a roof over their heads on a night like this."

Millicent put her hand to her mouth. She had to think of something.

The bandit turned his head her way. "I am sure none of you will be so foolish as to try to leave while we are in the cellar, Mrs. Copley. My partner is standing guard in the courtyard. Even if you did manage to reach the gate, the snow is still falling, and we are miles from any inn or town. You would freeze to death in a short time. I shall deal with you when I see that his lordship is comfortably settled."

Wetherby quickly glanced at Millicent's and Caroline's startled faces. With a growl, he lunged head first at the black-hearted jackanape, but Boggles caught him with one giant hand and stopped his flight.

"Ah, Lord Wetherby, no heroics please," the bandit said.

"You need have no concern for the ladies and the boy." He laughed. "I assure you, I will see to their accommodations personally." Then stepping aside, he gestured for Boggles to take the marquis below.

Millicent's worried eyes watched Wetherby disappear into the dark hole in the wall. "Are you sure he will be warm enough?"

Caroline placed her hands on her hips. "Oh, this is outside of enough. I will not permit you, sir, to continue this abominable behavior. I demand that you bring Lord Wetherby back up here and release us now."

The Bandit King held up his hands in supplication. "Ah, ladies, 'tis a pity that I shall be here only one night. You would have provided much needed amusement. But as to setting his lordship free, I am afraid that is impossible. Where will I get my income for this next year?"

Millicent put her arm around Caroline.

Rupert, knees quaking, bravely planted himself in front of the two women and recited over and over to himself, *"Women are frail things to be protected."*

"You are a scoundrel, sir," Millicent said.

"You are near the mark, madam," the bandit agreed. "But now I must think of something to keep you entertained and out of trouble while I am gone. Of course, there will be a few rules you will have to follow, but we shall speak of those in the morning when my men come in for breakfast."

"Your men?"

"My cohort will leave with me, but I have two stablemen who come for their meals. Peen, Tootle, and Boggles will remain inside the house."

The three men nodded their agreement.

Caroline stamped her foot. "I want to be shown to my bedchamber now."

Amusement colored his words. "You are in it, my lady."

Everyone took a sweeping look around the large open room.

The masked man looked at Caroline. "I suggest, your ladyship, that you count your blessings. I assure you, you would find the stables far more uncomfortable."

Caroline sniffed. "How dare you suggest I sleep in a kitchen? This is a big house. There must be nearly fifty rooms."

"And they are all uninhabitable," the bandit said. "There is no furniture, and the chimneys probably have not been cleaned in forty years. You would have to carry your own luggage, you know, for I will not have my men waiting on you. Why do you think I came to an abandoned house in the middle of nowhere? Each year, I choose a new hiding place in a different part of the country. One where no one would think to search. You may fix yourselves a space at the other side of the room by that small fireplace."

They all looked to where he pointed.

Millicent brought her hand to her throat. "But there is no privacy."

"I told the stablemen to fetch a couple of horse blankets to cut off a corner of the room."

As if on cue, a blast of cold air shot through the kitchen door. Two snowdusted men carrying ropes and blankets blew in just as Tooter and Boggles returned from the cellar.

The Bandit King motioned the men to the far end of the room. "Tooter and Boggles have been persuaded to give up their straw mattresses to you ladies. You will find your coach rugs over by the luggage."

By their scowls, the two men in question didn't appear to be the least bit pleased, but they, as well as the others, looked to where the tall man pointed. True enough, while they had been occupied with their concerns for Lord Wetherby, all the trunks and boxes from the coach had been brought in and tossed willy-nilly against the wall just inside the kitchen courtyard door.

"Where do you intend to sleep?" Caroline asked, eyeing him suspiciously.

"My partner and I have a space by the other small fire-place. We take turns being on watch during the night hours. Peen sleeps by his pots and pans. Tooter and Boggles have orders to stay where they can keep an eye on the door to the cellar. Do not fear, ladies, you will be amply protected."

Caroline commented with a questionable word under her breath.

The bandit paid no mind to her protest. "Breakfast will be at dawn. My partner and I plan to leave at first light."

"I never get up that early," Caroline complained.

"That is up to you. Peen serves two meals a day. If you miss breakfast, you will not eat again until nightfall. Now, ladies, I see that the blankets are hung and the men have dragged the pads over for you. I suggest you get settled in quickly. Peen seems to have supper about ready."

"I will need my night bag and the green trunk," Caroline said peevishly.

"You know where they are. You are free to help yourself."

Millicent coaxed Caroline over to the baggage. "Come, my lady, we only need our portmanteaux tonight. I think I shall feel much safer sleeping in my clothes, anyway. To-morrow we can sort things out."

They hurriedly searched for their bags and carried them to their corner behind the blankets.

The stablemen, Tooter, and Boggles were already seated, as was Rupert. Millicent was glad to see that Peen had re-moved the men's coats from the table before he placed the food on it.

"Bring my meal over by the fire, Peen," Caroline said.

The bandit strode over to her. "You will eat at the table with everyone else, or not at all, Lady Caroline."

Caroline pursed her lips and seated herself near Millicent and Rupert.

Millicent smiled encouragingly. "You must be famished, my lady. You haven't eaten since this morning."

Caroline stared at the crusted food clinging to the rim of the bowl. "This is disgusting!"

The bandit stood behind her. "Fie on you, Lady Caroline. You are too critical of poor Peen. He tries his best to put tasty meals on the table. Did it never occur to you that servants have feelings?"

Caroline snorted.

"If you had to work all day meeting the demands of those in command, you might change your opinion."

"Well, thank goodness, I don't have to."

There was a loud silence behind her.

Caroline gritted her teeth. "Well if I must eat here, why are you taking *your* plate away?"

"Because, dear lady, I permit no one to see my face. My friend will come in soon to eat, and I will take over the watch. He, too, does not wish to have his identity known." With that the bandit walked to the far side of the room, and sitting with his back to them, raised his mask and began to eat.

Caroline daintily picked a piece of meat out of the stew, then dropped it back in. Without a word, she left the table and, pouting, marched behind the hanging blankets.

There was nothing Millicent could do to stop her.

Rupert had no such compulsions, and was attacking his meal enthusiastically.

Millicent picked up a sticky spoon and placed it back down on the table. She decided it was far safer to eat with her fingers and sip the gravy from the bowl like the men were doing. The thick porridge, with huge hunks of meat and what could have been corn floating in it, was tasteless, but after looking at the cook's eager expression, she didn't have the heart to say so. Instead she smiled and said kindly, "It is most interesting, Mr. Peen."

The little man's eyes lit up and he offered her some bread. It proved hard, gritty, and burnt on the bottom, but she found it somewhat palatable when dipped into the broth and softened.

When she finished all that she could, Millicent broke off a chunk of bread, and scraping off as much of the black crust as possible, wrapped it in her handkerchief. Perhaps she could persuade Lady Caroline to eat a little. It was all they had.

Earlier, Millicent had seen Tooter go down the stairs to the cellar carrying a tray with a trencher and mug, and she wondered if Lord Wetherby was having as much difficulty as she in swallowing his meal. She yawned. Oh, dear, there had to be a way out of their difficulty, but now she was too tired to think clearly. Tomorrow. Tomorrow when she was rested, she would surely figure some way to see for herself if he was all right.

She found a bucket to use as a chamber pot and filled a bowl of water for Lady Caroline to wash in. She and Rupert would have to share a mattress. "I think it wiser if we keep our beds as close together as possible," Millicent whispered.

Caroline didn't object, and let Millicent lug her pad over nearer theirs.

Rupert ran over to the hodgepodge of trunks and boxes. He located his sword and his portmanteau, which he opened quickly. With a sigh of relief, he found the box with his mother's present still carefully wrapped among his nightclothes. He touched his journal. My, Lord Wetherby would have a lot of stars beside his name when they finished this adventure.

Running back across the cold floor, Rupert placed his sword beside the straw mattress and crawled under the fur robe beside his mother.

Caroline reached out from under her coach rug to the adjoining mattress. "Good night," she said, with a little tremor in her voice.

Millicent patted her hand. "Good night, my lady."

Rupert felt his mother's arms encircle him. "Don't be frightened, Momma," he said softly. "I shall take care of you." Millicent's arms tightened, and he snuggled closer. He had two fair ladies to protect now. It was a great responsibility, and he tried to think what his lordship would want him to do.

A few minutes passed. "We didn't say our prayers, Momma," Rupert whispered.

Millicent was mindful of the masculine voices murmuring only a few feet away. "Perhaps, tonight, we will say them to ourselves," Millicent said. "Like Lord Wetherby does."

In the cold cell below, Wetherby was not in a prayerful mood. He couldn't tell if it were day or night, the food had been atrocious, and he'd only eaten because he was near to starvation. Unless he practically sat on top of the brazier, he had to stay under the covers with his coat on to keep from freezing. His hands were no longer bound, but the chain on his ankle gave him little freedom to move about. They'd given him some candles, but nothing to read. There was no hope of breaking the lock. Even if he had a saw to cut through the pole that supported the beam, he'd only bring down the ceiling on top of himself.

Whatever possessed him to let himself be persuaded to take that spoiled, high-fashioned, clothes-horse Caroline to Wellington? They could have been safely on their way to Roxwealde Castle. One woman was bad enough, but being confronted by two—and a very determined little boy—he'd been overwhelmed. Who said women were frail things to be protected? It was men who needed assistance to resist them.

He cringed to think how foolish he'd been to send that message off to Copley telling him not to be upset if they were held up for a few days. There was no one, no one at all who would be concerned about them for as much as another week. By then, his father would have received the ransom note. The irascible old skinflint would probably refuse

to pay the price and let him rot in this hellhole for the rest
of his life.

He worried, too. Worried that Rupert would get himself
into trouble. Worried that Caroline would provoke the bandit
once too often. But most of all, he worried that he'd failed
miserably in his commitment to guard that unpredictable
woman he'd promised to protect on her journey to her
brother-in-law's. He realized how much he'd gotten used to
her. Her chatter. The way she wrinkled her nose when she
was trying not to laugh. Even the way she scolded him with
her eyes when he said *one of those words,* as her son put it.
Demme! If those imbeciles laid a hand on them, he'd kill
them.

His thoughts turned to Rupert. Wetherby couldn't help but
think how disappointed the little fellow must be in him—or
how many *X*'s he was probably marking down in his ledger
for failing to uphold the Code.

The next morning, the smell of bacon, burnt bread, and
strong coffee awakened Caroline, Millicent, and Rupert. It
was still dark, but they were all ravenous. They came out
cautiously, not knowing what their reception would be.
Tooter and Boggles lay snoring on one side of the big fireplace. The Bandit King and his masked companion were sitting at the table conversing in low tones. Their empty plates
showed that they'd already eaten.

Caroline took herself to the very end of the table, as far
away as possible from them. Millicent and Rupert followed
suit and took seats beside her. Peen came running with an
overflowing bowl of porridge, and in his eagerness to place
it in front of Caroline, he slipped on the greasy, stone floor
and spilled half of it down the front of her dress.

Caroline screeched.

"Oh, my goodness," Millicent said, handing Caroline her
handkerchief.

Caroline pushed the crusted dish away. "Bring me a clean bowl and spoon," she demanded. "This is not fit for a pig to eat out of."

Peen screwed up his face and looked in horror at the havoc he'd caused.

A deep voice traveled down the length of the table. "If you are not satisfied with Peen's cooking, Lady Caroline, perhaps you would like to take over that job yourself."

Tooter and Boggles woke up to the noise. Like two hungry dogs, they hurried to the table, seating themselves across from the women.

Caroline glared at them.

Boggles gave her a gap-toothed grin.

The bandit continued, "You need a lesson in manners, Lady Caroline. While I am gone, you will cook and wait upon my men when they come in for their meals."

Tooter hooted and nudged Boggles, who was already stuffing his mouth with food.

Caroline raised her chin defiantly. "I will do no such thing."

The bandit spoke cooly. "In any house of mine, everyone receives the rewards of their efforts. If you do not cook, you do not eat. It is as simple as that."

As that thought sunk in, Caroline's eyes widened. "But I don't know how to cook," she said miserably, her eyes glistening with tears.

Pity filled Millicent as she looked at Caroline, her hair rumpled, her fine dress stained with the porridge. "I do," Millicent said impulsively. "I will help Mr. Peen."

A chuckle came from behind the mask. "Ah . . . *Mr.* Peen, do you hear that? You have a kitchen helper."

The little man looked as if he wanted to jump up and down with ecstasy.

Caroline let out a sigh of relief and thanked Millicent with her eyes.

However, their host was not as benevolent. He walked over

and picked up a large black kettle from the worktable. "Since you cannot cook, my lady, and you have such a disgust for the state of the cookware, then perhaps you should be the one to clean it." He plunked the kettle right under Caroline's nose before seating himself once again.

Caroline pulled away from the food-encrusted pot. "I won't do it."

His voice became as smooth as honey. "Ah, but I think you will. If any one of you three does not do something for his or her keep, then all must suffer. *Mr.* Peen," he said, "remove Master Rupert's and Mrs. Copley's bowls, please."

The little man complied reluctantly. He even took the spoon filled with porridge from Rupert just as he was about to put it in his mouth.

Rupert watched his bowl being carried away, then looked sadly at Caroline.

"I think her ladyship is about to discover that any one person's selfish deeds affect those around her," the bandit said.

"Wait! Wait!" Caroline called desperately to Peen. "I'll do it—only give Rupert back his breakfast."

The masked man leaned back from the table and steepled his fingers. "Just think, Mr. Peen. In a single morning, you have acquired a kitchen helper and a scullery maid to clean your pots and pans. And, I might add, someone to scrub the floor clean, too. The way everyone has been slipping on the greasy flagstones, 'tis a miracle no one has broken a leg."

Caroline made a little choking sound.

Rupert had had enough of this bullying. "You cannot make Lady Caroline do such a thing," he said.

"Ah, but I can, because I am King here, you see. Isn't that right, Lady Caroline? In your household, you never question your right to order your servants about, do you?"

Rupert studied the black-robed man and leaned over toward Caroline. "I shall help you," he whispered hoarsely.

"You have loyal friends, my lady. I hope you realize how

fortunate you are." He turned to the boy. "That is very generous of you, Master Rupert. You may help the new scullery maid if you wish, but she must not shirk her duties. In fact, Mr. Peen, if any one of the three does not perform to my aspirations, you will refuse food to all. Is that clear?"

Peen wrung his hands and nodded.

The bandit pushed back from the table. "And here I was worried that I would not be a good host and couldn't find something to keep you all entertained while I was gone. Now you will not have a dull moment until I return from my errand."

"What about Lord Wetherby?" Millicent asked. "Surely you are not going to make him stay in the cellar all the time you are gone!"

"Alas, I feel that is necessary. I cannot have any of you getting in trouble by trying to help him escape. No, he will stay chained. I visited his lordship this morning. He has eaten well. Although he had some disagreement with what I am doing, I think he will eventually see reason in adjusting to his situation. Now if you will excuse me, we shall be leaving."

The bandit drew on his black coat with its several capes. As soon as he had pulled on his gloves, he exited with his henchman, leaving Caroline and Millicent looking helplessly at each other.

Twelve

Millicent was glad to have something to keep her busy. She suggested to Mr. Peen that he melt buckets of snow by the fire and fill a barrel to provide an unlimited supply of water for all their needs. She showed Rupert and Lady Caroline how to scour the pots and pans with sand, then rinse them with water. However, there seemed to be few foods to work with, and Peen prepared most of the dinner that proved to be as skimpy as that of the night before.

The next morning, Boggles fell down the cellar steps, splattering Lord Wetherby's food everywhere. Poor Caroline was given a bucket of water and a rag and told to clean it up. Tooter held a lantern over her head to light the stairs, giggling all the time. She could have killed him.

However, Millicent had her own concerns. "Mr. Peen," she asked politely, "will you please show me what supplies you have on hand?"

He led her to several sacks that were pushed against the wall.

"Dear heaven, that does not seem much to feed several hungry men. What is in them?"

He shrugged helplessly.

Millicent pulled one of the bags out. "It says barley, Mr. Peen. You had the words facing backward." She then turned all the bundles around. "Wheat flour, cornmeal, millet. See, someone has labeled all of them for you."

The little man studied the sacks hard and turned scarlet. "Don't make no difference. Can't read."

Millicent cringed when she thought of the flat, rock-hard bread they'd been served the night before. She began to suspect that he didn't know how to cook, either. "Surely there are more supplies."

Mr. Peen led her to a small, cold storage room off the kitchen. Mutton, chickens, and beef hung from hooks. She also discovered a barrel of apples and sacks of potatoes and other vegetables. The Bandit King had evidently planned for a long stay. She'd already noticed the herbs in the kitchen the night before. "What oils do you have?"

Peen took a cruet down from a shelf.

Millicent stuck in a finger for a sample. "It is a cooking oil of some kind. I'm not sure what, but it is not grease." She opened several other crocks and found brown sugar and molasses, honey, vinegar, and salt. "Oh, my, you have a good stock here."

Peen watched her with anticipation.

One look into those questioning eyes, and Millicent knew for certain that the timid soul knew nothing about preparing food. "I am sure you have your own way of doing things, Mr. Peen, but perhaps I can suggest a few recipes that our cook, Mrs. Woodhouse, taught me," she said.

He nodded happily, a little crooked smile lighting up his face.

"While you are busy chopping up some meat and potatoes for the evening meal, I can relieve you of the bread-making."

No argument came from Peen, who scurried out to the storage hut to get the needed supplies.

Thinking of how gritty Mr. Peen's bread had been, Millicent dug out the remnant of her torn veil to make a sieve. She sifted the flour into a large wooden bowl, fetched the kettle from the fireplace, and poured in hot water to make dough. "Now just a pinch of salt."

Suddenly, Millicent realize that she had an audience. Mr.

Peen had returned, and couldn't hide his curiosity. Caroline stood close, peering over Millicent's shoulder, and Rupert kept jumping up and down at her elbow.

"Momma, are you going to make some crumpets?".

She laughed. "No, we will simply start with unleavened bread."

Caroline set down her bucket of dirty water and wiped her forehead with the back of her hand. Her favorite velvet traveling dress was ruined: first by the porridge that Peen had spilled on her, and then because she'd torn the hem when she'd had to get down on her knees to scrub the slate floor. She now looked at the lump of flour and said, grimacing, "It looks a mess."

"But that is the fun of it," Rupert cried. "May I help, Momma?"

"Well, the dough has to be kneaded three hundred times, so you all can help by counting with me. When we reach one hundred, one of you may step in and take my place," Millicent said, watching Mr. Peen from the corner of her eye. His mouth formed a big *O*.

"May I be second, Momma?"

"First we will ask Lady Caroline and Mr. Peen if they want to knead the bread."

Mr. Peen, his eyes now like saucers, chewed on his lower lip and nodded.

Rupert tried not to look disappointed, but he failed miserably.

Caroline sniffed. "He can have my turn."

Rupert's smile returned.

While Millicent punched the dough, she and Rupert counted out loud. When it came Peen's turn to knead, he kept his gaze on Millicent's lips. He waited until she called out the number, then he repeated it in a near shout.

Finally, Lady Caroline's soft voice joined them.

As soon as Rupert finished his turn, Millicent retrieved a linen towel from her portmanteau and soaked it in water.

This she stretched over the bowl before setting it on the hearth.

Caroline, her eyebrows raised, followed her.

"Now," Millicent said, "we must wait until the dough rises before we knead it again. In the meantime, while Mr. Peen is putting the meat and vegetables in the cooking kettle, I might just make up an apple pudding to have with dinner."

Mr. Peen suddenly remembered his chopping chores and rushed back to the potatoes and other vegetables.

"How did you ever learn to do all that?" Caroline asked. "Didn't you have a cook?"

Millicent laughed. "The best. Mrs. Woodhouse started me out making biscuits and gingerbread men when I was a little girl."

"Goodness," Caroline said, "didn't your mother object to your working like a servant?"

"No, she thought it kept me busy and out of trouble. My father is mayor of our village and we had a steady stream of people coming to consult him. Mother often had to entertain them and their wives."

A few hours later, Caroline watched, fascinated, as Millicent plumped up the dough to just the right shapes to fit into two huge, oiled skillets. She then cut the tops lengthwise. "We must let them proof for an hour before we set them to bake."

"It swelled up," Caroline said, in awe.

Millicent laughed. "Would you like to try to make some bread?"

Caroline wiped her hands down the sides of her once-beautiful frock. "Do you really think I could?"

"You will never know unless you try," Millicent said kindly.

"I want to do it all by myself," Caroline said as she chose her flours and made her mixture. Rupert helped her count to three hundred.

Caroline's first loaf was hard as a rock, because she kept

taking off the towel to peek. Her second burned because she left it in the skillet too long. But her third loaf was just right, a hard crust with a soft and tasty center.

"Perfect," exclaimed Millicent.

Caroline brought her hand to her mouth, her eyes sparkling. "It is just, isn't it?" she said proudly, as the men devoured every bite.

"Now," Millicent said, "we will mix another batch so it will be ready to bake in the morning."

That evening after supper, Boggles, full of good food and too much ale, tripped over a stool, once again spilling Wetherby's food.

For the second time in one day, Peen had to fill the trencher all over again. The cook handed Boggles the lantern and told Millicent, "From now on, he can light your way, and ye will take Lord Wetherby's meals to him."

Boggles pouted, but went ahead to open the door of Wetherby's room for her. As soon as she was inside, he deliberately slammed the door, bolted it from the outside, and stomped back up the steps.

Wetherby couldn't believe his eyes. "Mrs. Copley?" She looked like an angel standing in the reflected light of the small brazier. He leaped to his feet and walked toward her as far as his chain permitted. "Here," he said, taking the tray and placing it on the floor. "I am afraid the only place for you to sit down is on my pad."

The room was cold. A candle flickered on the floor, and he wore his coat. After she'd settled herself Indian-fashion on the straw mattress, she was still shivering. "That odious man! I have been so afraid he might have hurt you."

Wetherby was moved by her concern, and settling beside her, pulled a wool blanket up over her shoulders. He searched for the words to set her mind at ease. "He will not harm me. The Bandit King would not allow it. Whatever else the renegade is, he has never hurt any of the gentlemen he kidnapped. Of course, I don't know what he will do if my father refuses to pay my ransom," he said, trying for a bit of humor to lighten the conversation. However, she didn't seem to get the point.

"My lord! Do not say such a terrible thing. Surely the duke will pay."

"Yes, well, I suppose he will. I am his only son . . . it is just that—"

"It is just what?"

"You might say we have had a few disagreements—mostly about my finding a wife of impeccable bloodlines to produce the next heir to the Lance family empire."

Millicent's heart fell. "Yes, I suppose you must marry *someday*."

Wetherby began to eat. "It just seems so disagreeable— being shackled to one woman for the rest of my life."

Millicent pondered that for a moment. "I cannot imagine my mother and father living apart from each other."

"You mean day after day, year after year?"

"Why, yes. Occasionally there have been times—like when my mother went to care for her sick sister up in Ashford. Mama was gone for two whole months, and we missed her sorely. Papa especially. But she said that Aunt Milly—I am named after her—needed her more."

He considered his mother's last illness, which kept her abed for months, and the fact that his father had visited her only twice. Wetherby had come more than that—three times. And yet, he'd considered that His Grace held his wife in high regard. He was always saying so. Hadn't he hired the best of physicians to attend her, and seen she had plenty of servants to supply her every need? But seeing the same face every day across the table, around the house, without becoming bored? That was a different matter altogether.

He suddenly realized how quiet Millicent had become. "I am sorry, forgive me. You were about to say something else, and I am afraid my mind wandered."

Millicent looked down at her hands. "I just said that I had expected Bertie and me to live the same sort of life when the war was over."

He didn't know why, but he took her hands in his. "I knew Captain Copley quite well. I have never known a more amiable, worthwhile fellow."

She glanced up at him, her eyes glistening with unshed tears. "You are a very kind man, Lord Wetherby. I am sure you will find a woman to love someday."

He was afraid it was getting to be a habit, but he wanted to kiss her, even though he knew he'd be taking advantage of her vulnerability. *Someone of your ilk probably would,* she'd said. He was totally reprehensible. No, not totally. He fought off the urge to take her in his arms, patted her hands instead, and placed them back on her lap.

She gave a nervous little laugh. "Did you like your meal?"

Wetherby looked at the empty plate. He'd eaten every bite without realizing it. "It certainly was an improvement over breakfast. Almost as if another person had cooked it."

"I told Mr. Peen I would help him. He is a very sweet man."

Wetherby looked to see if she'd become addled by this upsetting experience. "Sweet man? You jest."

"No, really. He has not had an easy life, my lord. He has told me all about it."

Wetherby really didn't want to hear about Peen. He wanted to hear more about *her,* but he would listen to anything—even take one of her scoldings—to keep her with him a bit longer. It was lonely down in this dark cell all by himself. "Tell me about him."

Millicent folded her hands in her lap. He was glad to see that she didn't seem any more eager to leave than he did to see her go.

"Mr. Peen told me he was orphaned when he was a child and was taken in by a family of smugglers on the Devonshire coast. His foster parents made him work like a slave, and since he was so small, the older boys beat him and made fun of him. They sometimes lent him out to farmers and then took every penny he earned away from him. He said that the Bandit King gave him his first honest job."

Wetherby made a choking sound.

"Are you all right?" Millicent cried with alarm. When Wetherby assured her that he was, she continued, "Mr. Peen allowed that he fibbed a bit, for he really did not know how to cook."

That was obvious to Wetherby by the first meal he'd been forced to eat. So Mrs. Copley could cook. "Now I know why the quality improved so greatly from one meal to the next. But it is you three that I am concerned about. They haven't made you do anything you didn't want to, have they? I mean . . . no one has forced you . . ."

Millicent cocked her head. "Well, Caroline may disagree with what I say, but no, I would not say that they have."

Wetherby stiffened. "What do you mean? Has Caroline not been treated well?"

"The Bandit King said she had to scrub pots."

Wetherby almost laughed. "Scrub pots? No one could ever make Caroline scrub pots."

"He left orders that if she does not, she gets no food." Millicent didn't add that neither would she or Rupert.

Wetherby guffawed with relief. "Thank God she was not hurt. If any of those scoundrels dares put a hand on her—"

A strange feeling of melancholy descended upon Millicent. She had guessed that Lord Wetherby was very fond of Lady Caroline, now she knew it. What man would not be? She was so beautiful—genteel—friendly. A diamond of the first water. Giving a nervous laugh, she said, "Well, I see that you have eaten all your supper. If I stay any longer, Mr. Peen may not let me bring you your meals."

No sooner had she said that than there was a pounding on the door. Boggles's irritated voice barked from the other side. "Ain't he finished with his meal yet?"

Millicent made to rise, and Wetherby jumped up to assist

her. He handed her the tray. When she reached the door, he tried to think of something to hold her longer. "How is Rupert?"

"Oh," she laughed, "he insists on helping Lady Caroline with her chores. He is quite taken by her, I am afraid."

Wetherby was surprised at how much he missed the little rascal. "Perhaps you can think of an excuse for him to come with you next time you bring my meal."

Millicent's eyes sparkled in the lantern light. "Rupert would like that above all else, your lordship. I shall have to think of something to get Mr. Peen to allow him to come."

The pounding resumed, louder this time.

"Yes, Mr. Boggles. I am ready to go," Millicent called out.

They heard the latch being lifted.

Wetherby was afraid he was beginning to feel sorry for himself. "I don't suppose you have anything I could read. It gets terribly dull having to converse only with oneself."

"Oh, it must," she said, sympathetically. "I have a book by Sir Walter Scott in one of my trunks that I think you may enjoy. *Rob Roy.* I shall look for it."

Boggles raised the lantern over his head and peered into the room. The lantern cast strange shadows upon his ugly face.

Wetherby watched Millicent go. It would be another twelve hours before he ate again . . . before he would see her again.

The following morning, Millicent brought Wetherby his breakfast. This time she knew enough to wear her wool pelisse. "I have not asked Mr. Peen yet whether Rupert can come. But I have brought you the book I spoke of." She settled down and waited for him to eat.

"Rupert said to tell you that he will put a star in the journal for you every night that you are in the dungeon. He said you would know what he was as talking about." Millicent waited for Lord Wetherby to give her a clue as to what her son had meant, but she soon realized that he wasn't going to.

Instead, he bypassed the subject completely. "How is Caroline?"

A trifle disappointed, she shrugged. "She is all right, though Boggles said she must scrub the stones in front of the hearth where he sleeps. I don't think she was too happy about that, because she has all the pots and pans from breakfast to clean yet."

Wetherby laughed outright for the first time since Millicent had brought him his meal. "I daresay Caroline hasn't done a useful thing in her life."

"It is outside of enough that you should make light of poor Lady Caroline's position. You just do not appreciate her hidden talents."

"I am afraid Caro has been spoon-fed since the day she was born."

Millicent raised her nose a trifle. "Did you like your bread, my lord?"

"What has that to do with Caroline?"

"She baked it." Millicent watched with satisfaction as disbelief, and then suspicion, passed quickly over his face.

"Good lord! Caro?" Wetherby guffawed. "I cannot believe it."

"I daresay, she was quite proud of her achievement, too," Millicent said smugly.

Boggles began pounding and shouting obscenities at the door.

Millicent held her ears. "That impossible man! I must think of a way for me to bring Rupert and get rid of Boggles all at the same time," she whispered, holding out her hands for the tray.

"I shall see you this evening," he said, kissing the inside of her wrist.

A shiver went through her. She was glad to see the sparkle

back in his lordship's eyes, but, oh, he was still a rogue. Loving one woman, while kissing another. The terrible thing was, she wanted him to do it.

That evening, Boggles and Tooter were already impossibly drunk by the time they had finished eating and went to sit beside the warm hearth. There they continued to drink, belch, and sing the most outrageous songs, calling to Caroline to come fill their tankards with ale as quickly as they emptied them. They laughed uproariously when she reluctantly complied.

Mr. Peen finished filling Wetherby's tray with food and looked helplessly at the two fustians.

Millicent saw her chance to have Rupert accompany her. "Both men are foxed, and in no condition to carry the lantern into the cellar," she said convincingly. "If either of them fell, the house would be set afire. My son is a strong lad, he can carry the light."

Rupert hurried to his mother's side. "I am that, Mr. Peen."

One look at Boggles and Tooter, and Peen agreed.

Rupert ran behind the curtain to get his sword. He took his responsibility seriously, and proceeded to lead his mother down the stairs. The corridor opened up into a much larger room, and off it were several doors—some closed—most hanging on broken hinges, or missing altogether. In the blackness of it all, some black holes seemed to go on forever.

" 'Tis the door on the right," Millicent whispered, as if she were afraid someone were listening.

Rupert had to put the lantern on the dirt floor and stand on tiptoe to reach the latch. With a bit of trepidation, he slowly opened the door. Once his eyes became accustomed to the dim light, he was overjoyed to see that Lord Wetherby was neither hanging by his toes from the ceiling nor being stretched on a torture rack. Only chained to a post, which really wasn't so bad when Rupert considered the alternatives. Relief shot through him, loosening his tongue, and neither adult got a word in edgewise for the first several minutes.

Then Lord Wetherby and his mother began to talk about grown-up things, and Rupert's imagination kept being drawn to the shadows on the walls and the black holes he'd seen running off the big storage room.

"Momma, may I go out in the passageway?"

Millicent started to protest, when Wetherby placed his hand on her arm. "What harm is there in it? He is getting restless." He then spoke authoritatively to Rupert. "Loyal knight, go outside and guard the entrance to my quarters."

Rupert snapped to attention, his eyes sparkling. "Aye, my lord. Code Number Two. Right?"

Millicent frowned. "Stay near, Rupert, and take the lantern, so I know you are there."

"Yes, Momma. I am not afraid of the dark, but may I have some candles, too? That will give even more light."

"Certainly," Wetherby said, handing him three tapers.

Rupert picked up the lantern and bowed his way out the door.

Millicent still wasn't sure it was a good idea. "He may hurt himself."

Wetherby assured her, "It is just a large, empty room. What harm can come to him?"

Millicent relaxed and waited for Wetherby to finish his meal. While she kept her eye on the yellow light outside the door, they talked about *Rob Roy*. They didn't stop until Millicent realized that the glow in the corridor hadn't fluctuated. If Rupert were using the lantern, the light and shadows would be moving, wouldn't they?

She didn't want Lord Wetherby to think her missish, succumbing to vapors. She said her good-byes, and taking the tray, left the room. The lantern sat about four feet from the door. There were no candles, and no little boy in sight. She quickly set the tray at the foot of the stairs and went back to bolt the door. Boggles was sure to check soon to see that she had done so.

"Rupert?" she whispered. There was no answer in the cellar, but sounds of a peppery commotion whirled down from the kitchen above. A shiver of apprehension ran through her. Picking up the lantern, Millicent turned in all directions. "Rupert!" she hissed, louder.

From above, Millicent heard Boggles bellowing like a bull, but it was Mr. Peen's shrill voice that called from the stairwell. "Mrs. Copley? Where are ye, Mrs. Copley?"

Millicent was beginning to have a terrible feeling that something awful was going to happen, when she saw the tiny flickering light of a candle growing larger as it made its way toward her.

"Momma! Momma!"

Millicent splayed a hand over her heart. "Rupert? My goodness, you did give me a start."

"I'm sorry, Momma."

"Wherever have you been?"

"I found a passageway."

"Well, after this, if you are going to have an adventure, I want to go with you. Is that understood?"

"Yes, Momma. But come, I must show you. It may lead to a way out of here."

Millicent held the lantern high. Several doorways opened off the wide room, but at the far end, it narrowed to a single corridor where she could see that the opening split into two directions. Curiosity and desire to investigate were about to win her over when there was a terrible crash.

Mr. Peen had tripped over the tray, scattering dishes everywhere. "Mrs. Copley!" came his frantic cry.

"Coming, Mr. Peen." Millicent put her face down near Rupert's. "I cannot come with you now. We must go back to the kitchen. I fear they are having a frightful row. Here, take the lantern, we must help Mr. Peen."

Millicent was assisting the little man up from where he

lay sprawled on the floor when a woman's scream spiraled down from the room above. It was followed by deep raucous laughter, then a loud crack, which sounded considerably like splintering wood.

"Oh, please, Mrs. Copley," Peen whimpered, "come at once, or I do believe she is going to kill them."

Thirteen

As the loud, boisterous voices rumbled down the cellar steps, Millicent leaned closer to Rupert. "I don't believe it wise to investigate just now, dear. If we delay much longer, the men may become suspicious and not allow you to come with me again. Perhaps we can explore further tomorrow, after we have brought Lord Wetherby his breakfast. You say you think there may be a way out of here?

"I am sure of it, Momma."

A little shiver of expectation ran down Millicent's spine. "Tomorrow it is, then. Now we must get back upstairs. We cannot leave Lady Caroline alone with those men."

"No, Momma, we cannot, but I have my sword. They shall not harm my lady."

Millicent and Rupert followed the agitated Peen to the kitchen, where they found Boggles and Tooter circling Caroline. She sat squarely on her jewelry box in the middle of her mattress, wielding a butcher knife, daring them to touch her.

As soon as the cowardly Tooter spied the others, he ran out to seek safety in the center of the large room. Boggles, however, continued to dance around Caroline just beyond her reach, spewing childish chants and holding Rupert's portmanteau in front of him in case she decided to test her aim. Trunks were open, clothing strewn helter-skelter. It was obvious that the men had been going through their belongings.

Rupert's eyes widened as he recognized his bag. He ran toward Boggles, shouting, "Put that down, you ruffian!"

"Ho!" guffawed the big fustian. "The brat says this is his, Mr. Tooter."

To his horror, Rupert saw the portmanteau fly over his head into the outer room. Tooter caught it. Rupert reversed his course, but again as he reached for his bag, Tooter whisked it back through the air to Boggles. Both women rounded on the renegade. The clumsy man tripped and turned a backward somersault over a stool. Rupert watched helplessly as his bag sailed over their heads and crashed against the bricks of the smaller fireplace.

While Peen stood in the background wringing his hands, Millicent and Caroline chased the big oaf from their sleeping quarters.

Rupert retrieved his portmanteau, then sat down on the hearth and opened it. With shaking hands, he unraveled the package. Shattered pieces of china fell onto his lap. He picked up a little hand and tried to fix it back on the pretty lady's wrist.

"Are you all right, Rupert?" Millicent called from the other side of the horse blanket.

"Yes, Momma," he replied, trying to block the pain from his voice. Rupert wiped a tear from his eye and looked around the room. What was he to do now? His mother's Christmas present was ruined beyond repair. He had to hide it. He couldn't take the chance of her asking questions, so he lovingly placed each chard back in the box, and stuffed it behind the pile of kindling that was stacked beside the fireplace. He'd no sooner finished concealing the package than his mother and Lady Caroline came back around the curtain and began to prepare for bed.

That night Rupert wrote his sad thoughts in his journal, then blowing out his candle, stuffed the book under the straw mattress and crawled into bed. For a long time, tossed and turned. His heart was heavy over the destruction of his mother's gift. The fact that he wasn't able to tell anyone about his loss only added to his misery, and he felt very much alone—even in his mother's arms. He couldn't help thinking how unhappy and lonely Lord Wetherby must be, too, down in the dark cellar all by himself. His mother and Lady Caroline, exhausted from their ordeal, slept soundly beside him. The thunderous snores of Boggle and Tooter and the high-pitched whistling twills from Mr. Peen told him that the men were not likely to awaken until morning unless the roof caved in upon them.

Carefully, Rupert wiggled out from under his blankets. He stuffed the journal inside his coat, put a pencil in his pocket, and quietly lit a candle. Boggles always left the cellar door open a crack so that he could listen for any suspicious noises from below. Rupert squeezed through the opening and made his way down the stairs. It didn't take him long to unlatch the door to Wetherby's cell.

Wetherby, growing more and more offended over his powerlessness, always slept battle-alert, one eye open, ears tuned to hear the slightest of sounds. The fire in the brazier burned low, but he could see that the figure silhouetted in the doorway was too small to be any one of the adults. He sat up. "Rupert?"

"I thought you might like to work on our journal," Rupert whispered, pulling out the book as he came nearer.

Wetherby raised his eyebrows. "I take it no one knows you are down here."

Rupert shuffled his feet.

"It will not go well with you if those barbarians find that you are not in your bed," Wetherby said, not unkindly.

"They won't wake up for hours. They are too drunk."

Wetherby winced. The lad was too young to know about the excesses of men. "Well, you are here now, and indeed I would like a bit of company. Light these candles in the fire and sit beside me," he said, patting the mattress.

Rupert happily did as he was told, and when the tapers were wedged into the dirt on the floor, he settled in and opened the ledger. For several minutes, the two heads leaned over the pages as Rupert explained what he had written. "My spelling may not be so good," he said hesitantly.

Wetherby was quite astounded with what he saw. There were no *X*'s beside his own name—only stars. "You make stars quite well," he said. "It must have taken a lot of time to draw so many."

Rupert pulled out his pencil. "Mr. Tipple taught me. See," he said, going up and over until he'd made five points.

"Isn't that something?" said Wetherby.

"Would you like me to teach you how, your lordship?"

"I would like that very much," Wetherby said, trying to keep a straight face.

Rupert showed him again. "Now you try it," he said, watching as Wetherby painstakingly traced over Rupert's bold marks.

"Oh, that is good," Rupert said reassuringly, "for your first try."

"You are an excellent teacher." Wetherby replied.

Rupert smiled proudly and wriggled a little closer.

Wetherby closed the journal, and Rupert was afraid he was going to be dismissed. "I am sure you have had many great adventures in your life, my lord. Would you tell me about some of them?" Rupert saw by the look on Lord Wetherby's face that he was too modest to brag. "Or perhaps you can tell me another story about the brave knights of old?"

That seemed to please his lordship more, because he immediately commenced weaving a daring tale about a young knight named Sir Jerome. He had fallen in love with the lovely Princess Alicia, who was being kept captive in a tower by a wicked gnome.

Rupert wished the knight had been called Wetherby and

the princess Millicent, but he feared he might cause his lordship embarrassment if he suggested it. Alas, all good things do have to come to an end, and as soon as the fair maiden was rescued against enormous odds and obstacles too numerous to relate in one short visit, Wetherby said, "I believe you had better go upstairs now before your mother discovers you are gone and rings an alarm."

Rupert nodded, hurriedly gathering up all that he'd brought. He only taken a couple of steps toward the door, when he paused and held out the ledger to the marquis. "Would you like to keep the journal, your lordship? It would give you something to read."

Wetherby realized the honor the boy was according him. "Thank you. I shall keep it safe," he said. He watched as the door closed. Then, running his hands over the weathered leather, he lay the book beside his mattress and fell into a restful sleep.

The next morning as soon as Wetherby had finished his breakfast, Millicent and Rupert set out to explore the passageways at the end of the cellar. The one to the right led only a short way before it ended, sealed off completely by fallen debris. The one to the left proved more promising until they came to a barrier of fallen dirt and rock, similar to the first.

Millicent's heart sank. " 'Tis no use, Rupert. It is the same as the other. Probably sealed off for years."

Rupert looked at his candle. "Momma! See the flame flickering? A draft is coming from up there," he said, making his way over the rocks. "Bring the lantern. I do believe I see a hole."

Sure enough, a narrow crack appeared. He started to wriggle through.

"Wait!" Millicent cried. "It may be dangerous."

Rupert's voice echoed back. "I am quite sure there are no dragons anymore for you to be afraid of, Momma. I've really known that all along." He hesitated a moment. "But I suppose there might be some pirates."

Millicent held the lantern high over her head. The beam revealed stairs going upward. "I doubt that, dear. However, I don't think you should . . ."

But Rupert had already crawled through the opening, his candle throwing only a small light on his surroundings.

"Wait for me," she ordered, just barely squeezing through the crevice.

Upward they went, excitement hurrying their every step, until they came to a small wooden door. Millicent placed the lantern on the landing and struggled with the latch until the rusty hinges, squeaking and groaning, gave way. A rush of cool, fresh air caught them in its grasp.

Millicent shivered as she peeked out onto a patchwork of brown and white. Much of the snow that had plagued them only a few days ago had melted. "You were right, Rupert. It is a way out. We must tell Lady Caroline and Lord Wetherby that we have found a way out of here."

"But Lord Wetherby is chained, Momma. He cannot escape," Rupert said, his growing anxiety showing on his face.

Millicent bit her lip. "Oh, dear. That is so."

"His lordship is a chivalrous warrior. He would tell us to be brave and go without him."

Millicent couldn't explain the sense of loss she felt when she contemplated leaving Lord Wetherby behind. "Yes, he would. There is no telling what those thugs would do if we were not here to protect him." Then and there she knew she had no intention of escaping without him. "We will consult Lady Caroline." she said with determination. "Surely between the three of us we can come up with a scheme to free Lord Wetherby from those jackanapes. But now 'tis better we go back. We dare not let Boggles discover us snooping around, or he will raise Cain."

* * *

Later, while all three prisoners were doing their morning chores, Millicent reported their discovery to Caroline.

"But we don't have the key to unlock his chains," Rupert lamented.

"If we can get the key—what then?" Caroline whispered, studying her red, callused hands with disgust.

Millicent saw the spark in Caroline's eyes and knew her faith in the fine lady had been well-founded. "Then we could all escape."

Caroline's eyes narrowed. "You leave that to me," she said, looking toward Boggles. "Now here is my plan . . ."

Millicent and Rupert listened with admiration as Lady Caroline outlined her scheme.

That evening, it took very little encouragement to get Boggles and Tooter totally foxed. As soon as she was certain the men were asleep, Caroline crept into the main room and easily cut the key from Boggles's belt.

Millicent and Rupert waited breathlessly behind the curtain for her to return. They had donned several layers of clothing: coats, capes, and walking boots. Millicent had made sure the door to the cellar was not closed completely when she returned from taking Wetherby his supper. They'd decided not to reveal their plans to him, until they knew for sure that they had the key.

But now—that feat accomplished—the three culprits stealthily made their way down the dark stairwell. Rupert had his sword, and Millicent had the key and carried a lantern, which she intended to light with the fire from Wetherby's brazier. Caroline was burdened with her heavy jewelry box, but she refused to leave it behind.

A few minutes later, they entered the cell. It wasn't the creaking of the door as much as the gentle words, that awakened the marquis.

"Lord Wetherby?"

He knew he had to be dreaming. However, the familiar sweet voice that he waited for with such anticipation each morning and night continued to whisper his name. He watched the three specters advance toward his bed. He was about to call her name when a more demanding order startled him.

"Ernest! For heaven's sakes, wake up!"

Wetherby sprang to a sitting position. "God, Caro! What are you doing here?"

"Well, that is a fine reception. Good Lord! You look as if you haven't shaved in days."

Wetherby ran his hand along his rough jaw. "I haven't had access to the luxuries you have been enjoying," he said sarcastically, taking note of her straggly hair and less-than-impressionable jumble of clothing.

Millicent could see his lordship was not overly joyed to see them. "Shh," she admonished, lighting the lantern. "There is no time for arguing. We have come to rescue you, my lord."

Wetherby was now standing, and pointed to the chain on his ankle. "How, pray tell, do you propose to do that?"

Millicent set down the lantern and falling to her knees, turned the key in the lock. The iron ring fell free.

"I'm afraid to ask how you got that," he said.

"Lady Caroline did it," Millicent said, then in hushed tones proceeded to tell him of their discovery of the passage-way and the door leading into the field.

"Did you give any idea to what would happen if we are discovered?" He held up his hand. "No, I can see you didn't. I only pray that you are right about the exit." Wetherby quickly pulled on his coat and was hurrying them to the door, when Caroline nearly dropped her heavy box.

"What is that?"

"My jewels, of course. I refuse to let that rude, masked thief have my valuables."

Deliver me from the vanities of women, Wetherby mumbled. "It will only slow us down and even cause us to be caught. You will leave it." He took the case and tossed it onto the mattress beside the ledger.

Caroline pouted, but complied.

Rupert, eyes pleading, picked up the journal and held it to his chest.

Wetherby started to shake his head, but on second thought took the book and stuffed it inside his coat. "It is not that big," he said gruffly. He handed Rupert a candle and lit one for himself. "Now, let us be gone before we are found out."

Millicent was already several paces ahead, carrying the lantern.

Wetherby caught up with her and reached for the light.

She refused to give it to him. "Rupert and I know the way," she said. "You and Lady Caroline do not. It would be more helpful if you brought up the rear to see that she doesn't fall."

Wetherby decided that now was not the time to argue, and upon reflection, it made more sense for him to stay behind in case their captors came in pursuit.

Which is exactly what happened.

Boggles's angry roar echoed through the hollow passageways, with Tooter's bugle call following close behind.

"Faster!" Wetherby urged.

Millicent looked back, and in so doing, stumbled over a fallen rock and pitched forward. The lantern crashed to the ground, the light going out with it.

"Momma!" Rupert cried in dismay.

Wetherby dropped his own candle as he leaped forward to catch Millicent.

She grimaced. "I am afraid I have sprained my ankle. Go on. Don't miss your chance to escape. I will be all right."

The angry voices of Boggles and Tooter sounded farther away than they had before.

"They have taken the wrong passageway," Rupert whispered.

"But not for long," Millicent said, the urgency showing in her voice. "They will soon discover their mistake."

Wetherby thought quickly. "Rupert, go on with Lady Caroline. I will not leave your mother. If the two of you escape, you can bring help." He handed Caroline his candle. "It will take Boggles and Tooter awhile before they find us. It is our only hope. Go!"

Rupert and Caroline hesitated only a minute, then fled down the final passageway, just as the thieves turned the corner and spotted them.

Wetherby raised his hands in surrender. He wouldn't take the chance of Millicent being hurt further.

"Hang it! The brat and the witch are getting away," shouted Boggles as he rounded on Wetherby and Millicent.

"The Guv woll have our heads if they escape," Tooter whimpered.

"Stoopid! Stay with these hoity-toities while I go after them other two," Boggles yelled at Tooter, before following the dim spot of light in the distance.

Up ahead, Rupert pointed with his candle and cried out, "Lady Caroline! There is the opening."

Caroline surveyed the black hole in alarm. "It is too narrow," she hissed. "I cannot possibly get through."

Rupert's faith in his princess was not deterred. "You can do it, Lady Caroline. I know you can!"

Caroline looked at the earnest little face below her. Yes, she very well might.

Rupert felt his heart thudding against his chest. "Quickly, I hear someone coming. I shall hold them off as long as I can," he said, handing her his candle.

Caroline looked with trepidation at the opening in the wall.

"There you are you, little brat," Boggles yelled, making a grab for Rupert.

Caroline climbed up over the pile of jagged rocks.

Rupert was quaking in his boots, but undaunted, he unsheathed his sword and faced his enemy. "On guard!" he cried, whacking Boggles across the shins with the wooden blade.

Swearing every foul oath he could think of, Boggles swatted Rupert out of the way, then clambered up after Caroline—too late. She'd already squeezed through the crevice.

Boggles couldn't even get one of his beefy legs through the narrow opening. He raised the lantern only to see a tiny pinpoint of light disappearing up the steps. Dragging Rupert by the scruff of his neck, he headed back toward Tooter and the other captives.

Rupert tried to break away. "Momma, are you all right?"

Millicent tried to reassure him. " 'Tis only a twisted ankle—but where is Lady Caroline?"

"She escaped," Rupert reported.

"Thank God!" Millicent said.

Wetherby could not believe what he'd heard. *She escaped.* Caro was showing a whole new side of herself. Perhaps his assessment of her had been wrong.

Boggles growled. "You," he ordered Wetherby, "make yerself useful and carry the jade up to the kitchen." Tightening his grip on Rupert's arm, he continued to pull him, sword and all, along the corridor.

Wetherby would have gladly pulverized both men, but with a woman in his arms and Tooter's gun at his back, he had little choice in the matter.

Wrapping her arms around his neck, Millicent closed her eyes and let out her breath. "If it had not been for my stupid blunder, you would all be free by now. You should have left me," she said.

Wetherby climbed the steps and held her closer against his chest to hush her. "Let me hear no more of that rubbish, madam." He wondered how, at a time like this, he could even be contemplating the softness of her. It was as he laid her gently on her mattress a few minutes later that the journal fell out of his coat and plopped to the floor.

Rupert made a dive for it, but Tooter was faster. Hooting like a ninny, he kicked the book across the floor.

"Shet yer trap, Tooter," Boggles bellowed, pinning Wetherby's arms behind his back. "We ain't playing games. He'p me with this sprig or we're in big trouble."

Rupert threw his arms around Wetherby's waist and glared at the two men.

Before the boy could get himself into more mischief. Wetherby whispered hoarsely. "Hide the book or those simpletons will tear it apart."

As Boggles and Tooter dragged the marquis to the far side of the room, Rupert retrieved his journal. Then, when no one was watching, he stuffed it behind the same pile of kindling that hid the remains of his mother's gift. He would retrieve it later after the men were asleep.

But alas, it was not to be. No more than an hour later, the Bandit King returned to the farmhouse, alone. He strode in confidently as if expecting to find the establishment running like a well-oiled machine, only to hear a cock-and-bull story of chaos and utter confusion. The marquis was chained to an iron ring that protruded from the large fireplace. Some terrible odor rose up from the black kettle on the hearth, strangling his throat. Mrs. Copley lay on her mattress with a bandaged foot propped up, while her son stood beside her, ready to unsheath his sword.

Boggles and Tooter exchanged looks that were both apologetic and terrified, while Peen busied himself noisily banging his pots and pans.

The masked man roared, "What do you mean, Lady Caroline escaped? Why didn't you go after her?"

"It was his lordship you said was the bait," Boggles sputtered.

"You bumbling fools! Don't you realize that if she gets help, it will not matter one way or the other if we have the marquis?"

Boggles gave a sickly smile. "Shouldn't be no trouble fer you. You got a horse. She don't."

"Hasn't any one of you bothered to stick his nose outside today? Snow has been falling for the last eight hours."

Boggles and Tooter looked first at their feet, then at the rafters in the ceiling. Everywhere except at their employer.

The bandit whirled on them. the urgency in his deep, rumbling voice unmistakable. "I must go after Lady Caroline. 'Twill be a miracle if she survives in this weather." He ignored Millicent's gasp in the background and continued, "It will take another two days for my business transaction to be completed. You are not safe here anymore. 'Tis imperative you move to another location immediately." There was a crash as a crockpot shattered on the stone floor. "Peen, quit hiding behind your kettles and get over here. I want you to see that these imbeciles do as I tell them."

The little man ran over and wriggled into the lineup between Tooter and Boggles.

The Bandit King marched back and forth in front of them, pulling on his gloves. "I shall deal with the three of you later. But now, every evidence of our guests must be removed from this house—and don't forget Wetherby's cell. As soon as the coach is loaded, I want you to head south back toward Exeter. Take our guests to the old inn where we had our first meeting. Blind Daniel will not betray me. Stay there until I contact you. And . . . I don't want one hair on their heads hurt. Do you understand me?"

The three men nodded like puppets on a string.

The masked bandit's anger cut the air like a Saracen's sword. "I warn you if you bungle *this* assignment, you will not receive so much as a halfpenny." He stared at them for one more agonizing moment before he slammed out the door, his final words ringing in their ears. "I shall deal with you later."

Fourteen

With the help of the two stablemen, the coach was loaded before daylight, and the three prisoners found themselves once again bound, gagged, blindfolded, and stuffed like sacks of flour among a jumble of trunks and boxes. Only Millicent had been given a small amount of consideration for her sprained ankle, and was carried to the carriage by Boggles—a humiliation she wished she hadn't had to endure.

Peen sent Tooter to clean out Wetherby's room in the cellar where he found Caroline's jewelry box. Squealing his delight, he ran up the steps two at a time to show Boggles. "Lor! Look yerr!" he giggled, his eyes shining brighter than the diamond necklace that he held up to the firelight.

Boggles smacked Tooter's hand, making him drop the necklace, then pawed through the collection of precious metals and sparkling gems himself. "I woll take care of these," he said, slamming shut the fine-tooled case and tucking it under his arm.

Tooter pouted but didn't challenge the larger man.

It was not long into the day before they were on the road leading from the old farm. When they came to the turn where they had posted the misleading signpost to Catscow Lane, Boggles dutifully turned the horses south.

Inside the carriage, Millicent found herself on the seat opposite Wetherby and Rupert. It was uncomfortable being seated with her arms bound behind her, and her ankle ached—

especially every time Rupert's feet banged against hers. He
was so young and impatient, but it seemed to her that he was
bouncing about far more than was necessary, until she heard
his squeal.

"Momma! I got my gag and blindfold off."

Millicent wanted to ask Rupert how in the world he'd done
that, but her own mouth was still filled with the dirty rag
Boggles had stuffed into it. It wasn't until she heard Wetherby's voice that she realized something was afoot.

"Press your back up against mine," Wetherby said. "Your
fingers are the nimblest. See if you can undo the knot on
the binding around my wrists."

Millicent strained to picture what was going on across from
her. Suspense, hope, and helplessness collided in her imagination.

Then Wetherby's words rang out. "You did it, you little
rascal."

She felt strong hands grasp her scarf and unwind it from
her eyes and mouth. They were not gentle hands, but they
were quick, and to Millicent they felt like those of a benevolent angel. She began to cry her relief, but before she could
do so, Wetherby clamped his hand over her mouth.

"Do not make a sound. We don't want our captors to know
that we have freed ourselves."

Millicent made out Wetherby's face in the dim light. It
was so close, she could feel his breath on her cheek. The
next moment she thought he was embracing her. A tremor
ran through her and she waited breathlessly for him to tell
her that everything was going to be all right. But alas, he'd
only reached behind her to loosen the rope binding her
wrists. She put her foolishness down to the excitement of
the moment. However, now that she was free, she felt much
more the thing and turned her attention to her son, who was
still doing far too much jumping about. "Rupert," she hissed,
"whatever you are doing, stop it. You are bumping my foot."

"I'm sorry, Momma. I was strapping on my sword. See? I found it on the floor of the carriage."

Sure enough, even in the dim light of the coach, Millicent could see Rupert confidently arming himself.

While the three prisoners consulted inside, an argument was crescendoing rapidly atop the high seat of the coach. Luckily, or unluckily—it depended on whose opinion one sought—Peen sat squeezed between the two men. Only his presence had so far kept his companions from being at each other's throats.

"It's all yer fault," Boggles spat out, cracking a whip over the heads of the four horses that were endeavoring to gain their footing in the rising snow.

"Ain't neither. If you weren't such a clumsy lummox—spilling everything you carry—that Jezebel wid never've gone down into the cellar in the first place."

Boggles reached over and tried to knock Tooter's hat off. "I told you he wud have our heads."

"Come, come, gentlemen," squeaked Peen from under their armpits. "We have a long way to go, and it is starting to snow harder."

Sure enough, the white flakes were descending with more and more rapidity, piling atop the already two feet that had accumulated over the night. But the struggling of the horses only made the men angrier, and the quarreling continued. Boggles reached over to smack Tooter again, and only ended up hitting Peen. As the little man grabbed for his hat, he jolted Boggles's arm, which made him jerk on the reins, sending the confused cattle off the now-invisible narrow lane and into a prickly hedgerow. The more they thrashed, the more entangled they became. The carriage tilted dangerously to one side, and was in danger of tipping over.

"See wot you done, Stoopid," Boggles bellowed. "Now we have to get them beasts out of this mess." With much maneuvering, he finally managed to get the frenzied horses to back up. "Get down and see if them nobs is still in one piece."

Tooter jumped off and ran back to the coach.

The minute the door opened, Wetherby came out fighting. Millicent thought he was magnificent. He landed a well-placed facer square on Tooter's nose, then rounded on the bellowing Boggles. Rupert grabbed his sword and followed. Tooter had recovered and lay siege to Wetherby from behind while trying to protect his backside from the whacking Rupert was giving him with his wooden stick.

It was not in Millicent's nature to stand idly by when she was needed. After all, she had an axe to grind with the ruffians as much as Rupert and Lord Wetherby did. With a flourish, she leaped to their rescue, only to find herself flat on her face beside the carriage. She'd forgotten her injured foot.

Poor Peen stood up on the high seat, rocking back and forth, wringing his hands, while his cohorts pounded the marquis into unconsciousness. "Oh, me, oh, my! Look what ye've done," he whimpered.

Both men stared down at the prostrate nobleman, blood running into the snow from the cut on his forehead. "The Guv will have our heads fer sure now," said Boggles, looking accusingly at Tooter.

"Oh, Momma! They have killed him," cried Rupert, kneeling beside his hero.

Millicent scooted over to Wetherby and cradled his head in her lap. His head was bloody, but he was breathing. "He has just been knocked unconscious, dear. He will be all right when he wakes up." She hoped she sounded convincing, but to hide her own worries, she rounded on the simpleton standing over her. "You were told no one was to be hurt," she scolded.

"Didn't mean to hit him so hard," Tooter whined, "but he was banging me face. He shouldn't have din that."

"Git into the carriage," Boggles demanded obnoxiously.

Millicent looked down at the lifeless face in her lap and swallowed uneasily. The indignity of it all brought back her courage. "And how, may I ask, do you think we can do that when I am crippled and his lordship is unconscious?"

"Gah! Sharp-tongued females," was the only reply she got from Boggles.

By now, Peen had climbed down, and he and Tooter managed to get Rupert and Millicent into the carriage. Tossing the comatose marquis in after them, Boggles slammed the door shut.

They had proceeded for another half hour before Tooter broke the silence. "Don't seem fair that we has to do all the work, and don't get no money."

Boggles stopped the horses. "That's the first smart thing I heard you say all day," he said. He reached under the seat and pulled out the jewelry case. "There's enough loot in this box to set us up to live like kings fer the rest of our lives."

Tooter stuck out his lower lip. "The Guv wouldn't let us keep it, you dummy. He wud come right to Blind Daniel's and wring our necks."

"Not if we head north instead of south," said Boggles, backing the horses around and turning in the opposite direction. "We can be on the north coast of Devon by tonight. With all the smugglers I know, we'll be on a boat and far away by the time the Bandit King knows wot's wot."

"More likely any mates of yers will take all the jewels for themselves."

"Not if we hide all the good stuff in our boots. What they don't know won't hurt 'em. We'll hand over the coach and tell them they can have all the loot if they take us up the west coast."

"And what do we do with his lordship and the biddy and her chick?"

"Hmm," Boggles thought a minute. "I say we do away with them. Who's to know?"

Peen gasped. "Oh Lor! Thee cannot do that."

Boggles snapped, "And have them fetch the authorities on us?"

"Surely if thee just leaves them somewhere where they wid not be found for a while, it wid give us time to get away."

Tooter giggled. "Like in a snowbank?"

Peen pulled his muffler tighter around his face. "If thee did that, they wid freeze to death."

"Do you want us to throw *thee* out with 'em, Peen?" Boggles threatened.

Shuttering, the little man shrank further down into his collar.

Only once did they stop to get some food and rest the horses. Due to their shortsightedness, the men had failed to bring any provisions with them. Millicent knew it was at Mr. Peen's insistence that she be allowed to go into the inn to freshen up.

"Jest herself," said Boggles. "The boy and the nob stay outside. She won't cry foul if we have her calf."

It was an unsavory, dirty place, smelling of stale tobacco and unwashed men. A coating of soot from the smoldering logs and cooking odors clung to the plastered walls like mold on week-old bread. Just the fact that she was a woman drew several crude remarks and made Millicent draw her shawl more tightly around her face. A worse lot she'd never seen. The only females were serving girls, and they gave her no more than a passing glance. She thanked her stars that her own bedraggled clothing and tangled hair bespoke nothing of a lady. If she had any hopes of slipping a word to someone of her plight, they were soon dashed. She hurried to the back room off the kitchen that was indicated by a slatterly-looking woman who was slapping food into trenchers from a large iron pot boiling over the fire.

It seemed that spirits were most on Boggles's and Tooter's minds for when Millicent returned to the common room, both men had two bottles tucked under each arm. Mr. Peen had secured a large mug of hot gruel and some bread for her. Millicent gave him a grateful look. She took only a sip and carried the rest out to Rupert, who sat inside the coach with his nose pressed against the window, anxiously awaiting her return.

Wetherby was still unconscious, and only a groan now and then showed that he was still alive. Perhaps it was better in the long run, Millicent thought, because men seemed to have a propensity for making matters worse when they were angry, and she was sure his lordship would be anything but pleasant when he awakened.

It seemed to Rupert as though they'd been traveling for ever so long, and the snow was coming down so fast the horses struggled harder and harder to make their way. As the path became bumpier and the drifts higher, the ride became increasingly rougher. He wondered if they were even on a road at all. Then the air cleared. The clouds parted, stars shined through, and a half-moon smiled down, painting a deceptively fairylike picture. Once in awhile a scraggly clump of leafless trees loomed on the horizon, but for the most part it was a white, barren landscape. In the distance, he saw a tiny yellow eye of light flickering. Then the wind ceased. No sounds now except for the heaving snorts of the horses, the creaking of their leather harnesses, and the deep growling voices that floated down from the driver's seat.

"The snow has stopped, Momma," Rupert whispered, "but I don't see any buildings out there."

Millicent tried not to show her anxiety. "Lie down and try to sleep, dear. Like his lordship," she added, trying to sound natural. "We must be rested for tomorrow." The marquis lay sprawled over the baggage on the floor, and she was not strong enough to lift him. She'd wrapped a cloth over his wound and covered him with the fur coach rug, hoping that when they reached their destination she would be able to persuade Mr. Peen to find a doctor for him. She tried to hold Rupert, but he wriggled free to look out the window.

"Do you think Lady Caroline is safe?"

"I am sure she is warm and cozy in someone's fine house," Millicent replied as reassuringly as she could. "The authorities are probably looking for us already."

Rupert didn't say anything for a few minutes, then sighed. "We are not going to get to Uncle Andy's for Christmas, are we, Momma?"

"There is still time, dear. I am sure the bandit will let us go as soon as he has his money."

"But Christmas is day after tomorrow."

Before she could answer, the coach came to a staggering halt. There was a commotion outside and the door flew open.

Millicent gave a sigh of relief. "Are we there?" she asked, hopefully.

Boggles laughed, a much more wicked laugh than Millicent liked to hear. "This is the end of the line, my lady," he said, grabbing her around the waist and heaving her from the vehicle. She tried to maintain her balance, but her ankle gave way and she tumbled into a snowbank. Rupert followed, his exit a little rougher.

"That was uncalled for, sir," she said, trying without success to rise. Millicent wasn't ready for what happened next, or she would have protested harder. Before she knew it, Wetherby was dragged through the door, coach rug and all, and dumped into the snow beside her, knocking her flat once more. With a great deal of effort, she held her indignation in check. After all, one couldn't expect much else from a fustian like Boggles, and any opposition from her would surely provoke him to more disgusting behavior. The important thing was to get Lord Wetherby into the warm inn. She looked about the bleak landscape in confusion.

The odious Boggles, still laughing, jumped back up to the driver's seat and with a shout to the horses, left the three travelers sitting alone in the snowbank beside a pitiful stand of trees. As they rode away, she heard a high-pitched, protesting squeal from Mr. Peen.

Occupied as she had been in searching for a dwelling—which she soon saw didn't exist—Millicent realized with a sinking heart that she'd failed to interpret Boggles's true intention. The bounder had meant all along to leave them there. She watched helplessly as the coach disappeared over the roadless hills into the starry night, carrying with it all their clothing and Christmas gifts.

So there they sat in the snow: a little boy, an unconscious man, and a crippled woman. Only one day before Christmas, and heaven knew where they were. They would surely freeze if they didn't get aid. Millicent held Wetherby's head gently to her chest and did the best she could to tuck the coach robe over both their legs. He was so still. If anything happened to him . . . It was then that Millicent recognized the warm sensation sweeping through her heart for what it was. Love. She'd fallen in love with Ernest Lance, the Marquis of Wetherby. She didn't want anything bad to happen to him any more than to her son.

But Rupert, clapping his hands together to keep them warm, was on his feet staring into the distance. "Momma, we must find help."

"Dearest, we will have to wait until daylight. I have no idea of where we are, and I cannot walk—and his lordship . . ." She didn't want to frighten Rupert with what she really thought. 'Twould be a miracle if anyone found us on a night like this.

"Oh, Momma, you are right. It *is* the time of year for miracles, is it not?" A moment of silence prevailed, broken only by Rupert's sigh. "But, I suppose God is quite busy tonight getting ready for all the holiday services."

Millicent held her breath in anticipation of what her son would think of next.

"Maybe God could use some help."

"Rupert, get over here and under this blanket before you

catch your death," Millicent admonished, more quickly than was necessary.

He squared his shoulders. "No. I will have to be the one to go," he said, a little waver in his voice.

Millicent watched the struggle on her son's face. "My goodness! Do not speak such foolishness. You are . . ." she started to say *only a little boy,* when she saw the look of defiance in his eyes. "What would his lordship say if he knew you planned such nonsense?" she said in a last desperate attempt to dissuade him from his folly.

"It is Code One, the most important of all—Faithfulness to one's God. Lord Wetherby knows all about that," Rupert finished, with a note of male superiority.

Knowing she was losing the argument, Millicent said a little defensively, "You are not dressed warmly enough. Besides, where would you go?"

Rupert looked back in the direction from which they had come. "I remember seeing a light from the coach back aways. It must have been a house. I shall follow the carriage tracks and ask for help."

The idea of letting her child out of her sight terrified Millicent.

Rupert made sure his sword was tucked securely in his belt. "I will be grown soon, Momma. Think how brave Lord Wetherby was when he was chained in that dark cellar all by himself. Think how hard he fought for us. I must show him that I can be brave too. You cannot go because you hurt your leg." He hesitated telling her that she was a frail woman and had to be protected, because that was a part of The Code that he still had trouble understanding. But now he had other, more important, things to attend to. "I shall not fail you."

Wetherby groaned and twisted restlessly.

Millicent drew him closer to try to warm him with her own body heat. She knew in her heart that there was no alternative but for Rupert to go if they were to get help for Lord Wetherby. "Then I shall pray for your safe return," she said, trying to keep her voice steady. "And, Rupert," she called after him, "pull your sleeves down over your hands to keep them warm."

Rupert did not hear her, for his thoughts were filled with the outlandish tales of gallantry that Lord Wetherby had spun for him. Fancying himself a knight of old, he stoically marched across the lonely countryside with only the moon and stars to light his way and the tracks of the coach to guide him.

Millicent's eyes strained to watch the small figure until he was no more than a speck of dust that disappeared over a snowbank.

Twenty minutes later, a very tired and cold little boy stumbled across a humble crofter's cottage that was overflowing with children's laughter. When the kindly farmer's wife opened the door, there were so many curious faces surrounding her that Rupert could not count them all. The family was getting ready for Christmas and the home was filled with the delicious odors of honey cakes, pies, and puddings.

Upon hearing Rupert's story of woe, Mr. Potter, a robust man with a thick red beard and arms as thick as oak trees, called to his two equally strapping sons, "Joshua . . . Samuel . . . don your coats and mufflers. Someone here needs help."

Taking no thought of their own discomfort, they came with Rupert to rescue the poor lad's parents, *Mr. and Mrs. Lance,* whom the boy said were freezing in the snow after having been set upon by thieves. Rupert thought the *parent part,* which he added to his already embellished tale of misfortune, was a very clever bit of frosting on the cake. Oh, yes. His bones may have been chilled, but his wit was only sharpened by all the excitement and adventure.

In no more time than it took a star to wink, Millicent found herself and Wetherby wrapped in thick, woolen blankets and carried into the comfortable cottage. As the warmth infused itself through her body, Millicent was only barely aware of all the activity their entrance had aroused. On the opposite side of the large room, a fireplace blazed invitingly. A long table and benches took up much of the floor space. She could hear the bleating of sheep and the lowing of cows through the walls.

Mrs. Potter shooed the younger children away and appointed the older ones to run errands. "Mary and Martha, fetch some bread and stew for the brave lad."

The brown-haired twins, round and sassy and already taller than their mother, good-naturedly did as they were told.

Rupert hailed that idea with much enthusiasm, and discarding his wraps, climbed onto the bench and fell to eating.

The woman then turned to Millicent, who'd been carried to a rocking chair near the hearth. "Now, don't thee be worrying yerself, dear. Yer son has told us all about your terrible ordeal. He is already eating a hearty meal—nothing wrong with his appetite—and my men are taking good care of yer man's wound."

Not until she heard that Rupert and Wetherby were being attended to was Mrs. Potter able to persuade Millicent into an adjoining bedroom where a small blaze burned in a stone fireplace. She undressed her as if she were a child and helped her into one of her own night rails. After *oohing* and *ahhing* over her bruised foot, Mrs. Potter redressed the swollen ankle before tucking her into the soft, toasty bed. She once more offered her guest a bowl of soup.

Millicent was too tired to take more than a few sips, and assured again that the other two were safe in the next room, she quickly fell into an exhausted sleep.

When Millicent awakened the next morning, she found herself staring up at an unfamiliar whitewashed low ceiling, crisscrossed by dark, hand-hewn beams. She let her gaze pan from one corner to the other. Last night she thought she'd never be warm again. Now, she felt as though she lay in a field of clover on a summer day. She heard the crackling of fire. Someone had already been in to light it. Slowly her memory returned. A woman's pleasant voice softly hummed "Hark! The Herald Angels Sing" in the next room. Children giggled. Then she recognized Rupert's runaway tongue. A sense of peace ran through her, and savoring the softness of the thick feather mattress, she snuggled down and tried to pull the comforter tighter around her. But it wouldn't budge. Millicent gave it another tug, then rolled over to see what held it. She gasped.

Tucked in beside her, a very familiar face lay upon the adjoining pillow, brown eyes watching her inquisitively. His head was bandaged and one eye nearly swollen shut, but still an insufferable, half-cocked grin was spreading across his face. Millicent sat upright. "You!" she exclaimed. A humiliating realization struck her. She had spent the night snug in bed with Lord Wetherby.

Fifteen

Millicent sealed her lips. She would never forgive him. Neither would she give way to a fit of the vapors, like some missish green girl. How dare he try to compromise her? She was no lightskirt. On second thought, Lord Wetherby had been unconscious when they had arrived at the cottage last night. There had to be another explanation of how he came to be in her bed.

Wetherby spoke from the right side of his mouth, which gave him a slight slur. "I shought for a minute that pr'haps I'd died and gone t'heaven."

Millicent eyed him suspiciously. It was plain as a pikestaff that if she was going to get a sensible answer, it wasn't going to come from his lordship. Yet, the jackanapes didn't seem the least disturbed at finding himself in bed with *her*. Millicent's gaze ran over his bruised face. It appeared that he might have a permanent wink etched upon his handsome features. She hoped not. What a disastrous happenstance that would be if his masculine beauty were marred. However, the comical picture of Rupert trying to imitate Wetherby's present lopsided expression triggered a totally unexpected response, forcing her to turn away from him to keep from giggling. She was becoming as addlepated as his lordship.

Perhaps she was being unfair. It had to be the delirium. After the hit on the head, he was not himself. Millicent would have to satisfy herself with that—for the time being. The fault was that she'd had no previous experience with rakes before she'd met Lord Wetherby, and therefore was amiss as to how to react to one who was obviously demented. So as not to unbalance him further, she decided the best course was to treat the whole situation lightly. Millicent cast Wetherby a sideways look.

The minute she glanced his way, he held his ribs, groaning, "Dashed funny—didn't notice a shing a minute ago—now, I feel like a coach and four hash run me over." His eyes closed and his head fell limp to one side.

Millicent, ashamed of her callousness in regard to all the bravery he had shown them during their perilous journey, leaned forward, letting the coverlet drop to her waist.

Wetherby's eyes popped open. "Did shoo know Mrs. Copley—'scuse the 'spression—shoo are a demmed attractive woman in th'morning?"

Millicent clutched her night rail at the neck. Of course, he didn't know what he was saying, she reminded herself. *Answer as if nothing is helter-skelter,* she told herself. "Lah! No more handsome than you, my lord."

Wetherby gingerly felt his swollen eye. *"Touche!"* he said, trying to sit up, only to fall back onto his pillow once more, his face turning white.

Panic gripped her, and Millicent began to massage one of his hands. "Please, don't try to get up. You are not at all well."

He began to stare at her in the oddest way. "Shoo will 'scuse me, Milli-shent . . . I may call you Milli-shent, may I not? It does seem that under the circumstances *Mrs. Copley* is a trifle formal."

Millicent quickly stopped her rubbing and jerked her hands away. He was laughing at her. Even after being knocked senseless, his lordship still remained a rascal. She was searching her brain for what to say next, when he furrowed his brow.

"I seem to have a vacant spot in my memory. I remem-

ber . . ." Wetherby threw off the coverlet and sat upright.
"Good God! Those runagates. Rupert! Is he all right?"

Millicent lunged across him just in time to grasp the edge
of the comforter before it fell to the floor. "Rupert is fine,"
she gasped, frantically trying to cover his legs back up. "After Boggles and Tooter left us in the snow, Rupert insisted
on going for help. He came across these good people, the
Potters, who rescued us. We are in their cottage now."

Wetherby sank back onto his pillow with a sigh of relief.
"Rupert did that? Hee'sh but a child."

"You should have thought of that before you filled his
head with all those tales of derring-do, my lord," she scolded.
"He just may have died out there in the cold." The thought
of her innocent son made Millicent more aware than ever of
her compromising predicament. She dare not let Rupert see
her. What explanation could she possibly give a little boy
for his mother being in bed with a man who was not her
husband?

Her question was interrupted by a knock. Mrs. Potter's
face appeared around the door. "Ah, prithee! Thee are awake,
Mrs. Lance."

Millicent pulled the covers up around her chin. *"Mrs.
Lance?"* she repeated dumbly.

The crofter's wife, her arms laden with a tray of sweet-
cakes and a pot of coffee, thrust the door open with her
ample hips. "Yer son has been very worried about thee and
his papa.

"His *papa?*" Millicent knew that she was beginning to
sound like a parrot, but she could think of nothing else to
say. To make things worse, the marquis lay beside her, hands
locked behind his head, grinning like an idiot. His attitude
certainly wasn't helping the situation one bit. Well, as soon
as she was alone with Mrs. Potter, she'd set things to rights.
But how could she possibly do that without making her own
position look worse?

Before Millicent could utter a coherent word, Rupert came

bounding into the room. "Momma, Papa, you must get up and see the Nativity Joshua and Samuel are setting up. Tommy says that Samuel carved it. Each year he makes a new figure and won't tell them what it is until they set up the whole scene and they are making bows and braids to put on the windows and Mrs. Potter says I may help decorate." He stopped to catch his breath.

Millicent stared at her son.

Chuckling, Mrs. Potter made way for the excited boy. Then, setting the tray on a table by the side of the bed, she checked Wetherby's bandage. "Now, now," she chided, "yer papa is in no condition to be gallivanting about. Hem had quite a beating."

"Come here, son," Wetherby said, exerting great effort to make both sides of his mouth turn upward at the same time. He failed.

Warily, Rupert looked back and forth between the two adults in the bed. He had called him *son*. It was only make-believe, of course, but his lordship seemed willing to play the game. He glanced hopefully at his mother.

Millicent pursed her lips and said nothing. So this was Rupert's doing. There was nothing she could do now—but just wait until she got him alone.

Rupert swallowed hard. From the warning in his mother's eye, he knew he had to move quickly before she spilled the beans.

Wetherby held out his hand like a lifeline and Rupert, grinning gleefully, ran to him. If Mrs. Potter hadn't been present, he would have jumped into bed with them. Then, they would be as they should be—a family. A momma on one side of him and a papa on the other.

Wetherby tossled Rupert's hair.

"You look terrible," Rupert said, frowning.

" 'Tish but a trifle inconvenience," Wetherby said. "A warrior muth 'spect a few battle scars."

Rupert stood up straighter and nodded solemnly. "I shall remember that," he said.

While Mrs. Potter turned her attention to Millicent, Wetherby whispered, "From the reports of shur brave and daring deeds, I do believe that another shtar will be forthcoming in your book, wouldn't shoo say?"

Rupert looked down at his feet. "I am afraid the journal got left behind at the farmhouse."

Wetherby placed his arm around Rupert's shoulder and gave him a hug.

By now, Mrs. Potter had rounded the bed to Millicent's side. "How's yer foot, Mrs. Lance?"

Surprisingly, Millicent had forgotten all about her sprained ankle. The swelling had gone down and with the new binding, she felt little discomfort. This knowledge made her disposition improve immeasurably, and she felt more inclined to let matters stand as they appeared for the moment. She looked warmly upon the kind woman.

"I thought thee would like something to eat in bed," Mrs. Potter said cheerfully. " 'Tis nearly noon. Thee has slept through the morning."

The smell of food raised Wetherby's spirits. "Are shoo as hungry as I am, m'dear?" he said. "I feel I haven't eaten for a week."

Millicent would not give him the satisfaction of looking at him. "Oh, no, Mrs. Potter, I prefer to eat in the other room," she said, springing from the bed only to look down in dismay at her night rail.

"Now, now," Mrs. Potter clucked. "Don't thee be worrying about yer clothes, dear. They were quite worn. I am sure 'twas due to yer terrible ordeal. Martha washed them this morning. Yer husband's, too. They are hanging by the fire. Thee are welcome to wear something of mine until yers dry." She took a gown and an apron from a peg on the wall and handed them to Millicent. "I'll leave now," she said, "so thee can dress. I know thee will be wanting to take care of yer husband's needs, too. The pot is here under the bed," she said, pulling the large lidded crockery out in full view.

Millicent's face turned crimson.

Without a backward glance, Rupert dashed out of the room ahead of Mrs. Potter.

Holding the garments, Millicent looked about frantically. There wasn't even a screen to hide behind.

"I shall close my eyes while shoo change," Wetherby said quite seriously, pulling a pillow down over his face to emphasize his sincerity.

Millicent flushed from head to toe. She didn't trust him one whit and as she dressed, kept looking back nervously over her shoulder. Her hair was quite hopeless. She stuffed as much of it as she could under the mobcap that Mrs. Potter had left for her. She had just started for the door, but she hesitated. Taking care of a man in delirium was one thing, but was he able to get out of bed by himself? "Do you want me to . . . to pour you a cup of coffee—or anything else?" she said, confused as how to finish.

"Just leave . . . Millish . . . Mrs." he mumbled some almost indistinguishable syllables from under the pillow, which she was sure she didn't want to hear anyway. "Whether shoo believe it or not, I am quite capable of taking care of m'self."

"Yes, my lord," she said, scurrying from the room, not at all certain of anything.

As soon as she left the room, Wetherby let out a low growl—a decidedly animal growl. Then the truth struck him senseless. He was in love. When had it happened? Was it this morning, when he had awakened to find her beside him? Or had it been in that dismal cell, when he'd counted every minute until he'd see her again? Or perhaps when he'd watched her give her money to a beggar? No, it had to be when she'd hit him with the snowball.

Who would have ever believed it? He, Ernest Lance, the

Marquis of Wetherby, had fallen in love. He'd found a woman he not only desired like no other before her, but whom he wanted to make his wife.

Surely his father would come round once he'd met Millie. *Millie.* It was the first time he'd permitted himself to think of her in such a personal way. He realized how much he would want to see that face next to his when he awakened each morning for the rest of his life. But from the way she'd glared at him, she obviously was not of the same opinion. How could he blame her?

Wetherby's head was spinning, and every time he opened his mouth he sounded like an idiot. Wincing, he tried to move his jaw from side to side. Boggle's facer had surely dislocated it. How could she possibly think of him favorably, looking like a ruffian dragged in off the streets? His courtship of Mrs. Copley would have to wait. Wait until he could do it properly. He never realized how much he depended upon his valet. He'd wait until Jespers had him shaved and dressed to the eyes—like a respectable gentleman. Then, he'd tell her how much she'd come to mean to him. He'd even get down on one knee to propose to her. Hell! Who was he fooling? He knew his father wouldn't give one inch in his requirements for his heir's wife.

Impeccable bloodlines, son. Make sure she's an heiress in her own right. Don't want a woman who is in awe of the title and wealth that will be yours someday.

Wetherby was afraid no amount of persuasion would ever change the old stick-in-the-mud, and he could see that his charm wasn't working any wonders on Mrs. Copley, either. What was it he'd said or done to put her in such a dither? He winced to think that at first when he'd awakened, he'd started to accuse her of deliberately crawling under the covers with him. The ploy had been used before, and as out-of-it as he'd been, he wouldn't have known the difference until too late. But she'd seemed as surprised as he had been to find them in the same bed—and he doubted that Mrs. Copley was capable of such fabrication.

At least she wasn't indifferent to him. He'd seen the flush creep up her neck. In fact, he'd watched it spread all the way to her toes. No pillow was going to rob him of that pleasure. He let out a whoop of laughter. If she'd known that he'd been peeking, he really would have been in the stew.

Now, Rupert—he was another matter altogether. There was the culprit, he was positive. His deceptively angelic face was like looking into a mirror. Wetherby had been accused of similar tomfoolery often enough when he was younger. The little devil would need watching when he got older, or he'd wreak havoc wherever he went. But the first thing Wetherby had to do was tell the Potters who he really was and find out where they were.

Millicent had no sooner shut the door than she heard the earthy howl. Such cavalier behavior! Ordering her to leave. The man had no conscience. That was outside of enough. What was he so out of countenance about? After all, it was *her* reputation that was in jeopardy. How could she have been so noodleheaded to even think she could possibly entertain tender feelings for such a rogue? If she hadn't known better, she'd have thought he was foxed, for a more disreputable countenance she'd never seen. Hair askew, four days of beard covering his face, one eye swollen shut like a bloody pirate. *Heaven help her! Even her language was becoming common.* She was beyond redemption. And now, trying to interpret the wild sounds he was making behind that door, she could only conclude that his mind wandered as well.

Suddenly, a sadness enveloped her like mist on a gloomy day. Even if she had felt any affection for the rascal, or he for her—a most unlikely occurrence—she knew that his father would never approve of a serious relationship between them. True, she was sister-in-law to a baron and her own father had a connection to a countess, but that was of little consequence to the likes of the Duke of Loude. Her family was not of the peerage, and the duke would say that she was not worthy of marrying into the Lance dynasty.

Millicent set her lips firmly and limped into the kitchen area. Who did the duke think he was to decide that a man like her father was not worthy? Edgar Francis Huxley, Esquire, was a good man. He'd been elected by the people of Cross-in-Hand to be their mayor. The duke hadn't been elected to anything. He'd only come by his title because it had been handed down to him. Well, if that was what the nobility judged a man's worth by—title and wealth—she wanted nothing to do with it.

By now, Millicent was in quite a state, and when she came upon Mrs. Potter coming up from the cellar, a sack of potatoes in her arms, she spoke a little more adamantly than she'd meant to. "I want to help you with the cooking today."

Mrs. Potter glanced down at Millicent's bandaged foot. If she thought her guest out of line, her round, ruddy face showed no sign of irritation. "Now, wouldn't that be nice. If thee truly want to be helpful, sit by the fire and stir the batter for the Christmas cake. But first, you'll be needing some breakfast. Martha," she called, "set the kettle to boil for Mrs. Lance. Mary, spoon up some porridge." The twins, as jolly and pink-cheeked as their mother, hurried to do as they were told.

The farmer's wife seemed determined to have her guest sit down, and taking her arm, steered Millicent toward the huge fireplace. "Now when thee has had something to eat, thee can tell me all that brought yer family to this sad state of affairs."

Millicent's ankle proved not to be as well-mended as she'd first thought, and after only a few minutes of standing, she found herself grateful to lower herself into the rocking chair. Mary brought her a large bowl and spoon, the smell of cinnamon and steaming cereal coming with her.

Millicent waved to Rupert, who was on the far side of the room playing with Tommy. She had the feeling her son was trying to avoid her—and for good reason, she had to admit. He kept swinging his sword, while Tommy flailed the air with a long stick. Finally he acknowledged her, and with dragging feet, started across the room. Tommy and his sisters followed.

Mrs. Potter leaned forward. "I am glad to see thee are feeling better this morning. But yer mister?" She clucked her tongue. "I am afraid he was not looking quite the thing, his face all swollen up like that. Last night, me mister kept hem up walking a bit before he put hem to bed. He also had me fix a posset to help hem sleep. I always keep barley water and herbs handy to tend me own. In fact, Mr. Potter insisted I make up a tisane, too—said it would take away the pain."

Millicent's eyebrows shot up. A mixture of an alcoholic drink and milk and another of herbs and barley water? A combination that would surely make an elephant noddy. No wonder his lordship was acting the clown this morning. But she would never think to be so boorish as to mention her suspicions to her hostess. She accepted the steaming bowl of porridge from Mary with a smile, and nodded as Martha placed a mug of hot liquid on the stool beside her. "You were all so kind to rescue us."

"Now, dear heart, 'twas nought. Thee are welcome to stay as long as it takes for Mr. Lance to get his senses back," Mrs. Potter said, seating herself on a highbacked, wooden settle, and facing Millicent. " 'Tis nought that us would not have done for any poor folk like us. Yer husband did sound a bit dotty, though, rattling on so," she said, with the lift of an eyebrow.

"He isn't like that all the time," Millicent hurried to assure her.

The good woman gave Millicent a sympathetic look. "Of course not, dear heart. It was getting his noggin cracked, I am sure. But, my oh my, someone certainly darkened his daylights. Such a mess—blood all over."

Millicent choked, spilling her drink.

"Oh, do watch yer coffee," Mrs. Potter warned. "I don't want thee to scald yerself."

Millicent took a deep breath to calm her stomach. "I'm sorry we put you to so much trouble. It was more than enough to ask."

Mrs. Potter threw up her hands. "Landsakes, child! With two growed sons as stiff-rumped as their father, I've patched up more broken heads than thee will ever see in yer lifetime. I did no more than wash and bandage yer man. Me mister stripped hem down and put hem in one of his nightshirts. I reckoned a good night's sleep was what he needed," she said, nodding knowingly. " 'Cept for the bruises on hes face, I'm sure hem will soon be feeling fit as a fiddle." She nodded toward her two sons and five younger daughters, who were coming toward them. Mrs. Potter put her arm around the littlest girl, Ruthie who snuggled up against her mother's skirt. "I'm just thankful I'm having a little respite before Tommy starts thinking hem has to lick every bully who crosses his path." Her eyes glowed with pride. "But, I suppose hem will take after hes father, too. Rough and tumble— me mister—but with a heart twice as big as any ordinary man. That's why hem said us dasn't think of letting thee leave until yer husband gets hes wits back."

They were interrupted by Mr. Potter's deep voice booming from the back doorway as he and his two big sons tramped in from the outdoors with armloads of kindling. " 'Twould be a sin against the Good Lord to cast strangers out into the snow on the eve of Christmas."

" 'Twould indeed," agreed Mrs. Potter, watching her older boys start to forage for any oddments left over from breakfast. "Joshua," she said, "before thee eat up all of the porridge, go knock on Mr. Lance's door and see if hem feels well enough to come out."

With a good-natured shrug, the young man laid down the bowl he was scraping, and headed for the bedroom door.

"Momma!"

Millicent jumped, startled to find Rupert standing at her elbow.

"Even if we cannot be with Uncle Andy for Christmas, being with the Potters is the next best thing—don't you agree, Momma?"

Mr. Potter looked back over his shoulder as he held his hands to the fire. "Thee were expected somewhere for Christmas, Mrs. Lance?"

Millicent put her finger on Rupert's lips to stop him from saying more. "Actually," she said, "we . . . we were headed for a residence in Devonshire—Roxwealde Castle. There was a party planned, you see."

"At Baron Copley's?" asked Mr. Potter.

Millicent was at a loss as to how the simple crofters would know of her brother-in-law. "Why, yes. I would have not expected you to have heard of him this far south."

"But us be in the north of Devonshire, Mrs. Lance."

Millicent mulled this over for a moment in her mind. "How can that be? I heard our abductor say that we were to be taken to a place near Exeter."

"My oh my! Yer man does muddle up things, don't hem? Poor man!" Mrs. Potter said sympathetically. "Why, thee are in the Devon moors on the border of the Copley property. Us are tenants of the baron's." Mrs. Potter clasped her hands to her bosom as a new insight presented itself. "Thee were going to a new situation at Roxwealde, were thee not? Us heard that they had opened up the old castle and were hiring new help."

Mr. Potter tightened his muffler and started out the door with Samuel. "Jobs be hard to come by in these parts. Me son here went up to apply for carpentry work, but they said they had already filled all the positions."

Samuel nodded.

Frowning, Millicent watched Joshua disappear into the bedroom.

Mrs. Potter shooed the children away. "Now, dear heart," she said, "I can see something is bothering thee. Do you wish to tell us what it is?"

Whether or not the Potters thought them a married couple or not, Millicent knew she must think quickly for some excuse not to spend another night in bed with his lordship. "Mrs. Potter, I wanted to talk to you about our sleeping arrangements," she whispered.

Mrs. Potter leaned closer to hear her. "Ay?"

Millicent took a deep breath. "May I have another room tonight? My husband is still not well, and he would sleep much better in a bed by himself. I worry that if I bump him, I may cause further injury." She thought that sounded plausible enough to take care of the situation, but she was mistaken.

"Oh, my! I am afraid that is impossible. We gave thee our bedroom, last night. 'Tis the only one in the house. See," Mrs. Potter said, emphasizing her point with a wide sweep of her arm.

Confused, Millicent took another look around her. The room was of good size, but there seemed to be children filling every crack and cranny. Near to where Tommy and Rupert were once again fighting imaginary dragons, the five littlest girls laughed and giggled as they strung brightly colored ropes around the windows. Mary and Martha chattered happily in the kitchen, and either Joshua or Samuel came stomping in and out of the barn, bringing in the aroma of livestock as he carried fresh straw to place around the Nativity scene. Besides the door to the animal shelter, there was the front entrance, and the door that led to the bedroom. Another exit off the kitchen area had to lead to the backyard. There could be no other rooms. "Then where did you sleep last night, Mrs. Potter?"

"In the loft with the girls," she said, pointing to the steep ladder-like steps leading to an opening in the ceiling. At Millicent's wide-eyed expression, Mrs. Potter laughed. "Now don't thee pay no nevermind about that," she said. "It brought back memories. 'Twasn't until us had five sprouts of our own before Mr. Potter added on that little room. Until then, the older children slept up above, and the mister and me stayed in this room with the new babe. It seemed large enough until our sixth little lamb came along. Now that Joshua and Samuel are growed men, they have made themselves a corner in the barn."

"It must be frigid out there."

"My goodness, no. 'Tis cozy as a mouse's nest up against the back of the fireplace. I can tell thee, they much prefer the company of critters to the chattering of their seven sisters and pesky little brother." With pride shining in her eyes, she looked across the room at the five little girls now playing ring-around-the-rosy with their ropes. "Poor Tommy. Hem ain't allowed to stay in the barn with his older brothers, and in his opinion, 'tis an insult to sleep with girls. So he makes his bed all by hemself down here. I tell thee, 'tis a rare treat for hem to have a lad his own age to play with. Hem and yer son slept on the hearth last night."

"How can we ever thank you for all your family has done for us?"

Mrs. Potter's robust laughter filled the room. "Yer husband should thank the Lord hem has such an understanding wife." She glanced around at the children and gave Millicent a wink. "I know what a temptation these men are. I will give thee some extra pillows to put down the middle of the bed, then thee won't have to fear hurting yer man."

Millicent tried to hide her embarrassment by intently scraping the last of the porridge from her bowl. "That will be very kind of you, Mrs. Potter." *Oh dear, now what was she to do?* Until Lord Wetherby recovered his wits, she could do nothing about her compromising situation. She would just have to keep herself busy and hope that a solution occurred to her by nightfall. She rose, casting a worried eye toward the bedroom door. "Mrs. Potter, I really do want to help in the kitchen."

Mrs. Potter gathered up her sewing bag and settled into her rocking chair by the fire. "Ain't that nice," she said. " 'Tis like I've gained another daughter. Now, I shall have time to get on with me knitting." Which is exactly what she did, and with needles clacking, she pursed her lips and concentrated on the pretty blue-and-green scarf she was making.

It was amazing what clean clothes and a hot meal did for one's constitution, Wetherby thought. Someone had even mended the tear in his breeches. By late afternoon, he announced that he felt well enough to come out of the bedroom, or so it seemed at first. But upon rising, his head spun and he nearly fell flat on the floor. The surprisingly gentle giants, Joshua and Samuel, were glad to help him dress. They did the best they could, but they weren't Jespers. Then supporting him between themselves, they saw him comfortably seated on the settle by the hearth.

Wetherby smiled and nodded magnanimously as one or the other of the girls left off readying the table for supper and brought a blanket and pillows to tuck around him. With a giggle here and a whisper there, they shyly stood watching his every move, as if they were expecting him to do something. He couldn't quite imagine what. Probably they had never entertained a member of the *ton* before.

"May I get thee something to drink, Mr. Lance?" Mary asked.

He shook his head, grinning his crazy, crooked grin.

"Or another pillow," Martha added. This time he nodded and indicated his right side, which rested against the arm of the settle.

Two of the younger girls raced to answer his request. Even Ruthie offered him her doll, a very used one from the looks of it, with its mouth gone and only one button eye.

"Her name is Bridget," she said.

At first he didn't know what to do with the doll, but as soon as he placed it on his knee, the child nodded solemnly. Then she stood, fascinated, her eyes never leaving his lips, while he told Bridget a story. Soon they were all laughing—for what reason Wetherby wasn't clear. To his own amazement, he found he was quite enjoying himself and made his stories more and more implausible, delighting in their reactions.

Rupert inched closer and closer, until Wetherby pulled him to his side. "How would you and Tommy like to hear about some very fierce dragons that I fought?"

The boys nodded eagerly, and as the girls pressed nearer, Wetherby added princesses to his tale. He knew his mouth was working faster on one side than the other, but it didn't seem to bother the children, who listened enthralled at every word he said. Soon he had them all *oohing* and *ahhing,* and clapping their hands. In wide-eyed wonderment, Ruthie leaned against his knee, never letting her gaze leave his face.

Millicent worked alongside Mrs. Potter and the twins in the kitchen. She was watching Wetherby so intently that she spilled gravy all down the front of her apron. She glared at him. From the way the girls were acting, she knew immediately that they were going to spoil him insufferably—the way he expected all females to do, no doubt. She banged the lid down on the kettle, but even that didn't get his attention. He only raised an eyebrow and went on entertaining his rapt audience. Well, she had to warn him that not only did the Potters believe them to be married, but now they thought them to be domestics going to Roxwealde to fill new positions.

On the pretense of rekindling the fire, Millicent hurried toward Wetherby. "Don't tell them who we really are—" She managed no more than a beginning to her waspy entreaty, before Mr. Potter, Joshua, and Samuel came in to supper. With a squeal of delight, Ruthie rushed to greet her father. And as little ones will do, she was waylaid halfway to her destination by the sight of her mother filling a plate with gingerbreads.

"Dash my buttons! Lance is up," Mr. Potter said, patting his smallest daughter on the head as he passed on to where Wetherby sat. "Thought thee looked too hearty a man to be kept down by a few blows."

With a sharp look at Wetherby and a shrug of her shoulders, Millicent retreated to the cooking area. He still chose to ignore her. Dreadful man!

"Potter, I believe?" Wetherby said, holding Ruthie's doll with one hand, while extending his other one to the farmer. "We are beholden to you, sir."

"Pithee, let's hear no more o'at." Mr. Potter said, eyeing the doll quizzically.

Wetherby shook his head. " 'Tis more than enough what you have done for us. It was not my intention to be such a burden to you. We will be on our way as soon as we can obtain transportation."

"Thee will stay until 'ee are well enough to go on," replied the farmer gruffly.

Millicent waved a wooden spoon in the air, trying to signal Wetherby from the kitchen. It seemed that so far he had not said anything about their situation to paint her as a fallen woman. She was thankful for that. But that didn't mean the obstinate man wouldn't make a slip of the tongue and somehow reveal their true identities. Then the Potters would know that they weren't man and wife. Wetherby was being impossible, of course.

It was right then and there that the devil sat down on Millicent's shoulder and suggested the appropriate solution in her ear. She glanced demurely at her hands. "Mrs. Potter?"

"Eh?" Mrs. Potter said, letting Ruthie help herself to a gingerbread.

The little girl stuffed the pastry into her mouth, then stealthily looked back and forth between the two women before she dared pilfer another.

Millicent lowered her voice. "There is something I must tell you about my husband."

Mrs. Potter placed a finger over her lips. "Say on, Mrs. Lance. Yer secret be safe with me."

With a gleam in her eye, Millicent leaned closer and spoke softly.

Sixteen

"Mrs. Potter, my husband is a simple man."

"So I concluded, dear heart. Thee need not hang yer head in shame. God makes some quicker than others, but I am sure Mr. Lance has many good qualities," she said, looking over at Wetherby.

Millicent sucked in her breath. "What I wanted you to understand, Mrs. Potter, is that he may say things at times that seem a little outlandish. I would not want him to frighten the children."

Mrs. Potter placed a finger to her lips. "Don't thee be worrying yerself now. The children are used to playing with Charlie Doodleby. He's a big lad—nearly four and thirty. Simple and quite harmless. I'll warn me mister to pay no nevermind to a word Mr. Lance says."

A slight smirk graced Millicent's lips. That brought a perplexed expression to his lordship's face, she was pleased to see. She smiled back. *That should put a spoke in his wheel,* she thought, turning her back on him to hide her laughter.

"Thou't's the spirit," Mrs. Potter said. "Always look on the bright side."

Millicent peered up meekly. "Oh, thank you, Mrs. Potter. I am so glad you understand." *Now let his lordship try to wiggle out of that one,* she thought smugly, chancing a quick glance at Wetherby where he sat looking like a large hairy bird nestled in its nest.

He grinned back crookedly.

To hide her amusement, Millicent made a pretext of wiping perspiration from her forehead with the sleeve of her dress.

This gesture consumed Wetherby with guilt. Odsbodikins! It did not sit well with him to admit to his weaknesses. He had refused to acknowledge to the Potters as well as to himself how badly he'd been hurt. He would have jumped up immediately to help her with the heavy chores, if he hadn't feared he would disgrace himself by falling flat on his face.

He admired Mrs. Copley for trying to put the best face on a difficult situation, when it was plain to see that she was shaking with fatigue. Had there ever been such a sweet and giving soul to grace the earth? It was almost more than Wetherby could bear to see her toiling like a kitchen drudge. He wanted to take her in his arms and tell her everything would be all right. When she became his wife, she would never work again. He would see that his sweet marchioness was clothed in the finest silks, and she would have a dozen handmaidens to wait upon her hand and foot.

Mrs. Potter picked up a large serving spoon and started toward the head of the table, where Mr. Potter was already sitting in his highback, beautifully carved chair. "Come, everyone," she called, "time to gather around for supper. 'Twill be a simple meal tonight. Bread and stew. Us don't want to spoil our appetites for tomorrow's yule feast."

Wetherby saw that matters had to be righted. He could clear up his own identity to insure that Mrs. Copley be treated properly, and still not reveal that she was not his wife. "Wait," he called, "I want to tell you who I really am."

Millicent, her face barely showing over the large crockery pot she held, shook her head violently. Her mouth formed a big round *No!* He could not help but notice her, so she could only surmise that he was purposely doing exactly what she didn't want him to do. Arrogant man!

Forcing himself up from the settle, Wetherby willed himself not to waver. "I am afraid I have allowed you all to be misled. I am really the Marquis of Wetherby, the son of the Duke of Loude." He was glad to see that in spite of Mrs. Copley's theatrics, all eyes turned politely his way. Aye, he may have never known anyone with such a kind and willing nature, but he feared that if Millicent continued her strange performance, the Potters would think her unbalanced.

Ruthie, her cheeks smeared with dough, stood staring sweetly up at Wetherby. "You're daft, aren't you?"

Mrs. Potter exchanged a quick glance with her husband. "Now, now, Ruthie, sweeting. Don't thee be pestering his *lordship.*" Then with no more than an if-you-please, she called over her shoulder, "Martha, bring the bread before you sit down."

Wetherby watched the younger children scramble over the benches. The adults were strangely silent. In shock, Wetherby looked toward Millicent, who was finding something of uncommon interest in the depth of the pot. *No one had believed a word he'd said.*

The little girls began to giggle; Tommy looked at Rupert, who sat with his mouth open; and the older boys elbowed each other.

Mr. Potter's strict glare silenced them. He then pushed back his chair, and rising, turned to Wetherby with a benevolent smile. "Come, my good man. A stomach full of Mrs. Potter's victuals will make thee right as rain. Josh—Samuel—help our guest to my chair. His lordship cannot be expected to climb over a bench, now can hem?"

Millicent looked everywhere but at Lord Wetherby. What had she done? Well, it served him right, the scoundrel. The man had no conscience.

Rupert squirmed for most of the meal, studying the situation, not daring to look at his mother. Things were going terribly wrong. He didn't know why she wouldn't play the game. She used to be so much fun. From the look of disbelief he'd seen on Lord Wetherby's face when he'd made his announcement, Rupert wondered how he could ever again raise his lordship's consequence in the eyes of the Potters . . . and most of all, his mother's.

Only Ruthie seemed unmoved by all the hubbub. "Hem tells good stories," she said, looking with unbiased admiration at Wetherby. "Better than Charlie Doodleby."

The other children hailed their agreement.

Mr. Potter nodded to Wetherby. "See? The Good Lord gives everyone a talent. Thee need not try to be someone thou were not meant to be."

Mrs. Potter added her accolades with hearty enthusiasm. "Hem is right, *yer lordship*. No one needs to be ashamed of what hem do best." Then she frowned and looked at her husband. "But it do seem a shame that the Lances may lose their positions because of their bad fortune. Can us do nothing to let Lord Copley know that the Lances are here and will come along as soon as they are well enough to travel?"

Lord Copley? It took all of Wetherby's powers of self-control to steel himself from choking on the bite of food he had just put in his mouth. Someone had set him up, and he knew it wasn't Rupert this time. His eyes zeroed in on Millicent, but she refused to meet his gaze.

"These are not easy times for the likes of us," Mrs. Potter commiserated. "Us poor have to help each other. The Quality have no such fears, do they?" she said, looking at Wetherby sympathetically. "They don't know what it is like to scratch a living out of the thin soil or dirty their hands in the service of others. But I do not envy them, for us are so much more fortunate," she said, looking about proudly at her children. "I hear their mommas give over the care of their wee ones to nurses, and the papas send their sons away to school when they are no older than our Tommy and yer Rupert. I pity them."

Millicent smiled weakly.

While Wetherby was trying to make sense out of this

strange commentary on his peers, Samuel spoke up for the first time since their repast had begun. "I will go, Mama."

Mrs. Potter shook her head. " 'Tis not even possible for us to get to the church in Danbury Wells for services this Christmas Eve."

"N'ought tonight," the young man said. "I can ride to the castle tomorrow to inform the baron that his new servants have met with a mishap."

Wetherby protested profusely. "What nonsense say you, Samuel? Tomorrow is Christmas. I will not permit you to miss your Christmas feast."

"I will leave after," Samuel said. "Old Darby can plow through a snowdrift as easily as he can through the moor's rocky soil. The castle is only a couple of hours away, and I can be back before dark."

A new idea presented itself to Wetherby, and he asked, "Do you have something to write on, so I can send a note to the baron?"

Mr. Potter's chest swelled. "My boy Joshua has writing materials. He has been studying with the vicar at Danbury Wells. Go fetch them, Josh. He can pen whatever thee tells him."

"I can write," Wetherby said, somewhat testily.

Mr. Potter blinked a couple of times, but nevertheless, finally nodded to Joshua, who brought Mr. Lance paper and pen.

Wetherby tapped his chin with the quill pen for a few minutes, contemplating what he should write. Then, setting down a few lines, he folded the paper and sealed it with wax from a candle that Mrs. Potter handed him. "You are not to let go of this paper until you can place it in the hands of Lord Copley himself. No one else. Is that clear?"

Samuel seemed so taken by Mr. Lance's tone of authority, that after he took the missive, he automatically stepped away, pulling on his forelock.

Millicent watched with misgivings. Lord Wetherby would give it all away if he weren't careful.

But in spite of Millicent's apprehensions, the evening played out comfortably on a congenial note. As soon as the table was cleared, they sang Christmas carols and Wetherby was persuaded to tell another tale.

Then Samuel brought out his newest figure for the Nativity. It was a lamb, beautifully carved in the finest of detail, so real that it looked as though it were breathing.

Ruthie was given the honor of placing it wherever she wished. After much deep contemplation, she set the animal atop the baby Jesus in his cradle, and stepped back with great satisfaction.

Everyone applauded—Wetherby most enthusiastically of all.

Mrs. Potter sat for a while, knitting, but as the hour grew late and Ruthie showed signs of falling asleep in Mr. Lance's arms, the good woman rose. Setting aside her needlework, she went into the kitchen area. "I do believe mugs of warm, spiced milk are called for. 'Tis a custom we have on Christmas Eve," she explained to Millicent. "The children expect it."

Within minutes, she returned with several cups upon a platter, and passed them around to the children. Finally—and not without protest—the girls were bundled off to bed. A second trayful was brought for the grown-ups, and they all raised their cups and wished each other merry. Soon after, Mrs. Potter climbed the ladder to tuck her daughters in and hear their prayers. The older boys excused themselves and left for their quarters in the animal shelter. Mr. Potter followed to give one final check to his livestock. Although they tried to stay awake, Tommy and Rupert were soon asleep on their straw mattress off to the side of the hearth.

Millicent sat on a stool facing the fire and slowly sipped the hot, spicy drink, trying to ignore the fact that she was alone with his lordship.

When he was assured that the boys were sleeping, Wetherby, still enthroned on the settle, tried to get Millicent's attention by staring a hole in the back of her neck. "And now, madam, would you mind telling me why you did not tell me we were on your brother-in-law's property?"

"How, pray tell, could I do that when you did everything within your power to ignore the signals I sent your way?"

Wetherby waved his arms about in the air. "You called these signals? I thought you were practicing for a pantomime at a country fair."

Millicent decided not to acknowledge his rude remark.

Wetherby thought he was being quite reasonable. "All I am asking is that before I believe I truly *am* ready for Bedlam, I would like an explanation of this farce. And, pray tell, whatever possessed you to tell them we were domestics? I've never heard anything so addlebrained in my life." One side of his mouth curled up as he spoke. "Though I have to admit—you did look rather fetching with that smudge of flour on your nose, *Mrs. Lance.*"

Millicent's hand went involuntarily to her nose. "You are disgusting," she said, turning her face away from him.

He chuckled. He *knew* that would nettle her. "I know," he said, shaking his head to keep from yawning.

Millicent bit her lip.

"Mrs. Copley? Are you laughing?"

Millicent fought the urge to giggle. There certainly was nothing funny about the situation. "Of course not. You are depraved."

"I agree," he said, putting his hand to his head. He was beginning to feel quite strange. He was sure he'd heard a muffled laugh.

"Truly, my lord, I did not know myself until this afternoon that we were on Andersen's estate. When Mrs. Potter mentioned it, one thing led to another, and she took it into her head that we were going to the castle to take on new situations."

Wetherby stared at her down his aristocratic nose. "Madam, how came you to think Mrs. Potter could believe such an absurdity?"

"How can you blame her? When did you last look in a mirror, Lord Wetherby? You do not exactly look like a member of the *haut ton.*"

Wetherby cocked his head to one side. *"Touche* again, *madame."*

Millicent set her mug down on the hearth. "Oh, do be serio-ush," she lisped, hiccoughing.

Wetherby raised his eyebrows. "I assure you, madam, I am serious—and now I want to hear the all of it."

"There is no time, Mrs. Potter is back," Millicent hissed, glancing over to where the farm wife had just checked the two little boys before coming their way.

Mrs. Potter sat down in her rocking chair and once more resumed her knitting. "I can see yer son has his father's eyes," laughed Mrs. Potter, looking at Wetherby. "Big and round and brown as chestnuts. Hem is such a comely child, I am surprised thee don't have more."

Two spots of pink appeared on Millicent's cheeks.

She looked so charming that Wetherby's good spirits returned. "Oh, we do plan on many more, Mrs. Potter, don't we, my dear?" He thought his quip quite clever, but Mrs. Copley didn't seem to see the humor in his jest, so he decided it wise to let the matter drop.

Suddenly, Millicent yawned.

"It sounds as though thee are about ready for bed."

Millicent made an effort to keep her eyes open. "That ish a very good suggestion, Mrs. Potter," she said, rising unsteadily. "If you will excuse me, madam . . . your lordship . . . I do believe I shall retire."

Heading entirely in the wrong direction, Millicent became confused and started to open the door to the barn, when Mr. Potter came in. With a little assistance, she finally found the bedroom and entered. "Good night, everyone," she called back over her shoulder.

Millicent stared at the mound of pillows down the middle of the bed. As Mrs. Potter had promised, two large feather pillows divided the bed in half. It dawned on Millicent that she'd forgotten to tell Lord Wetherby that there was only one bedroom. She quickly changed into her night rail. Well, it would serve him right when he found out he had to sleep on the floor in the other room.

But Millicent misjudged his lordship, for soon after, a male form stood silhouetted in the doorway. The scoundrel wove about in a disconcerted way, finally making his way to the bed. Millicent peered over the covers and held her breath. If she yelled, the jig would be up.

"What the hell is that?" Wetherby spouted. "It seems a mountain ridge has sprouted up across the bedscape."

As far as Millicent was concerned, a mountain the height of Mount Everest would not be sufficient. "Mrs. Potter put them there. She was only thinking of you, my lord."

"Of me? I doubt that she got the idea all by herself, Mrs. Copley."

"I told her I was afraid of bumping into you in the night and causing you more harm."

He sighed most pitifully. "You don't trust me."

"Not likely, my lord, especially after you had the affrontery to brag that we would have more children."

"Don't you want more children?"

"Yes, I would like more children—but that is not the point. We are not married."

"But you let them think we were," he said accusingly. "Even to telling them that we are domestics going into service at the castle."

Millicent bit her lip as she felt the jolt as he sat down on the bed. "I did not tell them that. Mrs. Potter only assumed."

His voice carried over the pillows. "Don't deny it. I heard you. Hah! Won't Copley have a laugh over that."

"You wouldn't dare tell him."

"Wouldn't I?"

She thought about that. "Well," she harrumphed, "you started it first by letting them think we were married. I had to think of something after they put us in the same bed."

"And talking of tall tales, how, pray tell, did the Potters *assume* that I was a noodlehead?"

"Well—that just happened." Millicent tried to stifle a laugh, but with no success. "I am sorry." she said burrowing her head into her pillow to hide the sound, but only making the bed shake more. "I am beginning to feel very strange."

Wetherby snorted, then burst out laughing.

"Shh," she hissed. "They will hear us."

"If I am any judge of people," said Wetherby, "the Potters will just think that you have overcome the barrier and climbed the mountain."

"Oh, you are disgusting!"

"I know that." Wetherby was not ready for the pillow that was flung over his face. "Mrs. Copley," he said, "if you do not stop this assault, I shall not take responsibility for the consequences."

A hand reached over the barrier to retrieve the pillow. Wetherby caught it and held it in his. He held his breath, waiting for her to snatch it away, but she did not. Slowly, he released her hand and watched it disappear onto her side.

For a few minutes the only sounds were sparks popping out of the ashes in the fireplace.

"Millicent? I . . . I would like to call you that, if I may," he said, his voice so low and serious that she could hardly stand it.

The sparks continued to crackle as they flew up the chimney. "Y . . . you may," she said, suddenly feeling very drowsy.

Wetherby yawned. "I want you to know that I would never hurt you. Do you believe me?"

Millicent nuzzled into the soft down pillow between them.

"Yes . . . and you know what else?" He didn't answer, and she was not quite certain he'd forgiven her for making him out to be a noodlehead. "I want you to know that I truly appreciated your trying to protect Rupert and me from those dreadful men—getting beaten up the way you were. That was a brave and very dangerous thing for you to do. And I want to thank your lordship, too, for not revealing that we are not man and wife," she confessed, shyly. "The Potters gave up their bed to us and are sleeping with the children in the cold loft. Did you know that?"

The maddenly stubborn man still lay on his side of the barrier, refusing to answer her. Here she was trying to tell him of her fears that he might die—ready to confess how much he'd come to mean to her—and the odious man didn't even have the manners to answer. It was more than enough. Millicent sat bolt upright and peered over the pillows. "Lord Wetherby!"

The dying embers in the fireplace reflected across his still form, his eyes closed and mouth slightly open.

"Lord Wetherby?" His steady breathing was like the steady rolling of ocean waves, and just as hypnotic. Strangely, Millicent's head seemed to disconnect from her body and fly about the room in dizzying circles. She flopped back onto her pillow and was asleep in a matter of minutes.

In the next room, Mr. and Mrs. Potter sat contentedly before the fire—she with her knitting, he with his pipe.

She looked up. "That Mrs. Lance—now there is a clever girl, don't ye agree, Mister Potter? She will do well in any kitchen anywhere. Lady Copley will be lucky to hire her." Mrs. Potter shook her head. "But Mr. Lance? Pool soul, I'm not so sure about hem."

"Hem will do well enough."

Mrs. Potter smiled a wee smile and began to hum.

Mr. Potter narrowed his eyes. "Mrs. Potter, I do believe ye have been up to yer tricks again."

"Now, Mister Potter, why ever would ye be saying such a thing?"

"Because, I know thee better than ye know yerself. I saw them young folks, weaving and a-yawning. Ye gave them a posset *and* a tisane all together."

"Well, I say that if they are to be getting on the right side of Lord and Lady Copley tomorrow, they needs a good night's sleep. Thee don't want them off on the wrong foot with their new employers, now do ye?"

Mr. Potter took a few more puffs on his pipe. "No. But now, Mrs. Potter, I do believe 'tis time us go to bed."

Mrs. Potter held the finished scarf up for inspection. Then, satisfied, rolled it up carefully and tucked it away in her basket. "I do believe 'tis," she said, glancing at her husband out of the corner of her eye.

A few minutes later, Mr. Potter gave his wife a push up the ladder. "I hope thee gave me one too, Mrs. Potter, or 'tis sorry ye may be that ye didn't."

Seventeen

Christmas morning began with a song. Wetherby heard someone in the other room singing "God Rest Ye Merry Gentlemen," accompanied by an orchestra of rich aromas that sneaked under the bedroom door. He opened his eyes to find himself looking at a sleeping figure beside him, so close that her hair touched his face. Somehow the pillows that divided them when they went to bed had ended up on the floor. Carefully, he removed her arm, which lay over him, and withdrew his own from under her. No matter how innocent he had been in the matter, he knew Millicent would have his head if she should find herself in his arms. He lay there watching her for a minute, when a wicked gleam appeared in his eyes, and he leaned over and kissed her. A little smile spread across her face, but she didn't waken. Rising stealthily, he replaced the pillows to their original line of demarcation, then made haste to dress before she awakened.

Wetherby rewound his bandage as well as he could and tucked the loose strands of cloth up off his forehead. Thank goodness, his brain no longer felt as if it were being squeezed in a vice, and the swelling around his eye had diminished. But each time he pulled a garment over his ribs, he grimaced. Wishing Boggles and Tooter to Hades, he silently slipped out the door into the main room of the cottage—only to find himself swept along by a whirlwind of yuletide activity.

Chirping bird songs—which sounded very much like children's voices—flitted about from somewhere on the far side of the room, and Mary and Martha bustled in and out of the kitchen area, now singing "Come All Ye Faithful." Fat dripped and popped from the goose roasting over the open fire, while the perfume of spiced muffins filled the air.

Wetherby targeted the wooden bench by the fire as his goal, hoping he could make the journey across the room without knocking into something. First he looked about to make sure Joshua and Samuel weren't in sight. He could not tolerate being coddled, as if he were a baby in leading strings, one more day. Then, boldly setting one foot in front of the other, he managed to reach his destination without falling on his face.

As he shuffled past her, Mrs. Potter raised her head out of the flour bin and called cheerily, "Merry Christmas, Mr. Lance. Did thee sleep well?"

Wetherby sucked in a deep breath. It was a mistake. Pain seared through his midsection, and the room seemed to slant crazily to one side. To save himself from pitching forward, he grabbed the arm of the settle. Once anchored to something stable, he felt much more the thing. Swallowing the less-than-polite expletive on the tip of his tongue, he forced a smile. "Never better, Mrs. Potter, never better."

"Glad I be to hear it. As soon as the pudding be finished, I will put a clean wrap on yer head. Thee made a mess of it, didn't thee?" she scolded. "In the meantime, do sit down by the fire and one of the girls will bring a bowl of hot porridge and cream. Hemself will be in a'fore long to keep thee company."

Wetherby had no sooner eased himself down than Mr. Potter emerged from the barn, stomped the straw off his boots, and took the space beside him on the settle. The younger girls raced to see who would be the first to reach their father, and Rupert and Tommy came over to inspect him.

"Your eye is open," Rupert said, matter-of-factly.

Wetherby's fingers went immediately to that area. "So it is," he said, smiling.

Tommy nodded. "Yer mouth ain't so crooked either."

"Thank you," Wetherby answered, not exactly knowing what the appropriate reply should be.

On the heels of the children, Millicent emerged from the bedroom, looking a little confused, a little sleepy, and strangely shy. Her hair flowed down her back and her clothes were the same as the day before. In fact, they had been the same for several days now. So it wasn't her attire that made her so appealing to Wetherby. But for some reason he couldn't explain, she appeared to him the loveliest woman he'd ever seen. He ran his hand over his stubble of beard. He would, of course, have to wait until he got to Roxwealde to be washed and shaved—dressed once more as a gentleman should be. Then, when he looked his most presentable, he would ask her to be his wife.

Millicent's cheeks burned. She knew that Wetherby was trying to get her attention, but she bowed her head and scurried into the cooking area. She remembered having the strangest dream during the night, but she was bound if she could recall what it was. She only remembered that she'd felt so warm and . . . and—Oh, my goodness, she couldn't admit which feelings had rushed through her, even to herself. Then she had awakened to find herself quite alone in the bed, hugging a pillow. She knew then that it had all been a dream. Lord Wetherby had not been there at all. But now, she dared not look at him, because she was afraid that her eyes would reveal what she was thinking.

Before Wetherby had time to refine on Millicent's behavior, Samuel and Joshua, loaded down with bundles of furze for the fire, blew in with a gust of cold air.

"Merry Christmas to all," Joshua shouted. "The snow has stopped. 'Twill be a bright day."

"No doubt o'at," Samuel agreed. "As soon as us eat, I be a-go to the castle."

Ruthie pulled on her father's sweater. "Me open presents first."

"And so thee shall, my little bug," her father said, turning his attention to his youngest daughter.

A multitude of *ayes* proclaimed that to be by far the most popular suggestion. Pandemonium followed, and bundles of oddly wrapped objects appeared magically from the most surprising places: from the loft, from behind the woodpile, and even from inside the bread bin; all accompanied by giggles and grins.

Tommy let out a yelp when he unwrapped two miniature carved horses. "Samuel made a wagon for me last year," he explained to Rupert. "Now I have the cattle to pull it."

Samuel had a lovely carved box for his mother, and for his father, a new axe handle. Joshua, from his small earnings at the vicarage, had provided the axe head, buttons and ribbons for his sisters, a new knife for Samuel, and a belt for Tommy. To his mother, he proudly gave a linen handkerchief trimmed with lace.

The men measured their heavy woolen sweaters across their chests. There were dresses and aprons for the girls, knitted gloves for Wetherby and Rupert. There were toys, of course: tops and whirly-gigs, a checkerboard and doll clothes. All homely objects, all handmade with care. All received with love.

Wetherby ticked off in his head the expensive gifts he'd bought over the years for his nieces and nephews. All ended up abandoned on shelves, neglected, broken, or discarded for something new in a few weeks' time.

Finally, Mrs. Potter presented Millicent with a lovely green-and-blue knitted shawl.

Millicent fingered the warm, durable wrap. "Oh, dear, I am afraid we have nothing to give to you."

Mrs. Potter brushed that aside with a wave of her hand. "Pooh! Pooh! Don't thee be worrying yerself about that, dear heart. Thee lost everything— but not each other. That is of more import."

Wetherby held his breath as he watched a fleeting change come over Millicent's face, and for an instant their eyes met and held—or so he thought. But he must have been mistaken in his interpretation, because he realized that her gaze had settled on her son, not on him. A feeling of disappointment ran through him.

But his despondency was short-lived when Mr. Potter handed Ruthie a doll, one with *two* eyes and a painted smile. He explained to her, "Samuel carved the wooden head, and yer Mama made her cloth body. Joshua bought the laces, yer sisters sewed her fine gown, and Tommy painted her eyes and hair and gave her a happy face."

After a close inspection of the doll's eyes, the little knitted shoes, and a peek under her skirt, Ruthie held her up for Wetherby to see.

"She is very pretty," he said. "What is her name?"

"Elizabeth!" scolded Ruthie, "Thee should know that."

"Of course. I stand corrected," Wetherby apologized, wondering what would happen to poor Bridget now. Then as he watched the child introduce Elizabeth, with great pomp and ceremony, to the older doll, his heart experienced a strange twist. He knew for certain that the less-than-beautiful Bridget would not be cast out or forsaken. The little mop-haired mother would love and cherish the used-up doll for the rest of her raggedy life.

Next, Mr. Potter cleared his throat and handed his wife a decorative ivory comb for her hair.

Mrs. Potter clapped her hands. "Did thee ever see the like?" she exclaimed, as though she'd been presented with the crown jewels.

Wetherby thought of the multitude of expensive baubles worth a fortune, which he'd lavished carelessly on his mistresses over the years. They'd thanked him in many ways most pleasant, none had ever looked at him the way Mrs. Potter looked now at her rough-hewn husband. A disturbing thought crossed Wetherby's mind. He, the son of a duke, was envying a rustic.

After the gifts were distributed, everyone gathered around the table, and Mr. Potter said a prayer. The Christmas feast began, and continued until one and all cried that they would surely burst if they ate one bite more.

There were only a few more hours of daylight left. Samuel hastily prepared for his ride to the castle.

"We are obliged," Wetherby said. "Don't forget my letter—and Samuel—see if Lord Copley can have someone come for us tomorrow."

The young man looked anxiously at his mother and father. Mr. Potter placed his hand on Wetherby's shoulder, Mrs. Potter shook her head, and Millicent, as Wetherby should have expected, began sending her nick-ninny signals again from the kitchen.

Enough was enough! Wetherby had about had it with the theatrics and he'd just decided to end the farce, when Mrs. Potter spoke. "There, there, now, Mr. Lance. Don't thee be fretting yerself. I'm sure his lordship will hold yer post. Thee know yer welcome to stay here 'til the snow melts. When yer well again, the mister will hitch up the wagon and carry thee all to Roxwealde."

Millicent hurried to his side. "I will take care of him, Mrs. Potter. It's all the excitement," she said, her eyes daring him to say more. "Come, dear, let us be reasonable and sit down."

Reasonable? She wasn't the one being made out to be a simpleton. Wetherby's sentiments of a few minutes ago took a quick turnabout, and he tried his hardest to give the termagant a set down with his eyes. But she obviously failed to see it, for she was too busy tugging at his sleeve. Wetherby said a few choice words under his breath, but nevertheless returned to the settle.

Mr. Potter pulled up a stool by the fire and took out his pipe. "Have thee ever farmed, young man?"

Taken aback by the question, Wetherby tried to think why Mr. Potter would think a marquis should be required to work in the dirt. Then the reality of his situation struck him, and he reminded himself that he was playing a role. However, as insulting as he felt the inference to be, a picture of his mother's neglected conservatory suddenly came back to haunt him. Drooping orchids, brown ferns, and spidery, leafless vines danced before him. The duchess would ring a peal over his head if she saw it today. "I have not been very successful with plants," he conceded.

"Houseman, then?"

Wetherby riveted Millicent with his eyes but she was again looking the other way. He was quite sorry she missed his censure. "No, sir," he sputtered.

Tommy held up one of his new wooden horses. "I'm going to be a woodworker like Samuel when I grow up. Can thee carve?"

"Why, no. I never have," Wetherby replied, wondering from whence the next attack on his ego would come.

"Never?"

Wetherby frowned. Although he'd attended Eton and Cambridge, he was beginning to feel that his education had been sadly lacking in some ways.

Potter shook his head. "Whatever do thee plan to do at the castle, then?"

Ruthie gave him an exasperated look. "Can thee not do anything?"

Rupert stepped to Wetherby's side. "He beats up ruffians, and he can tell stories," he said, defensively.

Wetherby looked at the clinched fists, the belligerent expression. Had he sunk so low that he had to be championed by a six-year-old boy? Enough was enough! Wetherby was about to set the whole fiasco straight when Ruthie said sweetly, "Tell us another story."

One of Wetherby's admitted faults was that he never could resist the request of a pretty woman. At first an uncomfortable feeling flooded through him, and he asked himself how he'd been reduced to an itinerant performer. Then he looked at the cloud of expectant faces surrounding him, and something happened within him. A wonderful thing. He didn't know where it came from, but he started to laugh and threw up his hands in mock surrender. He was rewarded by *hurrahs* all around. Even Joshua came to sit by the hearth to listen.

Wetherby glanced over at Mr. Potter and recalled the pride shining in the rugged crofter's eyes when he told him that his son Joshua was learning to read and write. Guiltily, Wetherby thought of how he'd wasted his salad days at Cambridge. Surely it would count for something when he occasionally took his seat in the House of Lords. However, Wetherby doubted that the practical Potters would look upon that as much of an accomplishment.

At least as a teller of tales, he had gained some degree of favor in their eyes. He looked about to see if Mrs. Copley was noting his popularity, but he was disappointed to see that she was so absorbed in washing the tableware that she seemed unaware that he even existed. He wondered what it was he had to do to gain her approval.

Ruthie raised her arms to be lifted up, and as soon as she and Bridget and Elizabeth were settled on his knee, Wetherby began his story. "Once upon a time there was a mean and terrible dragon who threatened to take Christmas away from a whole village in Devonshire. There was a family of brothers and sisters named Rettop. That is Potter backward," he explained, "and they vowed that they would drive the dragon away."

To his amazement, Wetherby found he was enjoying himself. Who would have ever thought that the Marquis of Wetherby would tolerate being surrounded by fidgeting children and holding a wiggly child on his knee? Maybe he *was* going daft. If so, it didn't seem to be any deterrent to his being considered top-o-the-trees by the Potter children. He could even see Mrs. Potter where she stood scrubbing the table, cocking her head to hear every tittle of the story he was relating. He grinned and looked over Ruthie's head to see if Mrs. Copley was listening. Unfortunately, she was now engrossed in sweeping the floor.

He looked down at Ruthie. She held her two dolls in her arms, her curly head bobbing up and down, her wide-eyed gaze never leaving his face. For what purpose, he did not know. Wetherby was beginning to feel as though he were being sized up by a stricter judge than any of the distinguished members on the King's Bench. When he finished his tale, the bigger children drifted away. After silently evaluating him for another long uncomfortable minute, Ruthie held out her raggedy doll to Wetherby.

"Ruthie wants thee to have Bridget," she said, looking up at him through her long lashes.

Overwhelmed by the gesture, Wetherby realized the honor and trust the little girl bestowed upon him. "Thank you," he said with great solemnity. He then settled the pitiful-looking doll atop his other knee, where it immediately fell over on its back. No amount of propping up could induce Bridget to sit upright, so he left her sprawled where she lay, her skirt in shocking dishabille. Undaunted by this display of unladylike behavior, Wetherby placed his right hand over his heart and continued his acceptance speech. "I shall cherish Bridget always, and I promise—on a knight's oath—to honor and protect her."

Ruthie hugged her new doll to her chest and with a snort, slid off his lap. "I wanted to get rid of her anyway," she whispered, with a smirk.

Wetherby blinked. He'd been duped by a three-year-old hoyden.

With not even a backward glance, Ruthie skipped across the room with Elizabeth and was seen introducing her to baby Jesus.

Wetherby glanced down at the disheveled doll lying limp over his knee, her black button eye staring blindly back at him. "At least, my dear Bridget, you are one female I don't have to worry about being fickle."

Millicent watched the entire scene surreptitiously. When she had seen Ruthie hold up her arms to Lord Wetherby, she'd held her breath. Oh, she had no doubt that he'd come back with some rebuttal that he thought quite witty. Instead, to her surprise, he'd lifted Ruthie up on his knee as if it were the most natural thing in the world for him to do. Millicent's heart leapt within her. But it was when Wetherby had accepted Ruthie's doll that Millicent knew she had fallen in love all over again with Lord Wetherby—at least the part of him that could captivate the heart of a little girl. How sweet to see the child whisper some secret to him and to see her innocent smile as she ran off to play. Millicent brushed a tear away with the back of her hand. She had been so overcome by her emotions that she dared not look his lordship in the eye. Silly woman. How could she even dream that he could hold her in affection in the same way?

It was outside of enough for her even to think of such a possibility. She'd heard that the Duke of Loude was a hard man, stiff-rumped and a stickler for the proprieties. He would never accept a wife of lower rank for his only son and heir. After all, Lord Wetherby must marry someone high in the instep. Someone like beautiful Lady Caroline.

Hopefully, tomorrow they would be at Roxwealde, and he would again be the Marquis of Wetherby, heir to a dukedom.

And she? Millicent sighed. She would still be the plain widow Copley. The daughter of a small village squire, the mother of a six-year-old boy who would one day go off into the world to seek his fortune, and she would be all alone.

A good many hours passed and darkness was nearly upon them when Samuel was heard riding around and coming into the stables next to the house. As soon as he entered the cottage, he reported that he had done as he was instructed and had not given up the letter until he could place it in the hands of Lord Copley.

"His lordship insisted I start back right away. Hemself said he would instruct his coachman to follow my tracks and catch me up on the road. They cannot be far behind."

It was no longer than half an hour when a great commotion was heard outside the humble cottage. Tommy reached the window first and let out a whoop. "Mama, Papa, a great coach and four has stopped out front."

Rupert, arms flailing, made a dash for the door. Disregarding his sore ribs, Wetherby leapt from the settle and caught him. "Don't say a word," he whispered close to Rupert's ear. "In my letter, I asked your uncle not to reveal our identities to anyone, not even the servants. We still have a distance to go tonight, so do not say anything in front of the Potters or the coachman to make them think otherwise. If we are stopped, the coachman will say that they are only transporting domestics." He could see that Rupert was disappointed.

"I wanted to tell Tommy before I went away."

"Let us pretend for one more day. How does this sound to you? We shall be knights in disguise going on a quest for the king. Until we are safely at His Majesty's castle, we cannot tell anyone who we are."

Rupert's eyes sparkled. Lord Wetherby was his old self again. Rupert liked the idea of calling his Uncle Andy a king. "Oh, jolly good, your . . . sir," he whispered back. "And can Momma be a knight too?" he asked, looking over at Millicent.

Wetherby tried to keep a straight face. "I believe that under the circumstances, we can permit that."

"I shall have to tell Momma, so she won't spoil things."

Wetherby glanced at Millicent, who again was doing her dance and motioning to him, all at the same time. "I don't believe we need fear that your mother will give our plans away." *They may very likely take her to Bedlam instead.*

They didn't have much to gather up for their journey, and their only delay was in the Potters' reluctance to see their guests leave.

When Millicent was all buttoned into her coat, Mrs. Potter placed her new shawl over her shoulders and gave her a kiss on the cheek. "Thee hold yer head up, now, dear heart. Yer husband's a kindhearted man, and I'm sure hem will do just fine in his new position."

It was as Wetherby was wrapping Rupert's new muffler tighter around his neck that he noticed something amiss. "Where is your sword?"

Rupert shuffled his feet. "I gave it to Tommy."

"But it is the only thing you saved, and it meant so much to you."

"Don't you remember what Momma said? *A gift has more value if you give something that is dear to your heart.*" He fished around inside his coat and pulled out a wooden horse. "Tommy gave me this. I told him that he needed it to pull his wagon, but he said that it is better that I have it. That way, every time we play with the horses, we will think of each other."

Unexplainably, Wetherby felt a lump in his throat. "Come," he said gruffly, " 'tis time to take our leave."

After much hugging and shaking of hands, the three travelers made their way to the waiting coach.

Millicent was the first to enter and the first to see the dark-clothed figure in the far corner. However, before she could cry an alarm, a gloved hand clamped over her mouth. *Heaven help us! We are being kidnapped all over again,* she thought, struggling against her assailant. But his hands were too strong for her to break free.

Wetherby and Rupert boarded behind Millicent. Before their eyes became well enough adjusted to the dim interior to realize her dilemma, the door slammed shut and the horses leapt forward.

Eighteen

Rupert was the first to get a good look at the other man. "Uncle Andy!" he shouted, throwing his arms around the baron's neck.

The moonlight coming through the small window was just bright enough for Lord Copley to make out his nephew's exuberant smile. "Well, I am glad someone recognizes me," he said, embracing the boy.

Everybody started speaking at once.

"Wait! Wait!" Copley laughed, trying to hug his sister-in-law, and at the same time shake the hand of his good friend.

Wetherby spoke first. "Samuel did not tell us you were in the coach."

"He did not know that I was. After that crazy letter of yours giving me your direction, then telling me not to reveal your true identity to the bearer, I feared more deviltry. I led the young man to believe it was only my servants who were bringing the coach to pick you up. Now tell me why you did not want the Potters to know who you really were. The family have been tenants of Roxwealde for several generations. You did not have to worry about their loyalty."

The coach bounced over a rut in the road. Wetherby hugged his ribs and tried not to think of the jolting they were taking. "It was not that, Copley," he said, through clenched teeth. "The Potters saved our lives. We will always be indebted to them. But at first, I did not know where we were, and, well . . ." He leaned slightly in Millicent's direction, the temptation to jog her out of her reticence compelling him to mischief. "One thing led to another and *somehow*—I cannot imagine why—the Potters came to the conclusion that we were going to the castle to seek positions there."

Millicent refused to rise to the bait. She merely cleared her throat and stared ahead—somewhere in the vicinity of her brother-in-law's chin.

Copley slapped his forehead with the heel of his hand and laughed. "Domestics? God! Ever since we received word that you had been kidnapped, we have been half out of our minds with worry, while all the time you were safely masquerading as ordinary servants?"

Rupert was happy to hear laughter again and eagerly added his opinion. "We had a great adventure, Uncle Andy."

Wetherby felt that they were not taking his injuries seriously enough. "It was not all that pleasant an experience," he muttered, as the coach proceeded along the gravelly road.

Millicent was inclined to be more to the point. "How *did* you know that we had been abducted, Andersen?"

"First, Jespers and your coachmen arrived with Lady Caroline's servants at Karkingham Hall outside Wellington. They were surprised that you were not there, but considered that you had stopped off at Sir Jonathan Bridges's. After all, you had planned originally to stay over. Three days later a farmer's wagon drew up at Karkingham with Caro wrapped in a horse blanket, perched atop a stack of straw."

Millicent clasped her hands, her voice full of concern. "Was she all right?"

Copley chuckled. "A bit bedraggled and quite angry, I understand. She does have a penchant for odd encounters, does she not, Wetherby?"

Wetherby exchanged glances with the baron, then began to shake with silent laughter.

Millicent gasped. It astonished her that the men found anything funny about poor Lady Caroline's narrow escape, but she also surmised that this was not the time to pursue their reason for hilarity. A man's sense of humor was vastly different from a woman's. From the corner of her eye. she caught Wetherby studying her. She tried to ignore the disturbing effect his closeness was having on her. "Go on, Andersen," she said primly.

Copley swallowed his laughter. "Caroline told the authorities the story of your abduction, but thought you had been carried south toward Exeter. That is where they have concentrated their efforts to find you. She has since returned to her father's house in Gloucester."

"Where she will most likely get a royal scold."

"Speaking of scolds, Wetherby. I thought you would like to know that your father paid the ransom, and I hear he is in a high dudgeon because you've caused him so much trouble. Now he is crying foul because you had disappeared and he is out the blunt."

"Poor Father. I doubt he will be any happier when he hears we have been rescued."

"The Karkinghams loaned Jespers and your men one of their vehicles so they could bring us the news."

Wetherby made no effort to hide his hostility. " 'Twas the Bandit King and his band."

"That is what Jespers said."

Wetherby shifted his weight to ease the soreness in his side. "It would give me great pleasure to track him down," he said through clenched teeth.

The baron could not have agreed more. "You and many others, but now tell me, why all the secrecy? You only wrote that you were well, and that I was not to reveal your true identities to the message-bearer. Did you fear that you were still in danger?"

Wetherby remembered Millicent's shock the morning she'd awakened next to him. "In a manner of speaking," he said, with a chuckle. He felt a kick against his ankle, but ignored it. She didn't seem the least bit impressed that he was trying to lighten the mood.

It was full night now, but as the moon rose higher, its light flooded the landscape. As if seeing him for the first time, Lord Copley narrowed his eyes and studied Wetherby. "When did you take to sporting a beard? And . . . God! Whatever did you do to your eye?" The baron leaned forward to better observe his friend. "I say, is that a bandage I see around your head?"

Copley's inquisition was annoying Wetherby, who thought his countenance had improved immeasurably over the last two days. Of course, he'd seen no mirror in the Potters' cottage, so how could he tell? He ran his hand over his face, dislodging the muffler that was wrapped around his head. Wetherby felt he'd suffered enough of Copley's scrutiny. "I feel fine." he snapped. " 'Tis the latest fashion in thieves' dens now, didn't you know? Beards and bandages."

"Cut line, Wetherby," the baron said, "I meant it well enough. Did they hurt you, Millie?"

"Momma sprained her ankle," Rupert reported happily, glad to have something of importance to add to the conversation.

The baron spoke sternly. "I want you to start from the beginning and tell me all."

For the next hour and a half, Copley heard a checkerboard recital—some from Wetherby, most from Rupert—of all that had happened since their abduction and rescue by the Potters. Millicent favored forgetting the whole incident and said so. However, for their own individual reasons, not one of the three confessed to the hoax that they had played on the Potters—that of letting them believe the Banbury Tale that they were the Lances: Papa, Momma, and son.

However, guilt was making Wetherby more and more aware of the woman beside him, and he lay his head back on the squabs and closed his eyes. But no matter how hard he tried, he couldn't shut out the sight of her. He had promised the baron that he would give his sister-in-law and her

son safe passage to Devon. He'd failed miserably in his mission,
he feared. She had never outwardly condemned him, but she'd
barely spoken a word since they'd entered the coach. Now, he
hoped her estimation of him had not been so badly tarnished
that he would have no chance to redeem himself. Well, he had
twelve days ahead of him to regain her approval. Plenty of time
to charm her. He'd often done it in far less time. He didn't think
she would reveal what had happened at the Potters', but there
was no way of telling what Rupert was capable of spilling. If
Copley found out that he'd been in bed with his sister-in-law,
Wetherby knew the baron would demand that he do the right
thing by her. But no matter how much Wetherby sought that
very consequence, he wanted more for Millicent to come to
him willingly. Perhaps his luck would turn at the castle.

The nearer they came to Roxwealde, the more he was reminded of Lord Copley's party almost two years ago. The
Merry Five, they'd called themselves. They had planned a
madcap weekend with some obliging little actresses from
Drury Lane. But when Copley had discovered he'd lost his
fortune and had only a few weeks to find himself a wealthy
wife, he'd made a turnabout and invited, instead, some of the
most sought-after young ladies of the *beau monde*. Lady
Caroline had been one of these.

However, the old monstrosity that his ancestor, Lord Percival Copley, the first baron, had built to resemble a Norman
castle, sat surrounded by rocky soil covered by bronzing
bracken and mottled bramble, treacherous boglands, and
granite outcroppings. Its sinister-looking twin towers were
enough to terrify the bravest souls. Hardly a setting for ro-
mance, until a sensible, young squire's daughter, Sarah
Greenwood, had switched identities with a notorious hostess.
She'd not only transformed the castle into a winter flower
garden, but she'd captured the heart of the baron as well.

The only thing that Lord Copley had failed to tell his
guests was that his pet lion, named Dog, was loose in the
castle. The baron, who had a soft spot for mistreated animals,

had saved the beast from being put down at the Tower Zoo for being too old. Dog, being the social creature that he was, turned up one night in bed with Lady Caroline. Ah, yes, thought Wetherby, that was an evening to remember.

"There it is!" shouted Rupert, his nose pressed against the window. "There is your castle, Uncle Andy."

The baron exclaimed, "I daresay, that *is* a wonder. Would you believe? 'Tis right where I left it."

Rupert didn't take his gaze off the tall four-storied granite structure. "Oh, Uncle Andy. You know what I meant. Momma says it is a fairy castle."

The coach drove around another curve in the carriageway to reach the circular drive, and for a moment, the castle appeared on Millicent's side. Glad to have something to take her mind off the disturbing presence of the man beside her, Millicent turned her head to look out the window.

Wetherby caught his breath. The silvery light of the moon had transformed her face into something fey, and he thought her the loveliest creature he had ever seen. He remembered at Copley's party, the castle had indeed cast a spell on nearly every one there. Four of the Merry Five had succumbed to Cupid's arrow. Wetherby had thought himself fortunate at the time that he was not one of them. He could not imagine any man wanting to be put into shackles. Now that he'd found the lady whom he wished would do just that, she seemed to become more and more agitated with him.

The old castle had worked its magic for his friends. Would it do so for him, now?

Copley swatted his nephew's bottom. "Aye, I was only quizzing you, Rupert. However, I think I should warn you all that I told everyone before I left that you were coming. So be prepared for an enthusiastic welcome."

Their arrival was just that. A celebration. The minute old Mr. Proctor opened the massive arched doors of the castle,

Lady Sarah Copley ran to embrace her sister-in-law, then Rupert, then Wetherby, who took the onslaught valiantly.

"I was so worried about you," Sarah cried.

Millicent and Rupert found themselves pulled in out of the cold and smothered in loving arms. Sarah's parents added their greetings to those of the servants who crowded around in the background.

Jespers was beside himself to discover that his master was still alive, and could not be faulted for shedding a tear or two.

When Wetherby was relieved of his muffler, Sarah spotted the bandage and blackened eye and exclaimed, "You look dreadful! Andersen, I insist you call a doctor."

Wetherby wished everyone would quit telling him how terrible he looked. "I've never felt fitter, my dear lady," he said, attempting to make a leg before his hostess. The truth was, Wetherby felt dizzy and swore that the floor curved up dangerously. He tilted his head to one side to make it straight.

His keen eyes narrowing, Lord Copley gripped his friend's arm when he saw him falter. "Come," he said, trying to hide any solicitous manner in his tone. "My wife will make milk-sops of us men if we let her." Then, tightening his hold, he directed Wetherby across the flagstone floor toward the fire.

Wetherby shook off Copley's hand. The long ride in the coach had done his injuries no good, and his head did feel queer, but if the women were not allowed to mollycoddle him, then neither was the baron. Wetherby glanced at Millicent as he passed her. She was lovely. He grinned at her. Yes, as soon as he was recovered and Jespers had transformed him into a figure of distinction once more, he'd court her in the style, with flowers and sweets and trips to the theater. He would take his time to make her love him. He would wine her and dine her and dance with her until the sun came up.

The Great Hall, with its flagstone floor, spread out before them. Christmas greenery festooned everything. Pine boughs, and sprigs of holly intertwined with red ribbons, encircled the columns that marched along both sides. Boughs of mistletoe were strung from doorways, and magic lanterns hung from poles extending from the balconies, casting their golden rays of enchantment over everyone.

Two dark oak stairways on either side of the hall spiraled up to the floors above, and at the far end, an immense fireplace spread almost the entire width of the room. It was said to be large enough to roast an ox in, but it now held a Yule log so big, it promised to burn far beyond the designated twelve days of Christmas.

Everyone was chattering at once, when they were all silenced by the roar of a wild beast. A great African lion raised his head from where he lay on the hearth.

"Dog!" shouted Rupert, running to hug his old friend. "You're still here."

The animal did not move from the spot. Beside him, a golden-haired child sat up from where he'd lain sleeping, his head pillowed in the thick mane.

Lord Copley laughed and picked up his son before handing him over to his nurse. "Dog is the only one with patience enough to put up with this rascal."

Sarah looked at Millicent's clothes and shook her head. "What a pity everything you had was stolen. Now, I know you will want to freshen up before we eat. As you see, we have been waiting for you to arrive before we had our Christmas feast." She indicated the other side of the fireplace where a long trestle table, draped with a white cloth, was already being covered with bowls of fruit and various dishes. "We have only opened the West Wing for the holidays, so you will all be on the same floor as my parents. I will let Jespers show you to your rooms while I select some clean clothing. One of Mrs. Potter's nieces is waiting abovestairs to attend you."

Wetherby's quarters were at the far end of the long hall. Big red bows decorated all the doors, and rope garlands of evergreens looped from side to side from the ceiling, along the entire length of the corridor.

It turned out that Wetherby and Copley were of a like size, and the clothes brought in fit him well. "I shall have to wait until tomorrow to shave, Jespers. A trim will have to do. Dinner is to be served shortly."

After he had dressed, Wetherby looked at himself in the mirror and was quite pleased with what he saw. Yes, he cut a fine figure. Mrs. Copley should be impressed. And now that he was going to reform and curb his wild ways, she should have no objections to his courtship whatsoever. "You know, Jespers, the beard does not look half bad. Rather gives me a pirate look, don't you think?"

So happy was Jespers to see his lordship, that he would have agreed if Wetherby's hair had hung to his ankles. He picked up Wetherby's dirty clothes with his fingertips and held them out at arm's length. "What do you wish me to do with these, your lordship?"

Wetherby wrinkled his nose. "Throw them out, Jespers."

The servant gave them a shake, and as he did so, a dirty cloth fell out. "What is this, my lord?"

Wetherby's eyes lit up. "What does it look like, Jespers?"

The valet turned it around. "A . . . a rag doll, my lord?"

"By Jove! You have hit it on the head, Jespers. 'Tis a memento to the fickleness of the female sex."

Jespers almost raised an eyebrow. "Do you wish me to discard it with the rest of your things, my lord?"

"Good heavens! No!"

Jespers, tip-top servant that he was, made no further comment and set the relic on top of the chest of drawers. The doll promptly fell over, face in her skirt.

Wetherby gave his cravat one last inspection in the mirror, then started for the door. "Oh, by the by, her name is Bridget," he said, leaving the room.

Millicent had just entered the hallway and was standing under the kissing bough. She looked lovely in a bright blue velvet dress, her shoulders covered by, of all things, Mrs. Potter's shawl. The knowledge of its simple origin and the honor she bestowed upon the friendship of a farmer's wife only made Wetherby love her more. He wanted to take her in his arms and smother her with kisses. But—he reminded himself that he was a reformed man now. Nothing on earth could move him to do anything to give her a dislike of him.

"Good evening, Mrs. Copley," he said, looking up for one whole minute at the clump of greenery above them. "Our hostess has very attractive decorations, would you not say?" Her gaze followed his, he was glad to see. Now she would realize what a true pattern-saint he was.

Millicent stared at the mistletoe. She knew full well what his lordship was thinking to do. Did the man have no idea of how humiliating it was to be grabbed and kissed with no more than a by-your-leave? A gentleman might—but a rake of Wetherby's ilk—no, never. If a man were so assaulted, he'd undoubtedly wish to place a facer square in the mouth of the offending party.

His lordship needed to be taught a lesson.

Millicent threw her arms around Wetherby's neck and pulled his head down until his lips met hers. She was not very strong, but she was determined—and—she had the advantage of surprise. She kissed Wetherby until she had no more breath in her and had to let him go.

His eyes showed shock, then wonderment.

Millicent was so jarred by what she had done, that she could do no more than clamp her hand over her mouth and dash for the stairs. She could not believe she'd had the courage to do it. Well, at least she had taught him a lesson. "There!" she threw back at him before running down the steps.

Wetherby stood stock-still, staring after her. "There? There, what?" he called after her, but she was already out of sight. Well, he'd done it now. He'd broken his resolve before he'd even implemented his plan, and lost any chance of getting her to believe that he was reformed. But wait! He hadn't kissed her. She'd kissed him! "Damn!" Now he wanted her more than ever.

Just before Millicent reached the Great Hall, she paused to collect herself. Her purpose, she told herself, had been to show him how disconcerting it was to have someone—someone of the opposite sex—someone handsome and witty and altogether too charming—forever kissing you for no reason whatsoever. But she had not considered the consequences on her heart. Taking a deep breath, she put on a pleasant face and took the last step to the flagstone floor.

After they had eaten, they all gathered around the fire. Percival, the Copley's baby, was brought down again for the opening of the presents.

Rupert sat on the floor at Millicent's feet. "I'm sorry, Momma, that I lost your gift. Lord Wetherby helped me pick it out, you know."

No, she had not known. His lordship had helped select her present? How had that come to be? Then she remembered all the whispering and confiding in the small villages they had passed through. And here she had thought his lordship was filling her son's mind with all sorts of unmentionable subjects. Had she misjudged him? Perhaps he wasn't as bad as she had made him out to be. She gave Rupert a hug. "That is all right, dear. Remember what Mrs. Potter said? *We have each other.*"

Millicent turned to give Wetherby a smile, but alas, he didn't see her. He was watching the baron pluck his son from his nurse's arms.

Lord Copley sat down on the settle and after balancing the baby on his foot, began riding him up an down.

Wetherby guffawed. "I never thought I'd see the day that Andersen Copley would be bouncing a baby."

"You know, Wetherby, it isn't all that bad. You ought to think about getting married yourself."

"I have."

"Well, well. Someone has finally captured the king of hearts. And may I ask what the lady's name is who has caught your fancy?"

Wetherby scowled. "No!"

"Ah," Copley said, winking at his wife, "I do believe his lordship wants us to play a guessing game. Is she beautiful?"

"Very . . ." Wetherby said. "The loveliest woman I have ever seen—and the most humble person ever to grace my life—and that is all I will say." But that was not all that he had to say. "She is also generous to a fault."

"Then she must not be suitable, if you are reluctant to name her."

Wetherby rose to the bait. "She is more suitable than any woman I have ever met—and—the bravest."

"Ah! A regular amazon."

Wetherby started to rise.

The baron chuckled. "A bit out of curl, are we?"

Sarah scolded her husband. "Now Andersen, leave the man be. You are embarrassing him."

"Hah!" said Copley. "That is just what I am trying to do, my dear. How many times has he had me at a disadvantage? Now, my friend, if you have found such a paragon, why do you not tell us her name?"

"Because she is so far above me that I do not know if she will accept my suit." From the corner of his eye, Wetherby saw Millicent stiffen. He couldn't interpret the expression on her face. She had to know he was speaking of her, so why didn't she look pleased? Any ordinary woman would be delighted to receive his praise. But, of course, Mrs. Copley was no ordinary woman. She chased dragons and threw snowballs, rode neck-or-nothing in a donkey cart, and out-witted thieves.

The baron was enjoying himself. "Well, now, we shall just have to make a list, Sarah, my dear—you are so good at that. Of all the eligible young debutantes who came out last year

which one do you suppose would be willing to have such a
rake for a husband?"

Wetherby winced. All the schemes he'd made to court Millicent were exploding like fireworks. When he had gone to
Cross-in-Hand to fetch her, he'd wondered how she had come
to take such an aversion to him. His encounter with her in
London had been no more than an introduction, so who could
have advised her otherwise? Now he knew. His so-called
friend Baron Copley had been spreading lies about him.

Millicent looked down at Rupert's golden curls and fought
back the tears. How could she stand to be around his lordship
for the next twelve days and not reveal her feelings for him?
He didn't have to name the object of his affections. 'Twas
obvious to anyone who knew her. "Lord Wetherby loves . . .
he loves . . . Lady Caroline," she said softly.

Rupert looked up with a start, thinking his mother was
speaking to him. But her eyes were on some distant point
among the evergreens hanging from the balcony. But he had
heard, nonetheless. Why was she saying that Lord Wetherby
was in love with Lady Caroline?

Millicent didn't notice her son's restlessness. Her mind was
on the shocking revelation she'd just heard. But she had to
agree with his lordship. He couldn't have found anyone more
beautiful, or generous, than Lady Caroline. The fine lady had
shared her gowns and jewelry with Millicent, and although
the task was quite hopeless, she'd even tried to teach Millicent
to flirt.

Rupert sat in a daze, surrounded by his own hopelessness.
All his scheming had served no purpose. All he'd hoped for,
and prayed for—everything—was going wrong. And it was
all his fault.

Nineteen

Lord Copley handed Percy to his nurse to take back to the nursery. "I don't know of any woman who would be brave enough to marry you, Wetherby."

Millicent flatly refused to hang her head. She knew that it was her ladyship of whom he spoke. Lady Caroline had been stouthearted enough to steal a key from a robber three times her size, and fearless enough to face the freezing cold to go for help. In Millicent's eyes there was no lady she thought braver.

Wetherby could take the jesting about his beloved no longer, especially when she sat in the very same room with them. Copley was acting abominably. 'Twas an aggravation to have a man who bounced a baby on his foot, telling his friend that *he* was not man enough to take charge of his life. There was a point when a gentleman had to declare himself. Wetherby narrowed his eyes. "You know, Copley, I just may propose to the lady and see if she will have me."

Rupert looked back and forth in desperation between the two adults he loved the most until he could stand it no longer. He didn't understand why people had to get married, for it seemed it certainly complicated matters. He'd chosen Lady Caroline for himself when he grew up. He had wanted Lord Wetherby for his mother. Now he knew he wanted his lordship for himself as well. He would have to sacrifice one or the other—Lady Caroline or Lord Wetherby. He loved his mother more than anybody in the world. He wanted her to be happy. His lovely gift that he'd saved for so long had been smashed. Now he could give her only one thing. Lord Wetherby.

Rupert had figured out a solution, but he knew he had to act quickly if all was not to be lost. He jumped up and cried, "Wait!"

All eyes followed him as he approached Wetherby. He tried hard to stand straight, hold his shoulders back, and not shuffle his feet. "My lord."

Wetherby glanced at the boy, not unkindly. "Yes, Rupert, what is it?"

Rupert bit his lower lip and tried to look his lordship straight in the eye, man to man, so to speak. "I am strong for my age, and I don't take up too much room, and I could help Jespers take care of you." He paused to catch his breath.

Wetherby's eyebrows shot up, then down again.

Rupert was not quite sure how one went about proposing. He reckoned it was sort of like praying. He fell upon his knees and steepled his fingers. "Lord Wetherby, if you will not marry Momma, will you marry me?"

Millicent's gasp was heard all the way across the room.

The look on Wetherby's face could not be described.

Confusion colored Rupert's cheeks scarlet, but he gathered his strength and continued, "Momma said that if two people liked each other well enough, they can sign a paper and live together for the rest of their lives. She said it is not hard when you love someone. And I love you."

As Rupert paused to catch his breath, Millicent's hand flew to her throat.

Wetherby looked over Rupert's head to where Millicent sat frozen to her seat. "I love you, too," he said.

Then, much to the amusement of everyone, Wetherby drew the distraught boy onto his lap and said, "I want you to know that I am very honored by your proposal, Rupert, but that is not exactly how it works."

"I am afraid I handled it very badly."

"Not at all, son."

Son! He called him son. Rupert could hardly contain his excitement.

Wetherby cast a warning look at Copley. "Since you are the head male of your family now, 'tis I who have to ask *you* for permission to address your mother."

It didn't take Rupert long to think the matter over. "Oh, yes, your lordship. I give it. I do. I told Momma that I wanted a father for Christmas, but she has not found anyone yet. But I am sure that I can persuade her to have *you,* my lord. You would make the best of fathers."

Wetherby was still watching Millicent, who was looking everywhere in the room except at him.

Millicent was beginning to wonder if all men took such a roundabout way to get to the point. If Lord Wetherby did not soon hurry over to where she sat, she was going to go to him.

While Rupert was trying hard to fight his inclination to throw his arms around Lord Wetherby's neck, that gentleman addressed the blushing Millicent. "Madam," he called quite loudly, "I do believe your son is sadly in need of a father. There is no telling what mischief the lad's ideas will lead him into if you do not obtain one for him in the very near future."

Millicent just knew that his lordship was in a delirium again. She tried to signal him to stop. That got no response. Then trying to hide her concern, she smiled vacantly at everybody in the room, including Dog. What would Andersen think? What would Sarah think? What would the entire world think?

Afraid that Mrs. Copley was going to go into one of her whirling dervish performances, Wetherby turned his attentions back to Rupert. "Master Rupert, I believe your mother is in a state of shock. So I shall have to ask you. May I apply for the position of being your father?"

Rupert threw his arms around Wetherby's neck. "Oh, yes, your lordship. I should like that above all else."

"Well, now that we have settled that, do you think we should go ask your mother if she will marry me?"

"Oh, yes, sir," Rupert said, hopping down. "I think that it would be best if you do."

Wetherby stood, and taking Rupert's hand, walked over to where Millicent sat. He was very glad to see that Lord Copley was speechless for once in his life. He suspected Millicent was laughing at him, and it made him a little uneasy. But the die was cast, and he couldn't very well act the coward in front of his new son-to-be. He knelt on one knee in front of Millicent. Watching Wetherby carefully, Rupert did the same, making sure that this time he put only one knee down.

Wetherby took Millicent's hand in his and put his other arm around Rupert. "My dearest Millicent, will you do me the honor of becoming my wife?"

"Yes," she said simply.

Wetherby kissed her hand and winked at Rupert.

Rupert could contain himself no longer, and popping up like a jack-in-the-box, shouted, "Oh, Momma. This *has* been a special Christmas, has it not? We did find a father for me after all!" He hugged Wetherby and his mother, then ran to his aunt and uncle, who were just rising to come over to congratulate the newly engaged couple. Mrs. Greenwood wiped her eyes, and Mr. Greenwood had the look of a man who still didn't comprehend what was happening. Dog yawned and lay his head back down on the warm hearth.

Wetherby rose, and pulling Millicent up to stand by his side, whispered in her ear, "Before we are inundated by our well-wishers, I want to tell you that you have made me the happiest of men. Not often is a man so lucky as to get a bride and a son at the same time. Merry Christmas, my darling."

* * *

Over a week had gone by, and Twelfth Night was still two days away.

Wetherby caught hold of Millicent under a sprig of mistletoe and kissed her soundly. A sudden donging of a clock made his head snap up. "Where is Rupert?"

Millicent sighed and placed her head on his chest. "I do believe he and Dog are hunting dragons belowstairs in the vicinity of the kitchen, although I suspect Dog's interest is more in Mrs. Proctor's hot cinnamon buns than in finding fire-breathing creatures."

Wetherby passed through an archway and started down the corridor. "I sometimes feel that even on cloudy days, I possess a second shadow. Do you suppose Copley will let us borrow the lion to keep tabs on our son for a while so we could go on a wedding trip?"

Millicent laughed. "I do not believe that will be necessary, my lord. Rupert needs to get back to his schooling. I received a letter from my mother yesterday, and they miss him."

Wetherby looked up at the mistletoe hanging from a banner pole. "I do not know if I can survive the next few days, my dear, if we stay here. There is a kissing bough in each room and several along every hallway. Even though I have complained profusely, Copley flatly refuses to take them down until after Twelfth Night."

"That is only day after tomorrow. We can leave from Danbury Wells right after the church service."

Wetherby took Millicent's hand and led her toward the library. "If it is all right with you, we will journey straight to Leicestershire, so you can meet my father. I want to get married as soon as possible."

"I confess, I do not think I can wait either. But, Ernest, I am so afraid His Grace will not approve our alliance."

Wetherby made sure that they were positioned directly under the mistletoe before he kissed the tip of her nose. "It will not matter one way or another."

"How can you say so?"

I have made my decision. I *will* have you. He cannot change the sucession." He gave her a long look. "You know, my darling, the first time we kissed—really kissed—I had the most peculiar sensation that we had done it before."

Millicent gave a half-smile. "Perhaps we had, my lord."

Wetherby tapped her chin with his finger. "I warn you. If we stay here, I will not be held responsible for my ungentlemanly behavior. Your lips do more to cause delirium than Boggles's and Tooter's fists ever did."

Millicent kept her arms around Wetherby's neck. "Then I shall just have to hold you in my arms for the next two days to make sure you do no harm to yourself."

"The agony will be worth it," he said, pulling her once more to him for another kiss. And when that one was over, another.

Epilogue

Before the Copley party departed Roxwealde Castle, a basket arrived addressed to Rupert. Inside was an automaton made of two exquisitely sculpted porcelain figurines, a man and a woman in court dress, embracing. When the mechanism was turned on, they whirled in a circle, dancing to the strains of a Viennese waltz. The present was a hundred times the worth of the little statue that Rupert had purchased. A short note in bold handwriting told him that the sender hoped it made up for the one destroyed. There was no signature. Rupert proudly presented it to his mother. He also found his journal lying at the bottom of the package, and immediately began adding stars to Lord Wetherby's list of brave and chivalrous deeds.

When Millicent and Wetherby visited the Lance family seat in Leicestershire, Millicent, with her sweet disposition and her endless patience, completely captured the heart of Wetherby's stuffy father. The duke said he had never been so well looked-after by his own flesh and blood. He challenged Wetherby by saying that if he did not marry the fair Mrs. Copley, soon, he would marry her himself. Being the obedient son that he was, and not wanting to cause his father any undue stress, Lord Wetherby made Millicent his wife as soon as he obtained a license.

Lady Caroline returned to London after a visit to her father's estate in Gloucestershire. Unfortunately, she did not recover her jewels. A short time later, a small package was delivered to her town house. Inside she found a perfectly formed black pearl.

The Bandit King was not caught, but neither was any other young nobleman kidnapped that holiday season.

Dear Reader,

Born and raised in Indiana, I now live with my husband in Maitland, Florida. I fell in love with Ireland and the British Isles when I visited in search of my genealogical roots.

In *A Father for Christmas,* I brought back John Teagardner, a character from my Zebra Regency *Lord Wakeford's Gold Watch,* published in June 1995. More importantly, my hero, the Marquis of Wetherby, my heroine, Millicent Copley, and especially, Master Rupert, came from my Regency *Charade of Hearts,* March 1995. Also brought back were Baron Copley and his wife Sarah, the hostess with the mostest. And, of course, I could not leave out Dog, the lovable lion. I hope everyone met my Irish heroine, Caitlin O'Mullan, the fairy sprite, in the short story, "A Matter of Honor," from the Anthology *Lords and Ladies,* May 1996, where she took the English Duke of Maitland on a merry chase. Coming up in February 1997 will be a short story in Zebra's Valentine's Day collection, *A Valentine Bouquet.*

I love to hear from readers. If you wish to write to me, I may be reached at P.O. Box 941982, Maitland, FL 32794-1982. A stamped self-addressed envelope would be appreciated.

Elegantly,
Paula Tanner Girard

WATCH FOR THESE ZEBRA REGENCIES

LADY STEPHANIE   (0-8217-5341-X, $4.50)
by Jeanne Savery
Lady Stephanie Morris has only one true love: the family estate she has
managed ever since her mother died. But then Lord Anthony Rider
arrives on her estate, claiming he has plans for both the land and the
woman. Stephanie soon realizes she's fallen in love with a man whose
sensual caresses will plunge her into a world of peril and intrigue . . .
a man as dangerous as he is irresistible.

BRIGHTON BEAUTY   (0-8217-5340-1, $4.50)
by Marilyn Clay
Chelsea Grant, pretty and poor, naively takes school friend Alayna
Marchmont's place and spends a month in the country. The devastating
man had sailed from Honduras to claim his promised bride, Miss
Marchmont. An affair of the heart may lead to disaster . . . unless a
resourceful Brighton beauty finds a way to stop a masquerade and keep
a lord's love.

LORD DIABLO'S DEMISE   (0-8217-5338-X, $4.50)
by Meg-Lynn Roberts
The sinfully handsome Lord Harry Glendower was a gambler and the
black sheep of his family. About to be forced into a marriage of con-
venience, the devilish fellow engineered his own demise, never having
dreamed that faking his death would lead him to the heavenly refuge
of spirited heiress Gwyn Morgan, the daughter of a physician.

A PERILOUS ATTRACTION   (0-8217-5339-8, $4.50)
by Dawn Aldridge Poore
Alissa Morgan is stunned when a frantic passenger thrusts her baby into
Alissa's arms and flees, having heard rumors that a notorious highwayman posed a threat to their coach. Handsome stranger Hugh Sebastian
secretly possesses the treasured necklace the highwayman seeks and
volunteers to pose as Alissa's husband to save her reputation. With a
lost baby and missing necklace in their care, the couple embarks on a
journey into peril—and passion.

*Available wherever paperbacks are sold, or order direct from the
Publisher. Send cover price plus 50¢ per copy for mailing and
handling to Penguin USA, P.O. Box 999, c/o Dept. 17109, Ber-
genfield, NJ 07621. Residents of New York and Tennessee must
include sales tax. DO NOT SEND CASH.*